D0445560

BOMBSHELL

Other Five Star Titles
by Barbara and Max Allan Collins:

Too Many Tomcats and Other Feline Tales
of Suspense
Blue Christmas and Other Holiday Homicides
Butcher's Dozen
Mourn the Living
Quarry's Greatest Hits

BOMBSHELL

BARBARA AND MAX
ALLAN COLLINS

Five Star • Waterville, Maine

This novel is a work of fiction. Names, characters, places and incidents are either the product of the author's imagination, or, if real, used fictitiously.

First Edition
First Printing: April 2004

Published in 2004 in conjunction with
Tekno Books and Ed Gorman.

Set in 11 pt. Plantin

Printed in the United States on permanent paper.

ISBN 1-59414-202-5 (hc : alk. paper)

Dedicated to
Stephen Borer . . .
. . . that most dedicated of fans

"I could tell Khrushchev liked me.
He squeezed my hand so long and so
hard that I thought he would break it."

—Marilyn Monroe, 1959

"It is a question of war or peace
between our countries, a question
of life or death . . ."

—Nikita Khrushchev, 1959

"I have little respect for money. . . .
Ideas excite me."

—Walt Disney, 1959

Authors' Note

The events described in this book occurred on the weekend of September 19, 1959. Some of what you are about to read is in the public record; some of it derives from recently declassified material—from both Russian and American sources—made available to the authors from various quarters, in part due to the Freedom of Information Act. Other information was culled from unpublished memoirs of various participants, including a State Department official, herein called "Jack Harrigan." Dialogue, whenever possible, is from these sources; other times the authors have taken the liberty of exercising their imaginations in what we are presenting as a novel.

Prologue

A BLINDING FLASH

The strobe of light—brighter than the simultaneous popping of one hundred million flash-camera bulbs—preceded the thunderous roar by seconds.

A young boy—clad in a plaid short-sleeved shirt and dark blue jeans with rolled-up cuffs, his blond hair sheared in a near-bald butch, his freckled face flushed from riding his bicycle in the hot sun—dove off the bike onto the green lake of a nearby lawn, where he belly-flopped, and frantically buried his face in the grass, covering the back of his head with his interlaced hands, protecting himself as best he could.

At the same time, across the street, a mother in a blue cotton housedress—she had been pushing a brown baby-buggy down the sidewalk past a row of neatly-kept clapboard houses with lawns cut as short as the bike-rider's butch—threw herself across the front of the open buggy, making a human shield for her baby, wailing within.

The deafening roar turned down its own volume, becoming a low growling rumble . . .

. . . and a mushroom cloud rose in grotesque grandeur, blooming beneath an awaiting heaven, life-choking smoke and debris shooting outward with insidious speed in every direction, a storm of rubble and rubbish, a manmade tornado fragmenting other harmless manmade objects into deadly projectiles, a rain of death that filled the little movie screen.

"Remember," a helpful if ominous male voice intoned, managing to be heard above the conflagration, as well as the rattle and hum of the movie projector, "in the event of atomic attack . . . *duck and cover!*"

Tiny eyes narrowed in young faces in the darkened classroom, heads nodding, filing away this priceless information.

"This action," the stern yet friendly voice informed them, "can save your life."

Light, ebullient music bounced along as if this were the end of the latest episode of "Ozzie and Harriet," and then swelled absurdly to greet the letters spelling out THE END, which forebodingly filled the screen, only to fade. The monster movie many of these children had seen at a recent Saturday matinee had ended similarly . . . only with a question mark tagged onto those final chilling two words.

Now the end-of-the-world cacophony was over, the only sound in the classroom the whipcrack of the celluloid film—*snap, snap, snap*—whirling around as the reel ran out. There was something scolding about the sound. . . .

Mrs. Violet Hahn—seventh-grade social studies teacher at Emerson Junior High in West Los Angeles—shut off the machine with a sharp click, making a few children jump, and the rotating film slowed, its snapping turning to soft, rather pathetic slaps, like a winded old man running out of energy. The teacher, looking matronly beyond her years in a drab tan cotton dress and brown oxford shoes, took a few steps over to a wall switch and turned on the lights with another spine-stiffening click.

Mrs. Hahn couldn't remember a single time during her twelve years at Emerson when her pupils had been so pin-drop quiet after the showing of an educational film, the usual likes of which admittedly included risible do's-and-don'ts—such classics as "Friendship Begins at Home,"

"Are Manners Important?" and "Alcohol is Dynamite."

Even so, she demanded complete silence during all the showings (anyone who broke this rule got sent to the principal's office), and so—afterwards—the youngsters usually unleashed their pent-up energy by poking fun at the "stupid" movie, or hitting each other, or throwing spitballs.

And this film—with its helmet-wearing cartoon turtle and Disney-like song—*had* been designed for decidedly younger audiences than junior high age. . . .

There was a turtle by the name of Bert
And Bert the turtle was very alert
When danger threatened him, he never got hurt
He knew just what to do . . .
He'd duck! And cov-er . . .

Even so, the response to today's film had been different. After all, it hadn't just been Bert the Turtle; it had also featured that sonorous, portentous narrator warning students to: "Always remember—the flash from an atomic bomb can come at any time!"

Mrs. Hahn crossed the polished wooden floor, its boards creaking with her every step, to the front of the classroom, where she turned to face her students.

Four dozen wide eyes stared back at her.

Perhaps the movie *had* been a little intense, she thought. It had certainly unsettled her. This wasn't a normal film day, with students instructed on good hygiene, or healthy eating habits, or acceptable lunchroom behavior. Or even one of the more disturbing documentaries, such as those about the animals that lived in the wilds of Africa, or the many fish that swam in the sea, or the tiny turtles making their way across an endless D-Day-esque beach, very few surviving the predators along the way. . . . Life and death was the underlying theme of many such educational films.

However, watching a panther track a gazelle, or a shark swallow a blowfish, was much more removed—and, from an adolescent standpoint, far more entertaining—than seeing a boy dive for his life and a mother sacrifice hers.

"Are there any questions?" Mrs. Hahn asked the class, making her voice sound matter-of-fact, hoping to take the onus out of the moment.

When no one responded, she added, "Or comments?" For if any student was truly disturbed, better to deal with it now, rather than receive an angry phone call in the middle of the night from some parent whose child couldn't sleep—or whose Johnny or Jane had awoken from a dream of a blinding atomic-bomb flash.

"Yeah," came a sullen voice from the back of the classroom. Harold Johnson, a dark-haired boy with piercing brown eyes in an acned pie-plate face, sat slouched at his wooden desk. He was bigger than the others—only because he'd been held back twice. "That 'duck and cover' is a bunch of junk," he said.

Mrs. Hahn raised her chin and looked down her nose at him. "What our film today tells us happens to be very good advice, Harold—lifesaving advice. So you'd be wise to remember it."

"Oh yeah?" he shot back. "If the Rooskies send one over, there ain't gonna be nothin' left *to* duck and cover under!"

A wave of nervous laughter rolled across the classroom.

"*Isn't* going to be *anything* left," the teacher said, correcting him tersely.

"There sure ain't," the boy replied with a nod.

Why must this boy always be difficult? He refused to do any studying and yet was always there with a smart-aleck opinion. She was going to pass him this year, no matter what.

"You know that flash of bright light?" he asked with a smirk, then went on before she could respond. "By the time you see it, you're already dead! Fried to a crisp. Ain't no time to duck and cover."

"Harold . . ."

"Okay, so maybe you do have time. But then what happens *after* a kid 'duck-and-covers,' huh? How come the movie don't go into *that?*"

"*Doesn't* go into that, Harold."

"Sure don't! Everybody's still lyin' on the ground, when we see 'em last. That's 'cause . . ." And Harold looked around at several girls seated near him, their eyes glued to him. With a delivery worthy of a Chiller Theater host, Harold finished his thought: ". . . they're all *corpses.*"

Laughter, squeals, and assorted sounds of dismay and delight rocked the room.

"Harold!" Mrs. Hahn said sharply. "Everyone!" The classroom quieted. "That's quite enough."

But the boy ignored her, and looked around at his classmates. "Hey, I oughta know," he told them, jerking a thumb back at his chest. "My pop was at Nagasaki right after they dropped the big one—the *A*-bomb!"

Another wave: this time *ooo*'s and *aahh*'s, rippled across the class.

Squinting, leaning forward, like a kid telling a ghost story around a campfire, Harold said, "The *lucky* ones were the ones what got killed. The *not* lucky ones? All their hair fell out!"

"Harold!"

But Harold had that *what-are-you-gonna-do, flunk-me?* attitude. "It'll happen to you, too! If the bomb drops . . .

radiation sickness! Your skin peels off from the heat—just like a snake—then ya start pukin' your guts up. . . ."

Seated across from the boy, Susan, a frail girl with red hair and homemade haphazardly-cut bangs, began to cry. And the rest of the children looked as frightened as school bus passengers after a sudden stop.

"Harold, stop it!" Mrs. Hahn commanded, stomping one foot.

"You asked for comments, Miz Hahn. I thought you wanted, uh, discussion."

She swallowed. "That's true. I do . . . commend you for your class participation, Harold. But you seem to have forgotten the lessons of last week's film—'Manners in Public.' "

Harold just shrugged.

Composing herself, Mrs. Hahn told the class as firmly as she could, "There are *not* going to be any Russian bombs."

Mary Ann Stein raised her hand; the perfect little brunette, a straight-A student, asked (when she had been recognized by her teacher, of course), "Then why did you show us this picture, Mrs. Hahn?"

Mary Ann was not being a smart-aleck—the girl was clearly shaken by the film and her classmate's comments.

"Even as unlikely as a Russian attack might be—" Mrs. Hahn began.

But Harold burst back in: "Last week the Rooskies shot a rocket an' hit the *moon*. Hey—don't kid yourself . . . we're *next*." He paused, then added, "An' now they got that fat boy, Krew-chef, comin' to town to spy on us."

Mrs. Hahn angrily marched down the aisle to the boy, and pointed a trembling finger at him. "Report to the principal's office," she ordered, "at once!" She hoped her manner was authoritarian and did not reveal that the boy's remarks had gotten to her, as well.

Harold smirked and shrugged and got up from his desk and sauntered slowly to the closed wood-paneled door, where he looked back at the teacher. But the smirk had wiped itself from his face, to be replaced by something else . . .

Fear.

" 'We'll bury you,' that's what that Rooskie fatso said," the boy told her, and for all his bluster, Harold's trembling lower lip and his teary eyes revealed his classroom behavior had been motivated not by orneriness but terror.

Then—embarrassed—Harold pushed open the door and disappeared out into the hallway.

The classroom fell deathly quiet again, punctuated by the sniffles of the red-haired girl, and one or two others. The cartoon with the cheerful "duck and cover" theme song and the cartoon turtle had scared the hell out of these seventh graders.

And their teacher.

Mrs. Hahn walked back up the aisle and planted herself in front of the chalkboard. "Class," she said, forcing her voice to be calm, "don't pay any attention to Harold. He's . . . he's just a prankster, trying to scare us." She squared her shoulders, hands clasped under her bosom, and pronounced: "President Eisenhower would *never* allow an atomic war."

Then she moved to her desk, pulled out the oak chair with a fingernails-on-blackboard screech, and sat down. "Now, take out your social studies book," she instructed coolly, "and turn to chapter four."

As the students rustled around in their desks, Mrs. Hahn glanced down at her notes on the forthcoming lesson; but her mind wasn't on them.

World War II had been the war to end all wars—hadn't it? Her husband had fought in the Pacific, coming home with nightmares and recurring malaria. She had lost her brother in Italy. The war to end all wars. That's what everyone said.

Of course they'd said that about World War I, as well. . . .

Could it all have been for nothing? Could the world end in a heartbeat—*always remember, the flash of an atomic bomb can come at any time!*

She gazed out the open window onto Selby Avenue, where on this beautiful Friday morning in September, in the entertainment capital of the world, cars and pedestrians bustled along in pursuit of the American dream.

Sighing, shaking her head, she made herself smile—for her students, for herself. President Eisenhower would never allow an atomic war. Wasn't that the reason he'd invited Nikita Khrushchev over? To sit down like human beings and reason together? To talk, to straighten all this silliness out?

An atomic war could *never, ever* happen!

Could it?

Then she withdrew into the class lesson, like a turtle into its shell, and went about her business.

Chapter One

BLONDE AMBITION

In bungalow number seven on the lavishly landscaped grounds of the Beverly Hills Hotel, the bustle of Hollywood had been banished. A goddess was—with the help of others—preparing herself for an appearance before those who worshipped her.

At just after nine a.m., Ralph Roberts—Marilyn Monroe's personal masseur—had just finished giving the celebrated actress a rubdown in a bedroom decorated all in white (with the exception of heavy black-out curtains). The man—handsome, muscular, heterosexual—and the woman—beautiful, curvaceous, blonde-all-over, naked—had exchanged only a few words, the massage all business, but for the pleasure the actress received from skilled hands.

In a corner of the room, a portable hi-fi—fit for the most pampered teenage girl—perched on the white-carpeted floor, spinning the latest of a stack of Frank Sinatra 45s. Later in the day the swinging come-fly-with-me Sinatra might have been heard in this snowy chamber; but at this early hour, the singer was crooning, "September Song," softly, lulling the actress into wakefulness.

In a blue t-shirt and chinos, Roberts—as tall as he was muscular, with wide Apache cheekbones and a perpetual smile—began putting away his oils and lotions in a worn leather carrying case, as the nude Marilyn lay stretched out on her stomach on the bed, her translucent, pale skin now pink, glowing, from the vigorous rubdown.

The two had known each other for only a few years, having met in 1956 at the Actor's Studio in New York, where they'd quickly become good friends. Robert's gifts as a masseur kept him working when his acting talents did not, and his easygoing manner and discretion made him one of Marilyn's closest confidants.

Whenever she called him for a massage—which was often (sometimes in the middle of the night when the Seconal or Demerol or Nembutal pills refused to kick in)—he always took her lead: if she craved silence (as was the case this morning), he was quiet as he worked his magic on her tense muscles. But if she desired some gaiety, his devilish humor could always make her laugh.

Sometimes, after a massage on the set of one of her movies, Roberts would help Marilyn with her lines, giving her the encouragement she always seemed to need, before she faced the camera.

"You did well with that diet," Roberts said, snapping shut his case.

"You're sweet," she murmured. "A liar, but sweet."

He sat next to her on the edge of the bed. Her eyes were closed as he said, "No, you have your figure back."

"Little too much of it."

"Anyway, you'll look fine for the shoot. Take it easy on the diet pills."

Her eyes flickered open, dark blue peering through lashes. "Don't you get tired of playing Jiminy Cricket?"

"Just be careful, Pinocchio. Chosen your co-star yet?"

She propped herself on an elbow, her breasts cushioned against the mattress, hair tousled. "Leaning toward Yves Montand. He has a one-man show coming up, later this month."

"Out here?"

She shook her head, tousling the platinum locks even further. "No, New York. Arthur's taking me. Arthur likes him—Montand played in *The Crucible*, in Paris."

"Kind of an unknown quantity, isn't he? In American movies, I mean."

She smirked prettily at her confidant. "Don't you think I can carry a picture by myself? On these little shoulders?"

Roberts gave her half a smile. "Those shoulders are already carrying one of the smartest minds in show business. . . . I imagine they can handle another movie."

"Are you fishing for a tip, Ralph? Or a role maybe? Maybe you just wanna fuck me."

He laughed, gave her an affectionate slap on her bare bottom, and went out, shaking his head.

As Roberts was heading out the door, two other members of the Monroe retinue entered: May Reis, Marilyn's personal secretary, and Agnes Flanagan, the renowned hair colorist.

"Marilyn," May said softly to her employer, who seemed to be slumbering again, "it's time. . . . Agnes is here."

May—fifty-five, a small, trim, oval-faced woman, businesslike in a simple navy suit, her brown hair cut no-nonsense short—had initially been Arthur Miller's secretary (following a stint with Elia Kazan). But after the playwright and the movie star married, and had moved into their East 57th Street apartment, it quickly became evident that Marilyn was the one who needed May's help more. Now May handled the daily onslaught of scripts and organized everything in Marilyn's life, from correspondence to grocery lists.

The nude Marilyn didn't budge. From his corner, Frankie was singing, "Five Minutes More."

"Marilyn, dear," the secretary tried again, "Agnes is

here. . . ." Taking Sinatra's cue, the star pleaded, "Just five more minutes," words muffled by the pillow in which her face was buried. "All right?"

But after a few moments, when May hadn't answered, Marilyn moaned and slowly rolled off the bed, wrapping herself mummy-like in the white top sheet, pulling its train along with her as she walked unsteadily toward the bathroom.

"I'll bring some coffee," May told her cheerfully, and exited the bedroom, closing the door off from the bungalow's living room, which had become a holding area for the entourage of specialists that would attend to the movie star on this very important Saturday morning.

In the bathroom, Marilyn plopped down on a white satin chair in front of a long make-up counter and mirror, gathering the sheet around her.

"I want it white, Agnes," she instructed the sixty-ish fireplug of a colorist, who had followed her silently in. "White as snow."

With a tiny smile, Agnes—who had heard these instructions countless times—nodded at Marilyn's wishes, placing her bag of bottles of peroxide and solutions on the bathroom counter, and set about her work.

"Not just . . . snow," Marilyn said, thoughtfully. Then she giggled. "*Siberian* snow."

Agnes smiled again. The stout woman knew all about white hair: she had her own, of course; but also she had long ago provided that famous platinum shade for Jean Harlow's tresses.

As a child, Marilyn—that is, Norma Jeane—had adored Harlow, sometimes sitting through her movies two or three times at a stretch, dreaming of one day becoming just like her. When the dark blonde Norma Jeane decided to give birth to a much blonder Marilyn, she had tracked Agnes down, bringing the woman out of retirement, using the colorist for her own movies and special appointments.

May returned with a hot cup of coffee, just as Frank was helpfully picking up the tempo with, "Oh, What a Beautiful Morning."

Forty minutes later, her hair freshly dyed, shampooed, and towel-turbaned, Marilyn stepped into a warm bubble bath drawn by her secretary. She slipped beneath the foamy surface, the fragrance of an entire bottle of Chanel No. 5—which had been poured into the running water—rising like a pleasant fog, and permeating her every pore.

Eyes closed, Marilyn soaked dreamily in the warm bath. Minutes, hours, days might have passed; she didn't care. Time was a concept she had never quite mastered and, anyway, this was her favorite place, far away from the murky second-hand baths she'd had to take in foster homes . . . and the reason she was always late.

"Marilyn, dear," May whispered gently. "Whitey is waiting."

The actress opened her eyes, a process that took perhaps five seconds. May was standing next to the tub, a rather shabby (though clean) white bathrobe in both hands, held out and open, as if to embrace her.

Marilyn frowned. Pouted. Put on her saddest eyes. "Just . . . a *little* bit longer. . . . Please, darling?"

Again, May didn't answer—her expression, though not unkind, as frozen as a cigar store Indian's.

Marilyn groaned, thinking, *Damn! Who pays the bills around here, anyway?*

But she kept this thought to herself, and—with a deep and oh-so-world-weary sigh—rose out of the tub, pale flesh pearled with water, Botticelli's Venus dabbed with bubbles, a well-bathed, perfumed martyr, and stony May helped her into the robe—a souvenir from *The Seven Year Itch*, now tattered and stained—the terrycloth soaking up the frothy bubbles still clinging to her moist skin.

Soon Allan "Whitey" Snyder—attired in his usual short-sleeved white shirt—was ushered by May into the bathroom sanctuary. Middle-aged, with a long slender nose, receding chin, and the inevitable blond crew cut that had given him his nickname, Whitey had been with Marilyn since the actress's first screen text at Fox, and together they had invented her "look," defining and refining, and re-defining it, over the years.

Marilyn took the chair once again in front of the mirror, the white robe—a security blanket that always traveled with her—casually hanging open. The actress was not a show-off, where her beautiful body was concerned—she was comfortable with it . . . just as she was uncomfortable in clothes.

"Let's make Marilyn," she said.

As the make-up artist began his familiar routine, Marilyn was quiet and withdrawn. It was nothing personal. Her mini-conversation with Ralph and dealings with May were all she could manage this morning. She knew Whitey understood that she was conserving her energy. It wouldn't be until the make-up artist had carefully applied the lipsticks—several different shades for contouring, because her lips were surprisingly flat—that together they would bring to life her creation, "Marilyn Monroe" emerging from Norma Jeane like a butterfly from its cocoon.

Whitey lined Marilyn's famous mouth with dark red pencil, and even as he was skillfully coloring it in, May entered again, and announced the arrival of hair stylist Sydney Guilaroff.

Discovered by Joan Crawford in 1935, the Canadian

Guilaroff—at age forty-nine—was still the most sought-after hairdresser in Hollywood. And for an event as crucial as today's, Marilyn insisted on no one but the best.

Marilyn, now in her movie-star persona, bid goodbye to Whitey, and greeted Guilaroff—ever dapper in a gray shark-skin suit and silk black tie—with a delighted squeal and out-stretched hand.

"I want something *different,* Sydney," Marilyn said, wrinkling her upturned nose. "How are the women wearing their hair in Moscow these days?"

"Under a babushka," he answered dryly.

Marilyn giggled. "Well, that won't do."

"I doubt today's honored guest wants to meet Marilyn Monroe," the hairdresser opined, "because he's longing to meet a typical *Russian* woman."

"You're right as always, dear." She plopped down on the satin chair, facing the mirror. Guilaroff removed the towel from her head and ran his fingers expertly, like an intelligent comb, through her thick, damp, naturally curly locks. Out in the bedroom, May was putting on another stack of Frank Sinatra singles.

"Let's style it straight, with a flip on one side," Guilaroff suggested, his narrowed eyes meeting her wide ones in the mirror.

"Okay!" she said, in the little-girl voice that belied the strong-willed woman possessing it.

While Guilaroff began setting the screen queen's hair in large rollers instead of the usual pin curls, his client coyly asked, "And how is Liz?" She knew the hairdresser had just come from Elizabeth Taylor's.

"Delightful as always," he responded. "All of my clients are sheer delights . . . you know that."

"I'm sure. . . . Any gray hairs . . . ?"

It was a game she played with Sydney, to get him to talk about his other clients. But no matter how much she cajoled him, or tried to trick him into candor, he never succumbed. Having coifed screen legends from Clara Bow to Doris Day, Guilaroff was rigorous about maintaining strict client confidentiality—whether to the press or his other patrons.

"I tell you what, Sid. . . ." And now Marilyn turned her head to look right at him, disrupting his work. "I'll give you permission to reveal to anyone you like that . . ." She looked side to side, then leaned toward him conspiratorially. ". . . I dye my hair."

He chuckled and, as she turned away, resumed his work.

She grinned cutely at him in the mirror. "Come on, Sid . . . just one little tidbit."

Guilaroff sighed dramatically. "All right," he said. "I give up. But just one."

Marilyn straightened, eyes bright. "Just one."

He bent and whispered into a perked ear. "After I finished with Elizabeth, working absolutely all of my magic, giving it my very best effort, and in spite of whatever extreme measures I took . . ." He paused.

Her eyebrows climbed the smooth forehead. "Yes?"

He shrugged. ". . . she looked simply fabulous."

Marilyn slapped at him playfully. "You're lying. She's a fat, hideous witch and you know it." And she slumped in the chair, half kidding, but nonetheless not pleased to hear of her competitor's beauty.

Though she barely knew Taylor personally—just to exchange strained pleasantries with, when they'd attend the same studio function or wind up at the same party—Marilyn disliked her fellow Fox star with an unreasonable intensity. Not so much because of Taylor's beauty—which didn't hold a candle to her own, she thought (usually)—but because of the high salary her brunette rival commanded.

Yet *who* was it that had pulled Twentieth Century's fat from the fire, time after time? Marilyn Monroe's movies had kept the studio afloat—despite the bad scripts that were frequently foisted upon her. Even a weak vehicle was strong at the box office, when it had Marilyn in it. Could Liz Taylor have survived *River of No Return*? Or *There's No Business Like Show Business*? Not hardly!

Anyway, that busty little munchkin couldn't carry a tune in a paper bag, and that *mannered* acting style of hers—well, really!

Marilyn had been crushed when she didn't get the ripe role of Maggie the Cat in *Cat on a Hot Tin Roof*. She could have torn up the joint in a rich part like that—done a *much* better job than the stilted Taylor. Even Tennessee Williams himself had admitted as much, when Marilyn cornered him at a party recently.

Anyway, Marilyn oozed sex—whereas Liz Taylor just oozed.

And now La Taylor seemed about to bring the whole goddamn studio to its knees with that exorbitant barge of a picture, *Cleopatra*, what with her outrageous demands and film-halting illnesses . . . how could any actress *be* so unprofessional?

The only reason Twentieth Century Fox remained afloat, at present, was Marilyn's latest box-office smash, *Some Like It Hot*.

Marilyn was just pondering what an interesting position this put her in when a knock drew her attention to the reflection of the bathroom doorway in the mirror, where a figure appeared unannounced.

Few men would have dared such a thing—even Arthur or Joe would have waited for May to present them. . . .

But this was—speaking of the devil . . . that is, the

Twentieth Century Fox variety—the president of the studio, Spyros Skouras himself, a tall, imposing, yet fatherly fellow, with thinning white hair and black glasses. The normally cool and collected president seemed quite unnerved.

"Dahling! For once in your young life, you must be on time!" Skouras delivered this lamentation to his star in his trademark Greek accent, which was no thicker than a slab of feta cheese.

"Don't *worry,* S. S.," she said slowly, drawing the words out, again mimicking Sinatra, who from his bedroom corner sang, "Don't Worry About Me." "Have I ever let you down?"

Skouras looked skyward, slapped his sides, though not in laughter. "Constantly!"

She gave him a million-dollar pout. "Don't be mean."

He shook a scolding finger. "This is big honor, today, young lady—for both of us."

"I know."

"World leader. Very important person."

"Oh yes," Marilyn nodded. "Almost as important as a movie star, don't you think?"

Skouras tried not to smile; he was very fond of her, despite the difficulties she brought to the sets of the movies he produced, and she knew how to manipulate him.

"Please," he said. "For once, my sweetness, my dumpling, hurry up your sweet tushie."

Her mouth pursed into the famous kiss. "I love it when you talk dirty. . . . Have you looked at those clips yet?"

She meant a reel of excerpts from Yves Montand's films she'd had sent 'round.

Impatiently, shaking his head, the studio chief said, "Yes, yes . . . he looks like charming man. But we can't use him."

"Why not?"

"He has *accent!* Turrible foreign accent."

"I think foreign accents are sexy."

He coughed. "We talk of this later. You must hurry!"

Guilaroff was putting the finishing touches on her stylish pageboy coiffure. "I won't be late," she said. "I'll be early."

Skouras groaned. "This I believe when pigs grow wings and fly."

"The longer you stay here," she responded sweetly, "the longer I'll be."

The head of the studio sighed deeply, and—dismissed like a child—turned on his heels and marched out.

Next came the dress—a little black-net number that had been whipped up by Marilyn's favorite designer, Norman Norell. It was rather transparent in the bosom, leaving little to the imagination, and perhaps too revealing for the occasion . . . but so what? She had a reputation to live up to, didn't she? And, besides, how often did a girl from the orphanage get to meet the premier of Russia?

A very cute man from the State Department had contacted her in New York several weeks ago—what was his name . . . Frank, Jack?—and told her that Nikita Khrushchev wanted to meet her on his first visit to the United States.

Her!

Little Norma Jeane Mortensen, who nobody had ever paid any attention to, shuttled from this foster home to that one. The State Department man . . . *really* cute, she wouldn't mind seeing him again . . . said Khrushchev had been taken with photographs of her—movie stills from *Some Like It Hot*—displayed at the American National Exhibition which had opened in Moscow in July.

The premier, on a history-making cross-country tour of America, was scheduled to make a stop in Los Angeles. Studio chief Skouras—who had been Marilyn's champion since her first contract at Fox, recognizing her special genius (even staying in her corner after she'd fled Hollywood for New York)—had cooked up the idea of throwing a luncheon at the studio for Khrushchev . . . Russia's biggest V.I.P. meeting Hollywood royalty. And while Marilyn wouldn't be the only star in attendance, both she and Skouras damn well knew which star would shine the brightest. . . .

Particularly since Marilyn was the only movie star Nikita Khrushchev had indicated an interest in meeting.

A few minutes later, in the bedroom, May stood by the door at attention, as if waiting for the changing of the guard.

"Time to go," the secretary said crisply.

They were alone in the white chamber; everyone else had gone . . . except for Frank, of course, who was singing, "You Are So Beautiful," the last record on the turntable.

Marilyn raised a champagne glass to her perfectly lip-rouged lips and took a final gulp of Dom Perignon. Then she adjusted her ample breasts in the low-cut dress, snugged the material around her considerable though always admirable posterior, and looked toward May for approval.

"You *are* lovely," May said, sounding sincere, even bestowing a small smile. They were words Marilyn never tired of hearing. She felt like a little girl who'd managed to do something right . . . something *good*. . . .

On the way through the living room, where stale smoke hung in the air like an acrid curtain and cigarette butts overflowed a coffee table ashtray, Marilyn was startled by another knock at the door—yet another visitor.

May, in charge of every detail of the morning's appointments, raised both eyebrows; she was, after all, the portal through which all must pass.

"Now who could that be?" the secretary wondered aloud.

Marilyn shrugged and shook her head, the pageboy flouncing in tribute to Guilaroff's artistry.

May crossed the thick white carpet and cracked open the bungalow door, enough to reveal a tall, slender man in a tailored brown suit and blue striped tie.

"Might I have a word with Marilyn?" he asked politely, his eyes darting past May to the movie star.

"Rupert," Marilyn exclaimed, surprised and pleased, moving to the doorway to greet the man. "How the hell are you?" To her secretary, she said, "It's all right, May. This is Rupert Allen. . . . Rupert is . . . was . . . my Hollywood publicist."

Suddenly, the awkwardness of it was unavoidable, and her surprise and pleasure turned to embarrassment. Since the move to New York, she'd had no contact with Rupert; their relationship had never been officially severed, but . . .

And now here he was, big as life, the man responsible for her first *Look* magazine cover, the real start of her rise to stardom. At age forty-six Rupert was, in the opinion of many, still the best press agent in Hollywood, and certainly among the most respected, with clients of such Tinsel Town renown as Bette Davis, Gregory Peck, Natalie Wood . . . and until recently, Marilyn Monroe.

There had been no falling out between them, just a . . . a sort of falling away. In New York, Marilyn had begun using a Manhattan P.R. agent, Patricia Newcomb. To May, Rupert was a stranger; to Marilyn, he was family.

May stepped aside to let the gentleman in; however, she gave him a gesture with a scolding forefinger. "Only a minute or two," she warned, "or Marilyn will be late to the luncheon."

"May," Marilyn said, "go ahead and wait in the limousine, would you?"

The secretary frowned at this suggestion, but did not argue, slipping out of the bungalow, leaving the two old friends alone.

"Do you mind if we sit?" Rupert asked, nodding to the white couch next to a beige stone fireplace.

"So formal?" Marilyn asked.

"I admit to feeling . . . a little awkward."

She sighed. "Good. We have that in common. But it's wonderful to see you, Rupe—"

"Please. Sit."

Marilyn complied, perceiving a problem, but she couldn't imagine what.

He settled into a soft chair opposite the couch where she sat. His smile was strained as he said, "I understand you're meeting with Chairman Khrushchev today."

She beamed at him. "Yes. . . . Isn't that wonderful? Can you imagine better publicity?"

"Frankly, yes."

"Rupe . . ."

"I don't think you should go."

Her smiled dropped. She couldn't believe she was hearing these words from the lips of such a renowned P.R. agent. Meeting Khrushchev, one of the most powerful men in the world, would be the ultimate publicity coup, an event covered worldwide in the press, from *Life* to *Pravda*.

And this publicity was coming at a time when she most needed it, when she was getting back into the Hollywood swing, after having exiled herself to what many considered the pretentious New York artiness of the Actors' Studio.

Amazed, she sat forward, eyes tensed, and—not confrontational, knowing Rupert always had his reasons—asked, "Not see Khrushchev . . . but why?"

His eyes were kind; his voice was harsh. "Because,

Marilyn, you're going to be used."

"No one uses me unless I want them to!"

He smiled, just a little. "Remember who you're talking to."

A bit of hurt, a tinge of defensiveness, crept into her voice. "Who's going to use me, then?"

"The government," the press agent said. "Or the CIA or State Department or somebody else who wants to get that chubby Russian S.O.B. into a compromising position."

Relieved, Marilyn waved that off with a laugh. "Oh, Rupe! I'm just going to *meet* the man. We're not going to bed or anything. I mean, you've seen him, right? He looks like Marjorie Main in drag!"

The publicist didn't smile.

"You're serious, aren't you?" she asked.

He nodded. "You don't always prize attractiveness in your men, my dear. . . . You've always been more attracted to power, and fame."

She stiffened. "Rupe, you're crossing the line, now. . . ."

"Frankly, I was thinking of your meeting with Sukarno."

Marilyn stood abruptly. "*Nothing* happened between us," she said emphatically, putting her hands on her hips. "How many times do I have to tell you, before you believe me? You're worse than my husbands!"

"Nothing happened? Okay. Fine. But something *could* have . . . and I believe the CIA put you next to Sukarno for their own purposes."

Rupe had a point. Sparks had flown between her and the darkly handsome President of Indonesia, Achmed Sukarno, at a reception held for diplomats a few years ago . . . right here at the Beverly Hills Hotel, coincidentally enough.

"I'll admit," she said, chin up, "that later that night, after the party, I called President Sukarno, for a private meeting. But I just wanted to know more about his country, which really isn't a country at all but a bunch of islands. You know how eager I am for knowledge. Do I have to tell *you* I'm not just another blonde bimbo?"

He arched an eyebrow, as if to say, *No, you're* the *blonde bimbo*. But all he said was, "And?"

"And," she continued with a toss of her sumptuously coifed head, "at the last minute I decided that I was too tired."

Rupert looked up at her sharply. "Hedda Hopper reported that you kept that meeting."

Marilyn frowned. "Jeez, Rupe . . . I always thought *you* told her that . . . for publicity's sake."

"No," he said, with a head shake, "I did not."

Marilyn sat back down on the sofa, puzzled, a cushion swallowing her bottom.

"You know," she said, eyes tightening as she leaned toward him. "There *was* a kind of click on the phone when I called President Sukarno that night. . . ." She lowered her voice to a whisper. "You don't suppose . . . the line was tapped?"

"After what you and Arthur have been put through by the House Un-American Activities Committee," the press agent said tightly, "do you have trouble believing as much?"

She was shaking her head now, risking Guilaroff's handiwork. "But why in hell would anybody care about the President of Indonesia meeting with some actress?"

"Not 'some actress,' dear . . . *Marilyn Monroe*." Rupert shrugged. "Obviously, to get something on him."

"Why? I just don't understand. . . ."

"Uncle Sam put Sukarno in power expecting Indonesia to go democratic," Rupert explained. "Then what does the ungrateful wretch do? He stops free elections and aligns himself with the communists . . . Russia and China."

Marilyn's eyes widened. "I didn't know that. I . . . admit I really haven't kept track. I thought Sukarno was one of the good guys."

"So did our government, early on. Now they'd use anything against him . . . even you. And if they feel that way about a comparative small fry like Sukarno . . . how do you think they feel about Nikita K?"

Marilyn put one finger to her lips and bit down on the platinum nail. She trusted Rupert. He was smart, and knew things she didn't. Yes, she always wanted to learn things, but her methods were pretty hit or miss. The press agent hadn't risen to his rarefied position without great instincts and greater knowledge.

Why did politics have to make things so difficult? If a man and a woman wanted to get together, why shouldn't they? Why couldn't people just be people?

"Now do you understand why I don't want you to meet with Khrushchev?" Rupert was asking.

Marilyn stood again. "I'm already ready," she said stubbornly, spreading her arms wide. "I've gone to a lot of trouble. My people have gone to a lot of trouble, too. And damnit, Rupe, I *want* to go. Khrushchev asked to see *me* . . . of all the stars in the Hollywood heavens . . . me."

"How do you know that?"

"The State Department said so. I mean, I don't want to go up against the State Department—you want me to start World War III or something?"

Rupert stood and his eyes drilled through her. "You know the press will skewer you," he said, not giving up. "They're going to dredge up all that commie nonsense about Arthur, and they'll drag you down with him."

Marilyn felt her face grow hot. "Arthur wasn't charged with anything," she retorted. "Anyway, I'm no communist

. . . I'm an American. I haven't even *been* to Russia!"

Rupert patted the air with his palms in a "calm down" fashion. "All right," he said. "Go if you want. Make the public appearance . . . but avoid anything else, no private meetings, no 'educational' rendezvous with the little fat man. And, please, Marilyn . . . be careful."

The heat had left her face, and a warmth for Rupert had taken its place. "I will, Rupe," she said. "I promise."

He put his hands on her shoulders, smiling, his eyes sad. "You know, no matter what happens, how much or how little we might see each other, that I care about you, very much. That I'm your friend, always will be."

Marilyn nodded, swallowing, touched by his concern. "Rupert?" She took one of his hands.

"Yes, my dear?"

"I'm . . . I'm sorry I haven't called you."

He shook his head, shrugged. "We've both been busy," he said.

It was so goddamn sweet of him to let her off the hook so easily.

"Let's stay in touch," she said.

"Let's." He gave her a tender smile. "Now . . . go knock 'em dead, Miss Monroe." He looked her over, and raised his eyebrows. "With that dress . . . what there is of it . . . you can't miss."

As Marilyn watched him go—pausing to toss her a little wave and smile, before slipping out—she felt a surge of melancholy roll through her, and linger. Then, taking a moment to summon back her movie star persona—that character she had created, that she played so well, and that to some degree she had become, leaving Norma Jeane behind—she put on her sunglasses and exited the bungalow and walked out to the waiting limousine.

Chapter Two

WELCOME TO L.A.

In a remote corner of Los Angeles International Airport, from the yawning mouth of a North American Aviation hangar, Jack Harrigan—his mental and emotional state a mix of detachment, concern, and fatigue—watched as an Air Force 707 landed in the heat-shimmering distance. The forty-two-year-old agent, assigned these days to the State Department Security Division, had flown ahead the day before from Washington to finalize preparations for the visiting Russian delegation, arriving at this moment on that jet.

At six foot two, Harrigan had a shaggy, rugged handsomeness—there were those who said he resembled a leaner Robert Mitchum, the movie actor—that made him almost too distinctive for the security division, which favored banality in its agents' appearance, the better to blend in with crowds. Among Harrigan's distinguishing characteristics were hazel eyes, singed eyebrows (age nine; fire-cracker), and a re-set nose (age twelve; fist-fight), false front tooth (age sixteen; hockey puck); one other deformity, only his ex-wife and a few other females knew about: a fistful-sized chunk of his left buttock was missing (age twenty-five; German mortar).

A sorry excuse for a welcoming committee had gathered at the hangar to wait quietly for the premier of Russia—and the sixty-some entourage accompanying him. This small assemblage was a pale shadow of the festivities that had been arranged for Khrushchev back east, when he flew in to Idlewild a week ago. Mayor Wagner of New York rolled out a literal red carpet, complete with waving banners, effusive speeches, a huge cheering crowd, and three blaring brass bands.

Mayor Poulson of Los Angeles—that pain-in-the-ass prick—felt differently about having a communist dictator delivered to his bailiwick, viewing Khrushchev with the warmth reserved for a bastard child found in a basket on a doorstep.

As the plane began to taxi toward him, Harrigan stood motionless in the noonday sun's withering heat; but behind the black sunglasses his trained eyes were darting from the handful of put-upon perspiring dignitaries lined up across from him, to the press corps held back behind a cop-guarded barricade, to the small crowd of citizens who'd been aware of Khrushchev's coming, and cared enough—for whatever reason—to witness the historic moment.

Harrigan was cataloguing every movement, scrutinizing every face, looking for any hand-held objects that weren't fountain pens, cameras, or little American flags . . . and looking for certain kinds of faces, hot with rage or, even more dangerous, cold with rage. . . .

Just because the crowd was paltry didn't mean the agent could let his guard down, not for a heartbeat; it only took one person—in one heartbeat's time—to pull out a gun and assassinate Khrushchev, and send the United States to the edge of a precipice beyond which was an all-too-real nuclear abyss.

Yup—just another day in the life of Jack Harrigan.

And had Harrigan deemed to remove his sunglasses, to take a better look at the meager mob, something else would have been revealed about the agent: dark circles under his eyes, indicating the lack of sleep and abundance of stress he'd endured this past week, which had begun dubiously—a bad omen, for those who believed in that kind of thing (and he did)—with the initial arrival of the Russians on American soil.

The Soviets had put down at Andrews Air Force Base, fifteen miles southwest of Washington D.C., in a huge Russian Tupelov jetliner. The use of that airplane—considerably longer and taller than its American counterpart—was a disaster in and of itself: when the metal debarkation staircase was wheeled up to its door, the ramp was too short. It was a scene out of a slapstick comedy: chaos broke out on the ground, while Khrushchev and company were left cooling their heels, until some poor bastard finally found a common household ladder.

When the Russians finally climbed ignobly out, and down, like sweethearts eloping in the middle of the night, Nikita Khrushchev was not in the mood for love; the dictator was red with rage. The press had a field-day snapping him and the portly missus, her dress wrapped tightly around her legs for modesty's sake, coming down the ladder. Harrigan, working closely with the Secret Service boys (until recently he'd been Secret Service himself), saw to it that any film—whether news organization or civilian—was confiscated.

When a reporter pal of his had bitched, Harrigan said, "No way I'm gonna let World War III start up over some fat Russian broad gettin' embarrassed . . . but don't quote me."

Various pomp and circumstance had awaited the Russian premier and his people at Andrews—the usual twenty-one-gun salute, President Eisenhower on hand, honor guards, ten bands massed to play both the Soviet national anthem,

"Soyuz Nerushimy Respublik Svobodnykh," and "The Star-Spangled Banner." A motorcade through the Maryland suburbs into Washington had been followed by a full-dress parade down Pennsylvania Avenue.

But none of it took the bite out of the ramp-and-ladder incident: strike one for the Americans—not at all an auspicious beginning to a last-ditch peace mission between two nations on a nuclear collision course.

At one point early on, when the Russians had still been aboard the Tupelov jet, Harrigan—watching from the sidelines as the catastrophe unfolded—thought he detected a small, smug smile briefly purse Khrushchev's thick lips, as the dictator peered from the plane's window at the Americans below, running around like ants that had their colony disturbed.

Surely the Russians knew the specifications of U.S. commercial jets. Had they built their plane bigger on purpose? Was this a cunning chess move, designed to make the Americans start off the trip with a blunder?

Later, when an obviously embarrassed President Eisenhower asked Khrushchev to leave the huge Tupelov behind at the base, and offered one of the Air Force's new 707s for the rest of the premier's cross-country trip, Harrigan again could only wonder: Had that been Khrushchev's plan all along? Just how much national security would be compromised in the name of hospitality?

Harrigan of course had been briefed extensively on Khrushchev at the State Department. There was no denying that this man—however much the roly-poly despot might seem a thug or peasant-risen-to-power—was a smart and formidable adversary. He'd have to be, to have survived the bloody purges of Stalin.

Now Harrigan had had a week to form his own opinion of the Russian ruler, and found him to be a complicated man, whose disposition could turn on a dime, like a big precocious child. Amusing and warm at one moment, Khrushchev was an erupting human earthquake the next: shrewd and ruthless, and about as subtle about his wants and needs as a sailor on a three-hour pass.

At the moment, however, Harrigan was not the least bit interested in the inner workings of Nikita Khrushchev's mind and what made this bomb of a man tick; he was concerned—make that panic-stricken—over the perils of making it through the last leg of what he considered to have been an ill-advised trip in the first place . . . a trip that had only deteriorated further with each stop along the way.

While in New York, the premier infuriated the United Nations delegation—Chiang Kai-shek's democratic Nationalist China had refused to attend—who had generously allowed him to give a speech before the General Assembly. The Russian guest had repaid this gracious gesture by delivering a tirade punctuated with bellicose blustering and outright threats.

Still, Harrigan had noted, there had been a suggestion that what Khrushchev wanted most was peace. . . .

Khrushchev—surprisingly dapper in a blue serge suit with gray tie and gold stickpin, two medals on his lapel—had taken the U.N. podium with his personal interpreter at his side, a handsome if vaguely sinister-looking young man named Oleg Troyanovsky. As Khrushchev spoke in his native tongue, his voice grew sharper and louder. The interpreter was able to soften the premier's inflection, but not his words, which warned of world destruction unless the cold war came to an end, and disarmament began.

"Over a period of four years," Khrushchev suggested, "all states should effect complete disarmament and should no longer have any means of waging war. Military bases on foreign territories shall be abolished, all atomic and hydrogen bombs destroyed. . . ."

The delegates had no argument with that. But how? Khrushchev never said.

Twice before—in 1927 and 1932—the Soviet Union had proposed total world disarmament of this kind, but on both occasions the rest of the world had recognized the proposal for what it was—a one-sided attempt to get every other nation to cast its armaments aside . . . while Russia refused adequate supervision to demonstrate that they were doing the same.

Khrushchev concluded his seventy-two minute speech by condemning the assembly for not allowing Mao Tse-tung's Red China to join the United Nations. Nationalist China on Formosa, he told them, was all but dead, "a rotting corpse that should be carried out." Delegates shifted uncomfortably in their seats, disgruntled murmurs rising among them.

After the media reported the speech, the mood of the general public—who previously had been guardedly polite toward the Russian leader in Washington and New York—began to shift ominously; and by Chicago, crowds had become downright hostile, as Khrushchev continued his lecturing on the evils of capitalism and of eminent Soviet domination.

There had been an electrified charge in the air as the motorcade whisked the premier along Chicago's Michigan Avenue amid signs that read: FISH AND GUESTS SMELL IN 3 DAYS!, GO TO THE MOON, LEAVE US ALONE!, and RUSSIAN ATROCITIES IN HUNGARY MUST BE ANSWERED! The lynch mob mood concerned Harrigan enough that he'd flown back to Washington that night to meet with his State Department boss, on whose shoulders rested the enormous responsibility of safeguarding Khrushchev.

For decades, the Secret Service had protected not only

the president of the United States but any visiting dignitaries. Recently, however, a new security division had been formed in the State Department to handle the ever-increasing number of foreign guests; the world was growing smaller, it seemed, even as living on it grew more dangerous.

Many of these agents, Harrigan included, had been culled from the ranks of the Secret Service. Protecting Khrushchev was their first assignment. Harrigan wished they could have gotten their feet wet with a much smaller fish; but they were stuck instead with this big barracuda.

"I think we should cut the trip short," Harrigan told Bill Larsen, his chief.

He and Larsen had known each other for over ten years, working the White House Detail together. They had both gone after the coveted top spot in the new division, but Bill—Harrigan's senior officer by a few years—had landed the position, putting a strain on their friendship.

Seated behind the massive, cluttered mahogany desk in his executive office, Larsen—middle-aged, brown-haired, average, even undistinguished looking (always a plus in this work), wearing a rumpled Brooks Brothers suit and a twelve-hour stubble—gave Harrigan a hard stare.

A portrait of Eisenhower peered over the shoulder of Harrigan's former colleague/new boss, as if Ike were curious to hear Harrigan's thoughts, while an American flag stood at attention in the corner. A wall clock with the division seal read just after midnight.

"I say we go straight from Chicago," Harrigan said, "to that photo-op farm in Iowa. Get our boy grinning with his fellow pigs and then put his big ass on his big-ass airplane and ship him back to Siberia or wherever-the-hell."

Larsen thought about that for a moment. "Skip L.A. altogether, you mean."

"Skip it. Why borrow trouble?"

Larsen thought some more; then he slowly shook his head. "Ike won't like it."

Harrigan sat forward, put a hand on the desk. "Fuck Ike," he said, with a sneering nod at the portrait. "Would Ike like some more ugly incidents? Maybe he'd like a dead premier for supper, and atomic war for dessert?"

"Are you on amphetamines again, Jack?"

Harrigan sighed. "Bill—it's getting hot out there . . . and I'm not talking about the goddamn weather."

"I know . . . I know." Larsen sat and brooded; then he pounded his desk with a fist. "Goddamn that fat little bastard! Why can't he just keep his big mouth shut? Doesn't he know anything about diplomacy? Can't he just sit back and look at the scenery and shut the hell up?"

Harrigan sighed, shrugged, nodded. "Even his own people can't control him. He's like Al Capone or something."

"Al Capone we could put in jail—this jerk we have to wine and dine." Larsen let out a weary blast of air. "Maybe the president could broadcast an appeal. . . ."

"For what?"

"Patience on the public's part. To cut the guy some slack, the way you do some hick from the country who shows up at the family reunion with the manners of a billy goat."

Harrigan smirked. "And how does that work, exactly? You think Nikita's people won't tell him what the prez is saying about him in the press?"

"Ike could simply imply that—"

"That the public should just ignore the commie dung being flung their way?"

A small shrug. "It could work."

"Yeah, and if we all believe, really *really* believe, maybe

Tinkerbelle won't fucking die." Harrigan shifted in the chair. "Anyway, that's not the real issue here, Bill. We have the most volatile man in the world heading into the most volatile city in the world. . . . And I'm not getting the support I need from the mayor."

Larsen's eyes tightened as he sat forward. "What do you mean?"

"You know how many men Poulson's giving me? How about a hundred?"

Larsen's eyes ping-pong-balled. "Jesus Christ! We had *three thousand* agents in Washington—*two thousand* in New York!" The division chief leaned back in his chair, looking like he'd been poleaxed. "Why do I think that prick Poulson would just love to have Khrushchev take a bullet on his turf?"

"I don't know. Because he would?"

Larsen stood, leaning forward, hands touching the desktop. "Jack, I'll call Mayor Poulson personally—I'll remind the S.O.B. which side of the bread the politics is buttered on."

"Good. Thank you." For that much, at least.

Larsen was saying, "You'll have more men than a damn *hundred,* or I'll have his honor's head on a stick."

"Either way that goes," Harrigan said with a smile, and shook hands with his old friend, "sounds good to me."

With the meeting over, Harrigan stopped at a water fountain to take a pill; then he spoke to another burning-the-midnight-oil agent in the hallway for a moment, just small talk between co-workers, and was heading down the shining tile corridor of the State Department building, when Larsen suddenly called him back to his office.

"Hey!"

Harrigan walked back and stood before Larsen, who was poised at the doorway.

"I just got word from Central Intelligence," the chief said.

He looked shaken, standing there rigidly. "One of their agents in Formosa is warning of an assassination attempt."

Harrigan's eyes narrowed. "Target K?"

"Target K," Larsen said.

Well, it looked like Khrushchev's speech to the United Nations had reached the ears of Nationalist China.

"That's just great," Harrigan said tersely, "that's just swell—well, hell, why don't I round up every Oriental in the greater Los Angeles area, and call it even!"

Larsen shook his head, ashen. "I'll see that you get that manpower."

"You'd better," Harrigan said. "Or there could be a new man in your chair."

"Maybe, Jack," Larsen said, kidding on the square. "But it sure as hell won't be you. . . . Anything else I can do for you?"

"Sure, Bill."

"Name it."

"Pray."

The Air Force 707, bearing Khrushchev and his entourage, rolled to a smooth stop in front of the hangar, and polished metal glistened in the California sunlight. Immediately, the ground crew pushed the heavy aluminum staircase-on-wheels to its door, which after another few minutes opened slowly, with theatrical melodrama.

First down the steps were three of Harrigan's men from the State Department Security Division; on their heels were four of Khrushchev's personal *Okhrana* guards, elite uniformed members of the KGB, the Russian spy agency. Then came the premier himself, wearing a lightweight tan suit; he was smiling, waving his homburg hat, apparently in a good mood. *Thank God for small favors,* Harrigan thought.

Close behind him was plump, pleasant Mrs. Nina

Khrushchev, attired in a simple navy dress, being helped down the steps by her twenty-four-year-old blond, blue-eyed son, Sergei. An older son might have been on Nina's other arm, if his plane hadn't been shot down in flames back in World War II by the Germans.

Next were Khrushchev's two daughters, Rada and Julia, both in their early thirties, one blonde, the other brunette, fetchingly framed in the jetliner's exit doorway, debunking any notion that Russian women were strictly shotputting babushkaed beasts at the Olympics. The two sisters were downright pretty, Harrigan thought.

Finally, bringing up the rear, were the bureaucrats and intellectuals, the entourage Khrushchev insisted he have with him: Foreign Minister Andrei Gromyko, Ambassador Mikhail Menshikov, Atomic Energy executive Vasily Emelyanov, Minister of Education Vyacheslav Elyutin, and, among others, the editor of *Pravda*, Pavel Satyukov.

The mayor of Los Angeles, Norris Poulson—a beefy bucket-headed character with dark hair and dark-rimmed glasses, his black suit a perfect choice, if he'd been attending a funeral—stepped forward to greet Khrushchev.

"We welcome you to Los Angeles, the City of Angels," Poulson said, with all the enthusiasm of a white Southern sheriff meeting his daughter's colored boyfriend, "where our city motto is that the impossible always happens."

Well, Harrigan thought, that was easily the dumbest goddamn city motto he'd ever heard.

Everyone waited for the mayor to continue—some minor speech seemed appropriate, some small recognition of this important personage in their presence. But only an embarrassing silence followed.

Khrushchev's smile dropped, his eyes narrowed. Holding a four-page speech in his hands, the premier—who obviously knew damned well he'd been insulted—growled only one line from it, before stuffing it angrily back in his pocket. Oleg Troyanovsky didn't bother to translate.

Harrigan clenched his teeth and cursed the mayor under his breath; it was clear Poulson had intentionally snubbed Khrushchev, who was now moving briskly, angrily, past the small crowd of stunned well-wishers.

One of the crowd—a dark young man in a short-sleeved white shirt and denim tie—called out in Russian to Khrushchev, stopping the premier in his tracks. The young man appeared to be of European stock, with just a tinge of Asian in the eyes—or was that Harrigan's imagination running wild, in light of the Formosa threat?

The agent tensed as he moved quickly between the two, prepared for anything, his coat unbuttoned to give easy access to his shoulder-holstered .38. But Khrushchev only smiled back at the young man, providing a wordless non-response to whatever it was the youth had said.

Harrigan would have to ask the translator later. Right now, however, the urgency of the moment was to get the premier and his entourage safely into those waiting, bullet-proof limousines.

As the caravan of cars slowly drew away, Harrigan—in the limo directly behind Khrushchev—looked back at the hangar, where the press and the small crowd were drifting in this direction or that one, dispersing . . .

. . . except for the young man in the white shirt, who intently watched them go, eyes unblinking, smile frozen.

Harrigan filed the face in his mental cabinet and settled back in the seat, hoping to Christ that Mayor Norris Poulson was wrong about Los Angeles.

That it wasn't the city where the impossible happened.

The goddamn possible was bad enough.

Chapter Three

POETIC JUSTICE

The notion to kill Khrushchev hadn't come slowly; it arrived to him in one swift instant—not a thought, but an impulse, a need, a duty. . . .

In America he was called Jonas Veres—Veres Jonas in his native land (Hungarians used their last names first)—though he was not yet accustomed to it, slow at assimilating, a reluctant exile. It was difficult to realize he had been in the United States for almost three years already, coming here following the revolution in Hungary in 1956.

Before the bloodbath, Jonas had been a student at the university in Budapest, where he would often pass time at the Writer's Union, and dabble in poetry. . . . But his major passion was history.

Through history he learned the tortured but fascinating facts about his country's convoluted past—a past riddled with foreign invasion and suppression, first by the Asian warlord Attila the Hun, then the Romans, Turks, Austrians, Germans, and now . . . the latest in a seemingly endless chain of invaders . . . the Russians. A joke that circulated the campus among the students was: *What time is it . . . and who's ruling us now?*

Perhaps it was inherent in the temperament of the Hungarian people—peaceful and happy—that they seemed so susceptible to conquest. Or maybe it was their willingness to make the best of a bad situation, a positive attitude that had a negative result by keeping them from attaining the freedom they so longed for.

Those days were over. The "gentle" people had had enough of rape and pillage. And of course invaders always seemed to forget that when they rape the women of a victim nation, they sow their warrior's seed into the blood of the conquered people.

Jonas had been only eight years of age when Hitler was defeated by the Russian Army in the spring of 1945; with this victory, there was great hope among the people of Hungary—hope that they would regain their land, so brutally taken in the war, and at long last be able to govern themselves.

But Stalin crushed that hope—along with any resistance to the new communist regime he had installed—and the Russians ruled with a force that made the Hungarians practically long for the vanquished Germans. The irony was not lost on a college-age student of history like Jonas: the liberators of the Hungarian people had suddenly became their captors.

Almost overnight, street signs came down and old accepted names changed to new strange Russian ones; and, too, Soviet emblems quickly replaced Hungarian ones, shattering any sense of place, shredding national pride, even as schools began teaching the Russian language, twisting the Hungarian tongue in yet another unmerciful torture. Farmers lost their land, merchants their shops, and the workers any rights, as Russia moved like a hungry beast over the picturesque land, devouring everything in sight, a greedy monster spouting (between bites) nonsense about the "good of the people," destroying a nation's heritage in the name of collectivization and Soviet domination.

Bad led to worse: next came the witch-hunts and executions by the Russian Secret Police—the dreaded NKVD—of any "criminal" (real or imagined) who dared to criticize the new Russian government. Was it any wonder the people all but prayed for World War III to break out? If only the Americans would defeat the Russians, perhaps Hungary could again rise from the ashes . . .

Then two things happened to bring back a glimmer of hope: Stalin died, and neighboring Poland revolted.

Jonas, like all Hungarians, watched in awe as the crisis between the Polish citizens and Moscow—with Nikita Khrushchev now at the helm—boiled to a head. The result was astonishing: Khrushchev agreed that Russia's satellite country could "choose its own path toward socialism," and did not send in his troops!

A bolstered Hungary took this cue, and on October 23, 1956, staged its own revolt, in the belief—the hope—that they too might win such concessions.

The riot had ignited like spontaneous combustion, thanks to impassioned students like Jonas, and what had started on campus quickly spread throughout the country—writers, artists, teachers, laborers, merchants, peasants, even children, all picked up arms supplied to them by the Hungarian Army, who sided with the populace in the effort to drive the Russian government out. NKVD agents were shot on sight, and the few Russian tanks that did dare enter the cities received Molotov-cocktail welcome parties.

And now it was the Russian street signs that came down, the Soviet emblems defaced, while statues of Stalin were toppled and spat upon and sledgehammered and even riddled with bullets. But the fervent patriotism—incited by Jonas and his fellow student rebels—had a righteousness that did not lose its high ground: there was no looting of broken store windows—even the professional thieves abstained.

And after three intense, frenzied days of fighting,

Hungary was rid of the communists. Elated, the people of the often-invaded land—for the first time in hundreds of years—went to sleep that night a free country.

Jonas woke the following morning in bed next to his girlfriend, Eva. She too was a budding poet, her father a cobbler, much as his had been a baker; a year younger than him, a slender fair-haired blue-eyed beauty, Eva seemed nearly waif-like in comparison to the norm of Slavic zaftig farm girls. And for all his artistic and scholarly leanings, Jonas had something of the warrior in his blood—the Hun in his ancestry could be seen in an angular face Eva insisted had a pleasing "exotic" quality.

"The Magyar in you," she had reminded him that wonderful night, "it shows."

"Don't speak foolishness," he laughed.

"They were fierce tribesman, you know. A thousand years ago they made a kingdom, here. Maybe you will be a poet king. Maybe you will help forge freedom. So few poets can make history. . . ."

Such talk came only after many cups of their nation's sweet, delicious wine. Of course students shouldn't have been drinking in the dormitory, a violation of university policy. . . .

As was spending the night together, which was an infraction that could have had both students expelled; but this was the new Hungary, and many such rules fell by the wayside that glorious night, including their previous precautionary use of birth control. With the promise of freedom, it suddenly seemed all right now to risk bringing another life into this better world.

As morning sunlight streamed in through the slatted windows of the tiny dorm room, Jonas was enjoying the warmth of Eva's nude body, running his hands along her slender curves, mentally composing a poem to her charms as he drifted in and out of consciousness. Her long brown hair smelled of smoke from last night's bonfire; but the acrid scent was perfume to him, a pleasing reminder of how the students had made a pile of communist books and propaganda pamphlets they'd ransacked from the Party's bookshop, and hauled into the street, and set aflame.

Suddenly the door to the dorm room burst open.

"Jonas!"

Pluck, a younger classman—his pale, smiling face dominated by wild eyes so brown they were almost black—was standing in the doorway. The boy was wearing a Soviet Secret Police hat with the emblem torn off, his brown hair sticking out from underneath it like straw.

"Our resolutions are written!" Pluck blurted. "We're taking them to Parliament. . . ." Then he noticed Eva, who was hastily pulling a sheet up over her head, due to his unexpected entrance, and the boy shyly added, "Oh . . . hi, Eva."

Eva giggled, muffled from beneath the sheet. She drew the bedding back, just enough to reveal her face. "Good morning, Pluck," she said with a smile.

The happiness in the room—unaided by wine, merely a heady mixture of elation and youth—was as clear and obvious as the sunshine lancing through the shutters.

Jonas leaned on an elbow. "When are we marching?"

"Right now, you silly goose! Hurry up!"

And Pluck shut the door.

"Such language," Jonas said, and burrowed under the blankets, cupping one of Eva's firm, round breasts. "Maybe they could do without us today. . . ."

Her blue eyes held his, her full lips made a kiss that was also a smirk. "Do without the poet king? Stuff and nonsense."

"I'm no king, my sweet. Just another student."

"And think of what we students have done. . . . Don't you even want to know what the student delegation has come up with?" And rather formally, she removed his hand from her small, perfect breast, then gave him a playful smile. "There will be plenty of time for . . . poetry . . . later."

On Rakoezi Avenue in front of the dormitory building, Jonas bent over and picked up a leaflet dropped by one of the students. Eva, buttoning her dark wool coat against the cold morning wind, leaned against him, peering at the paper.

"Multi-party democracy. . . . ." Jonas was reading. "Freedom of worship, press, and opinions . . . public ownership of industry . . . return of the land to the peasants. . . ."

"This too is poetry," Eva said. "What about neutrality?"

Jonas scanned the paper. ". . . Hungary non-aligned with any other country."

Eva's eyes widened.

They both knew this was a bold step. By demanding neutrality, the Hungarians would be asking even more from Moscow than the Polish had, daring to demand that the door to the West be pushed open wide.

Jonas slipped an arm around her and Eva smiled at him, and he at her. He gave her what began as a peck of a kiss and turned into a long, passionate embrace.

Their lips parted, but their eyes did not. "Let's catch up with the others," Eva whispered, touching his mouth with a fingertip as he tried to kiss her again.

Jubilantly, holding hands, they hurried along the wide street where shopkeepers were already busy cleaning up debris and repairing broken windows. His father in Szeged would be doing the same, as would hers in Miskolc. Here and there lay remnants from the recent battle: a burnt-out Russian tank, sprawled like a dead beetle, an overturned Army truck, its broken headlight eyes looking stunned; in the middle of an intersection stood a life-size statue of Stalin, its arms outstretched as if directing traffic, but its head knocked off, at its feet.

At this, they looked at each other and laughed.

Just past Republic Square, they caught sight of the student delegation—nearly one hundred in all—approaching the steps of the Parliament Building, where a de facto government had hurriedly been put into place.

He and Eva were walking arm-in-arm, with a bounce in their step, when they first heard the brittle mechanical sound, shattering the peaceful morning, and it took several seconds before Jonas recognized it as machine gun fire.

The crowd of students—at first confused, then yelling and even screaming—tried to scatter, but were cut down by Russian soldiers materializing from all around them like uniformed ghosts. The hand-held machine guns made a terrible drumming, and the students marched to it, the air misted red with blood, the cobblestones streaming with it, crimson battle ribbons of dying surrender.

Within seconds, they were all dead—*all of them*—many still clutching the white resolution papers, now speckled and spattered with red.

Half a block away, Jonas and Eva froze in their tracks—they did not seek cover . . . they were not in the path of the invaders; like Stalin's headless statue, they stood there, stunned and horrified, witnessing the massacre like some abstract theater piece, a grotesque ballet of blood.

But this was nothing abstract—not when their friends were dying. Eva gripped his arm and turned away when a boy fleeing toward them turned out to be Pluck, his eyes wide not with enthusiasm but terror; then his body was riddled with bullets, flung to street like so much refuse.

The machine guns stopped.

The street was scattered with puppets whose strings had been snipped; the acrid stench of gun smoke floated on the wind, a ghastly echo of last night's bonfire.

Some of the soldiers prowled the perimeter, while others—snouts of their machine guns curling smoke—began climbing, two-at-a-time, the steps of the Parliament building—to assassinate the renegade government inside. Jonas and Eva were taking this in when, over the top of the building, a Soviet MiG fighter came streaking down.

Jonas grabbed Eva's hand, spun her around, and pulled her roughly back down the street.

"Truck!" he said, meaning the overturned truck could provide a barrier from bullets.

He wasn't sure she had heard him, though she kept pace at his side; he could hear the plane bearing down on them. Behind them, bullets chewed up the street and spat up powdered cement, spraying their feet. The bullets were stitching the street at their back as they dove behind the truck, Jonas throwing his body over hers.

"Oh, God . . . Oh, Jesus . . ." he moaned, on top of her, like last night. "Where did the hell did they come from. . . ."

But the body beneath him was so motionless, not even trembling with fear, that he knew. He knew.

He raised himself up enough to look down at Eva, who was on her back, blue eyes staring and empty and, yes, she was dead. Then before he could even sob, much less cry out in anguish, he felt his head explode, or seem to—the butt of a Russian rifle had come down on the back of his skull, to put him temporarily out of his misery, and he lay on her one last time.

When Jonas regained consciousness, he was on his side on a flatbed truck, arms and legs bound, face encrusted with dried blood, like the crisp sugary surface of a pudding. He wasn't alone: the back of the truck was filled with other boys, some of them very young, all of them bruised and bloodied.

Jonas's tongue was so dry he couldn't speak, but a youth next to him, who was similarly bound, answered the question he could not pose.

"They're taking us to Russia," the boy whispered, his eyes large and frightened. "For rehabilitation."

A burly Soviet guard near the cab stirred and moved toward them.

"Shut up down there," the guard snarled in Russian, pointing his rifle threateningly at them. His eyes were as black as Pluck's and as dead as Eva's.

Jonas lay his throbbing head back down and closed his eyes. When he awoke again, it was dark. He was still in the truck, bouncing along a rutted dirt road. He soon realized, due to his position, that he could probably throw himself off the truck—his first thought was to try this, not to escape, but to die. Something else deep inside, burning like some foul food that refused digestion, pushed him instead toward escape and survival; he did not know it yet, but his life had a new engine now—not history, not poetry, not freedom, not Eva . . . revenge.

Slowly, inch by inch, he moved his bound body toward the edge of the flatbed, and when the guard wasn't looking, took a deep breath and rolled off.

A peasant woman found him along the roadside the next day, took him in, and dressed his wounds. After a few days, he set out on foot for Austria. There, the American Embassy helped him—along with hundreds of others like him—get to the United States, where he remained in New York, working at various menial jobs, his childhood baking skills proving helpful. . ..

But with each passing day he became more restless; America was a great country—they had freedom, though they did not seem to appreciate it—and, anyway, it wasn't *his* country. And the language was hard to learn.

He hopped a train, sharing a boxcar with hoboes, fitting in fine, eventually landing in Los Angeles because that was as far as the rails could take him. Then the Holy Cross Mission helped him put down some roots—an apartment, a bakery job—which gave him some semblance of peace. But at twenty-three Jonas could never really see himself finding a wife better than Eva, or raising a family, or even becoming an American citizen. No matter how hard he tried, these universal visions, once precious to him, would never materialize. Something had died with Eva; the only thing still alive in him was that hot coal of revenge, which never went out . . . cold as the rest of him might be, it always glowed hatefully at his core.

No, his notion to kill Khrushchev had not come slowly; it came in one swift instant . . . like the instant it had taken for the MiG bullets to kill Eva. It was a reflex—a doctor's hammer to a patient's knee. When his co-workers in the bakery began to talk of "that fat commie fucker," "that Red bastard," Jonas perked up.

Khrushchev is coming, they said.

All right, then.

Khrushchev is coming . . . Khrushchev will die.

At first, Jonas thought he might have to return to New York to assassinate Khrushchev; he had enough money saved to take a bus—hopping trains would not be necessary, this time. But soon the American press was thoughtful enough to provide the premier's travel schedule, which included a stop in Los Angeles.

How wonderful freedom of the press was!

His parents had been Roman Catholic, but when Jonas went off to the university, he had abandoned the church; like so many students he found notions of existentialism interesting, and considered himself an agnostic.

Now, in America, and for the first time in many years, Jonas went to a Catholic Church and prayed—thanked God for this gift. He did not, however, take confession.

Jonas watched the hearse-like black limousines pull away from in front of the hangar at the airport in Los Angeles. He thrust his hands into the pockets of his flour-soiled chinos, fingering the press-pass card he'd lifted off a *Newsweek* reporter. His fellow reporters had been nice enough to mention among themselves that Khrushchev was going to a luncheon at Fox Studios later, and that a civic dinner would follow at the Ambassador Hotel that evening.

Getting into Fox Studios would be hard—they had a gate, and guards, and everyone knew everybody. But the hotel? That was a public place; so much was unguarded in a free country. The hotel would be easy, with so many guests and restaurant patrons. . . .

Jonas caught a bus at the airport that took him downtown, boarding another one going to West Los Angeles, where he lived on the fifth story of a rundown brick apartment building in which only a few less languages were spoken than at the United Nations.

In his tiny kitchenette, he placed the stolen press badge that read, "John Davis, *Newsweek*" on the table next to a black Kodak camera with silver flash attachment. He opened the camera and inserted a small revolver in its hollowed-out interior. The pistol didn't look very threatening—like a starter's gun at a track meet—but pressed against Khrushchev's temple, it would be up to the noble task.

Then, taking a piece of butcher paper, Jonas printed a note for the authorities to find. He didn't want his adoptive American country to bear the brunt of his actions.

Satisfied, Jonas went into his bedroom where a new brown serge suit, white shirt, diamond-patterned beige tie, and tan hat awaited, spread out like a sartorial feast on the threadbare bedspread. The outfit had taken much of his savings, except for the change in his pocket. But that was all right; after tonight he would have no further need for money.

He'd studied the photos in the recent *Life* magazine of the pressmen covering the dictator's trip . . . of what they wore . . . and newsreels at second-run movie houses and news programs on televisions in store windows . . . of how they acted, these American reporters. He practiced their brash stance and obnoxious smirk in the bathroom mirror, until he thought he'd gotten it right. He was no actor, but he had been in the arts; he was creative.

Jonas pulled out the loose change in his pocket. There was more than enough for him to call a taxi, and arrive at the Ambassador in style.

But that would be later.

He checked his watch.

There was plenty of time for a long, refreshing nap.

And, sunlight creeping in the shuttered windows, Jonas slept better than he had since that night with Eva, who entered his dreams and kissed him and called him a poet and a warrior.

So few poets, after all, can make history.

Chapter Four

A SELF-MADE MAN

Boiling with rage, flesh white as dead skin, Nikita Khrushchev sulked in the back seat of the limousine, seated between his wife Nina and translator Oleg Troyanovsky, as if they were indulgent parents on either side of their fat little boy, a spoiled brat denied a toy. The perpetually pleasant Nina remained placid, despite the rude treatment the Russian entourage had just endured at their arrival in Los Angeles; Oleg, who had a cynical streak, accepted this fate with typically cool detachment.

The sleek, black Lincoln sedan transporting the Khrushchevs and their translator—followed by four other limousines—traveled swiftly out of the airport, heading into the city and a luncheon that had been scheduled at some motion-picture facility. Nikita had prepared a gracious, amiable speech that he'd intended to grant the crowd that would greet him when he came off the Air Force plane. . . . He would have told these citizens how happy he was to be in Los Angeles, and the positive things he hoped to accomplish in their sunny city. He was going to say—quite cleverly, Nikita thought, a peasant delighted by his own poetry—that the city's smog was like the cold war: both must be abolished if the two countries were to continue breathing. . . .

But then that *vyesh brakovanaya* Mayor Poulson had insulted Khrushchev—the premier of Russia!—by dismissing him with a paltry, one-sentence introduction. This was a slap in the face, missed by no one—not a personal affront, no—this was not a matter of Nikita's ego being bruised; rather, a display of public disrespect to Russia itself.

With some satisfaction, Nikita had noted the embarrassment on the faces of the American dignitaries, and of that fellow Harrigan, the agent in charge of protecting the premier and his family. The State Department man's eyes had tightened and so had his hands, clenching as if he wanted to punch the mayor right in the *zhiloudak*.

Now the sedan sped along streets in the bright California sunlight, which shimmered on the leaves of palm trees and other exotic plants, winking off the windows of tidy little houses; it seemed an automobile sat in every driveway, and toys no child in Russia could ever afford lay discarded on sidewalks and in yards, like so much trash. Not one iota of this decadence escaped Nikita's view, though even Nina and Oleg might never have guessed just how much his peripheral vision was reporting to him, as Nikita remained motionless as he rode, a statue of himself, seemingly staring straight ahead.

As he had on the entire American trip, Nikita steadfastly refused to acknowledge the abundance of riches around him. To do so would be to admit that Russians didn't have such material things, and—though the Russian people were of course above such degenerate consumerism—this could be taken as a sign of weakness.

Besides, Nikita Khrushchev was not a stupid man—he was no fool. He knew very well that this was all just a show that the Americans had put on, along pre-selected routes, carefully orchestrated to impress and deceive him; no country on earth was really so wealthy.

Unfortunately, his two daughters and son—sitting opposite him in the limo—were leaning forward with bright eyes, children at the circus, pointing at the sights, whispering excitedly, all but drooling on the car's bullet-proof windows. Nikita shot Sergei a stern, reproachful look, and the young man glanced meaningfully at first Rada, then Julia, and all three then sat back, hands folded in their laps. Good children all (and though they were in their twenties and thirties, they were to him children), the trio followed their father's example.

Nikita sat staring forward—and yet missed nothing, out of the corners of his eyes . . . like the strange sight of a little girl rotating a plastic hoop around her waist. Of this he made a mental note; the toy looked affordable, although why any child—American or Russian—would want such an object he could not fathom.

More than anything, the premier was painfully aware of the absence of any crowds along their route. Poulson must have banished the well-wishers inside, Nikita felt certain, no doubt under threat of being shot should they show the visitors any hospitality whatsoever. Or was it that even a string of shiny limousines zipping through the streets could not attract any attention here—not in this city of decadence, where a gross indulgence like a limousine was apparently a common sight.

For the most part, Nikita had felt buoyed by the welcome the Russian party had encountered previously on the American trip—the crowds had been numerous and receptive, some even cheering. People were people, after all—the press insisted on referring to the Russians as "communists" but Nikita did not look at Americans and think of them as "capitalists." He saw people, only people, of flesh and blood, of hopes and dreams, weak and strong, kind and . . . sometimes . . . unkind. As the Russian saying went, no apple was safe from worms, like the maggots in Chicago with their signs condemning him for his action in Hungary.

★ ★ ★ ★ ★

The invasion of that satellite country—a necessary but unfortunate foray to crush the counter-revolution—was not his decision alone, and had caused Nikita great anguish.

When word reached him in Moscow that the Hungarian Communist Party had fallen in Budapest at the hands of the students and intelligentsia, Nikita's first reaction had been not to meddle, but to monitor the crisis . . . he hoped to follow a similar tactic to the one he had taken, the year before, with Poland. Nikita believed that the cream—that is, the communist party—had a way of always rising to the top.

And if truth be told—although telling such a truth would have been political suicide—the premier could certainly understand how the Hungarians could be gripped by unrest and unhappiness, subjected as they'd been for years to the harsh rule of Stalin, and that foul henchman of his, Rakosi.

But why hadn't they simply re-organized themselves—peacefully—as had their Polish brothers? Instead, communist party members were made examples of, brutally murdered, and strung up in the vandalized town square, and then outrageous demands had been made—not just freedom, but neutrality!—which had made it impossible for Moscow to look the other way.

In handling the crisis, Nikita fell back on a tactic he had learned long ago—a tactic that had saved his life more than once . . . like the time Stalin had sent for him in February of 1939. . . .

To be summoned in the middle of the night to the dictator's dacha just outside the capital—which the insulated Stalin rarely left—could mean many things, most of them bad, many involving death, often the death of the one summoned. The young Khrushchev, then First Secretary of Moscow City, had survived more of these invitations than just about anyone in the Party . . . but with each new summons, Nikita's odds worsened.

Without so much as a greeting, the burly, big-headed head of the Communist party came directly to the point. In his bedclothes, his eyes wilder than usual, thick black hair unkempt, massive mustache in need of a trim, Stalin had the look of a madman. This was largely because, as Nikita well knew, the dictator was indeed mad.

"Comrade," Stalin said, with an intensity worthy of reporting the infidelity of his mate, "someone is poisoning the horses in the Ukraine."

"Oh?" was all Nikita said. With Stalin it was always better to listen than to be heard. To be heard was to have an opinion, and to have an opinion was to risk much too much.

Pacing, Stalin flailed his arms like a drowning man. "All over the countryside, the peasants are reporting their horses falling like dead flies."

"I see."

Clearly vexed, Stalin asked, "Do you know what this means to our country? The dire ramifications?"

Nikita did. Horses were needed not only for farming, but for the military, as this was before American trucks had arrived.

Stalin's eyes narrowed and he leaned close to the smaller, younger man. "An enemy is under my nose."

Nikita nodded thoughtfully, twitched his own nose, but said nothing.

Now Stalin paced again, shouting, "It is an enemy of the people doing this!" He pointed a thick finger right at Nikita.

But Nikita—his mind filling with images of his wife, his children—merely waited.

Stalin continued: "I want them found, and I want them punished!"

"All right then," Nikita said calmly.

Folding his arms, apparently reassured by his trusted associate's composed reaction, Stalin said, "I have already had a professor at the Kharkov Veterinary Institute look into this matter. Nothing! Then I enlisted the minister of the Institute of Animal Husbandry—he too failed miserably."

"Just the same," Nikita responded, with a small shrug, "I would like to speak with them . . . before I conduct my own investigation. They may have insights."

Stalin shook his head dismissively. "Impossible," he said. He threw his nose in the air and snorted—one of his favorite mannerisms. "They've been shot."

Nikita somehow managed to conceal his horror, asking casually, "But why?"

"Because it turned out they were involved in the poisoning conspiracy—you can read their confessions to the NKVD, if you like."

"Ah," Nikita said, nodding, understanding. If someone couldn't solve a problem for Stalin, they conveniently became part of said problem. And the secret police could convert God to the Devil, and vice versa.

"You will put a stop to these poisonings?" Stalin had posed this as a question, but clearly it was an order.

"I will do my best," Nikita responded with a curt nod, and as much confidence as he could muster; but all the while wondering how he could do any better than the minister of Animal Husbandry.

"My good friend," Stalin said with a smile that would have curdled milk, "I knew I could count on you," and the dictator placed a fatherly hand on Nikita's shoulder—the same hand that would sign his death warrant, should Khrushchev fail this mission.

Before leaving for the Ukraine, Nikita called upon the president of the Academy of Sciences, and with his help put together not one, but two teams of top Soviet scientists to study the problem of the dying horses, theorizing that, should this brain trust also fail, Stalin surely wouldn't have them *all* shot.

Would he?

After months of careful study, both teams—operating separately—came to an identical conclusion: the horses were dying from ingesting a fungus that grew in wet hay.

When Nikita presented his findings to Stalin, the dictator's eyebrows first grew together in a frown, then shot up with surprise.

"Really?" the dictator commented. "Wet hay?"

"Yes, Comrade Stalin," Nikita replied, with cool confidence that masked terror. He knew that his contradiction of the dictator's theory of an enemy "poisoning conspiracy" was perilous.

Stalin thought about this for endless moments; finally he shrugged. "Well, then—there must be no more wet hay. . . . You will see to it?"

Again a curt nod for his dictator. "I will see to it, Comrade."

Nikita was dismissed.

There was no mention by Stalin (and certainly not by Khrushchev!) of the poor professor from Kharkov Veterinary Institute or the minister of Animal Husbandry . . . or a number of others involved in the nonexistent conspiracy, about whom Nikita learned later . . . all of whom, prior to Nikita solving the mystery of the horse sickness, had been eliminated as "enemies of the people."

This strategy—obtaining a consensus before making a decision—Nikita had also brought to the unpleasantness in Hungary, flying to neighboring Czechoslovakia and Rumania, then on to Yugoslavia. To do this in the necessary timely manner, he had braved a fierce thunderstorm, his life spared only by the wit of the pilot—their reconnaissance plane had not been so lucky.

Surprisingly, the leaders of the satellite countries unanimously felt Soviet troops should be sent in to restore order in Hungary—as did the entire Presidium of the Central Committee in Moscow, to whom Nikita had returned with his report.

But before sealing Hungary's fate—and to cover his backside—Nikita sought one final opinion . . . from Chinese leader Mao Tse-tung, chairman of the world's second most powerful communist party, and Russia's chief ally.

Over a staticky phone line, through an interpreter, Nikita told Mao of the revolt, and asked the chairman for his opinion, his counsel. After a moment, Mao said that whatever decision Nikita made would be a wise one—a typically sly reply.

Shrimp would learn to whistle before Mao Tse-tung said what was really on his mind. Nikita was glad he'd sought this "counsel" over the phone, and saved the airplane petrol. In truth, Nikita despised the Chinaman, who was shrewd, not smart, that big balding head home to a small brain, reflected in close-set eyes that told nothing, and a smile as meaningful as a porcelain doll's. But it had taken Nikita a number of years to realize this grinning panda was a treacherous "ally," never to be trusted.

Once, at a meeting between the two leaders, Nikita had proposed, "With all the trade going on between us, it would be helpful to have a road to China through Kazakhstan."

Mao's tiny eyes had brightened; he seemed immediately taken with the notion. And the chairman announced, "Then I will allow you to build it!"

"Now, just one moment," Nikita responded. He pointed out to the chairman that China's border was rugged; creating such a road would mean cutting through mountains and building bridges. "We couldn't possibly afford that, alone," he said. "No, my friend—we should each take care of our own side of the road."

"All right then," Mao agreed cheerfully.

So the Russians had begun their share of the work. But well into the extensive construction, Mao again requested that the Russians build the Chinese span of the road, and Nikita reminded him of their original agreement.

"All right then," Mao agreed. Cheerfully.

And when the Russians finally reached the border of China, they found no road under construction, no builders, nothing even in the planning stages; now Kazakhstan had a lovely new road—leading to nowhere.

Nikita especially hated Mao's stupid slogans. The panda kept trying to foist these idiotic aphorisms on the entire communist party, using the press to publicize the likes of "Imperialism Is a Paper Tiger." Hardly! Only a fool would think such a thing. Capitalism was, if nothing else, a deadly predator—the only thing "paper" about it was their money.

More recently Mao had set the Chinese to chanting, "Let a hundred flowers bloom!" What in hell did that mean? Perhaps this held significance to the Chinese, but not to any Russian. If it meant—as Nikita guessed—to encourage new and different ideas, to allow art and culture to "flower" in their own way . . . well, what sort of dangerous nonsense was that, for a true communist to spout?

Soon, however, it became clear that Nikita's interpretation was exactly what Mao's slogan meant; but its sinister purpose was not to *allow* tolerance in new thinking, rather to draw out these "different" flowers . . . the better for Mao to cut down, and trample in the dirt.

Clever, Nikita would have to admit; but how could he trust so ruthless a man? Hadn't one Stalin been enough for one lifetime?

In recent years, the fissure between the two communist leaders had widened to a chasm. Intelligence indicated the Chinese dictator was furious about Khrushchev's conciliatory trip to the United States; and Nikita in turn was becoming increasingly aggravated by Mao's incessant pestering for the plans to the A-bomb.

Even the thought of it—China with the bomb! Mao with a button to put his pudgy finger on! *Ahstahrohzhnuh!* Comrades or not, the notion chilled Nikita. If he were ever foolish enough to comply with Mao's request, it would be like the old Russian saying: "The fox kissed the hen—right down to her tail-feathers."

When Nikita warned Mao of the responsibility of having such a weapon, and the retaliatory destruction waging such a war would bring, the Chinaman had only laughed.

"Even so," the panda had said, "there would still be three hundred million Chinese left!"

A more dangerous man, Nikita had never met—Stalin included.

Rather than this deadly ally, the premier would far rather deal with his enemy, Eisenhower, any day of any year. The colorless American president, at least, said exactly what was on his mind—that is, once something had been placed there by that pompous bastard John Foster Dulles, who was always passing the president schoolgirl notes and whispering in his ear.

Last week, in Washington, Eisenhower had seemed tired to Nikita—almost ill of health; perhaps that was why the president hadn't accompanied the premier on the cross-country tour. Whereas the war with Hitler had strengthened Nikita, it appeared to have taken a toll on the former warrior, "Ike." Russian intelligence—not always reliable, but worth considering—had passed along information of a serious heart condition, which now appeared to be true.

If so, a healthy Nikita might be able to take advantage of a weakened Eisenhower at week's end, when they were to meet at the fabled Camp David. No Russian had ever been invited to this "camp" before, and it struck the premier as a strange custom for world leaders to indulge in . . . maybe it was this American pioneer heritage they trumpeted so—Davy Crockett, Daniel Boone. Should they have brought their own sleeping cots, he wondered?

Nonetheless, despite their opposing positions, Nikita sensed the president was a genuine, decent man. At the close of World War II, as Berlin had been about to fall, the Americans—under the orders of General Eisenhower—halted their offensive, allowing the Russians to step forward and take the city. This was in recognition of the rivers of Soviet blood spilled at the hands of the Germans.

This show of generosity Nikita would never forget. Nor could he be sure he would have done so magnanimous a thing for the Americans, had their roles been reversed. And it gnawed at the back of Nikita's brain, this incongruity—that these selfish decadent Americans could be possessed of such a large heart.

The limousine bearing Nikita and his family cruised along through a commercial section, where some storefronts looked shabby (even the Americans couldn't hide everything) and pedestrians—women in cotton dresses and men in lightweight suits—occasionally glanced at the passing sedan, their faces perking expectantly.

"They think we must be movie stars," Sergei said to his father with a little smile.

"And when they find we are not," Nikita said, "you see their disappointment?"

Nikita folded his arms and snorted. Even if they were too ignorant to recognize the most powerful leader of the world—their precious "Ike" had fallen to second place behind him, since the launching of Sputnik, and recent rocket to the moon—the premier certainly must have looked like someone important in his expensive, tailored clothes (the best his government could buy from the Western world, for this trip—no Moscow haberdasher could have managed them).

A self-made man, born poor in Kalinovka, Nikita took care not to repeat a naive blunder he'd made six years ago when he attended the Geneva Summit—the first time he met with the leaders of the so-called "free" world: the United States, England, and France.

While the head men of the other three world powers each arrived in impressive new four-engine planes, he putt-putted in, in a beat-up two-engine Ilyushin, making himself look like the peasant he at heart still was—and putting the Russian contingent at an immediate psychological disadvantage.

When Nikita and then-Prime Minister Nikolai Bulganin disembarked in their saggy, baggy summer cotton suits—Bulganin looking like a Model-T motorist in his long coat and goggles—and on the tarmac joined Eisenhower, Eden, and Faure (in their impeccable, expensive, tailored woolen suits), Nikita had felt a shame of station that he had never before experienced. He could see the veiled contempt in the eyes of the other world leaders—except perhaps the kind-visaged Eisenhower—and could almost read their minds:

"Why should serious sophisticated men like ourselves pay any attention to such clownish country bumpkins?"

In his political life, Nikita had made his share of mistakes; but he never made the same one twice.

The limousine had been stopped at a red light and was beginning to slide on through the intersection when a tremendous *thump* shook Nikita's side of the vehicle. Startled, everyone in the back of the sedan jumped, as a man—*where had he come from?*—threw himself against the car, plastering his face against the rear window, a dirty, hawkish countenance, long-haired, bearded, an American echo of the insane Rasputin, pressing and distorting his features against the thick glass, smearing it with saliva, banging on it with grimy hands, his shouts muffled.

Nikita, leaning protectively over his wife, was jolted again as the sedan screeched to a stop.

Within seconds, the State Department man, Harrigan—having leapt from the car following them—wrestled the man quickly to the pavement. And within a few more seconds, the limo windows revealed that Nikita and his family were surrounded by more security men, both American Secret Service and the premier's own uniformed KGB agents.

With the danger now past, Nikita ascertained that his family members had not been injured by the sudden stop; then he peered out the vehicle's window at the beggar-like man in tattered clothes, who was being dragged away by two of the plainclothes agents at Harrigan's direction.

The State Department agent opened the back door of the limousine and poked his head inside.

"Everyone all right?" Harrigan asked. His voice sounded calm, but Nikita could see excitement dancing in the man's hazel eyes.

Oleg Troyanovsky translated.

Everyone nodded numbly.

"That was just an indigent," Harrigan explained with a shrug that did not entirely conceal his chagrin. "You know, a poor homeless wretch. California has more than its share, because of the warm weather."

Troyanovsky reported what the agent had said.

Surprised and pleased by the agent's candor, Nikita grunted and spoke to the translator, and Troyanovsky turned to Harrigan.

"The premier said we have the homeless too . . . only in Moscow they freeze."

Nikita watched closely for the agent's reaction. He wanted to know if the man understood Russian humor.

And perhaps he did: Nikita thought he caught a tiny smile . . . or was that just a twitch?

Nikita again spoke to his personal translator.

"Mr. Khrushchev," Oleg said, "saw something very interesting in Washington last week. . . . Men running alongside President Eisenhower's limousine."

There was a pause as Harrigan considered this, the eyes widening, the excitement gone now.

"Yes," Harrigan said, with a nod. "The Secret Service does that to provide the president with extra protection."

This was translated for Nikita, who replied (and Oleg conveyed this to Harrigan): "Would this extra protection be, for example, to keep a homeless man from assaulting the president's rear window? Upsetting the president's family, perhaps?"

Harrigan paused again—and he smiled . . . that tiny smile again, lingering past the twitch stage into unmistakable if gentle amusement.

The agent asked, "Would the premier feel more comfortable if we did that?"

Oleg spoke to Nikita.

Nikita nodded.

"Tell the premier it will be our pleasure," Harrigan said, and backed out of the sedan and closed the door. As the agent began to organize the other plainclothes security around the car, Oleg rolled down the window.

"Please use some of our own men, as well, Mr. Harrigan," Oleg called out. "Mr. Khrushchev thinks they are getting too fat on your rich American food."

Harrigan chuckled, and grinned; he nodded to Khrushchev, who smiled and nodded back.

Soon—as the procession of limousines, surrounded by trotting American and Russian agents, moved slowly on toward the movie studio—the sidewalks began to fill up with people. They ran out of the shops and houses, to point and gawk. A V.I.P. was passing!

Nikita settled back with a self-satisfied smile, and Nina—who knew him so well—beamed at him, eyes twinkling.

The premier of Russia didn't need that son of a bitch Poulson to draw a crowd!

Chapter Five

THE WRONG ROOM

As Marilyn Monroe's limousine whipped into the parking lot of the commissary at Fox Studios, the movie star's eyes widened in shock and her mouth dropped in dismay—her mood, anxious though positive, seemed suddenly poised to plunge into despair.

The lot—but for a handful of cars, expensive ones in personalized spaces, sunshine ricocheting off their smooth metallic surfaces—was empty. Tumbleweed might have blown through.

"Oh, damnit," Marilyn moaned. "After all that effort—we're late! The party's over." She could just cry! When would she ever learn? Why had she taken so long to get ready?

But her unflappable secretary, May Reis—seated next to her, like a plainclothes cop extraditing a prisoner—was, as usual, cool; cucumbers had nothing on her. The trim, brown-haired woman shook her head and patted Marilyn's knee. "No, no my dear—we're early."

Marilyn's eyes tightened in thought, as if this word—"early"—was foreign to her.

May continued, with a gesture to the empty lot: "The others simply haven't arrived yet."

Marilyn's eyes popped open again, as she regarded her secretary with astonishment. "Well, what do you know about that! I *am* on time." She grinned and gave May a gentle elbow. "When has that ever happened before?"

May smiled tightly. "Never, dear."

Marilyn's longtime Los Angeles chauffeur, Rudy Kautzsky—looking jaunty in his black suit and cap, as perfect for his part as if Central Casting had sent him 'round—helped the glamorous star out of the back of the limousine, wishing her luck by way of a wink and "thumbs up."

"Thanks," she said, and kissed the air in Rudy's direction.

Along with the chauffeur, May remained behind in the car. Like an overly cautious mother, she'd only ridden along to make sure that Marilyn made it safely inside the door. The secretary had learned long ago that her employer—whom she adored—was a vulnerable, distracted creature capable of losing her way across a living room. May need not have worried—not today. Marilyn Monroe might have been the current blonde bombshell, but—when she set her mind to it—that bombshell was a veritable guided missile. Today was important to her—flattered by the premier's desire to meet her, Marilyn felt proud she could serve her country as Hollywood's ambassador, and in some small way forge good will between two world powers who seemed on such a terrible collision course.

The big bland room that was the studio commissary—where normally stars, studio bosses, and crew members alike gathered for lunch or coffee at dozens of scuffed round tables—had for today's event been transformed into an elegant Parisian restaurant. No soundstage set could have rivaled the "Cafe de Paris," with its linen tablecloths, sterling flatware, and sparkling crystal. From the ceiling hung hundreds of colorful balloons and streams of crepe paper, and in the center of each table perched a lovely floral arrangement with a French flag—the tricolor justifying the red-white-and-blue theme that pretended to salute one country while invoking another.

A half dozen or so reporters were milling around by the entryway, in a haze of cigarette smoke, waiting for the event to start, when Marilyn approached.

One of the newshounds was saying, ". . . so the one-legged jockey says, 'That's all right, honey—I ride side-saddle!' " He was a tall, thin hawkish-looking man Marilyn had never seen before. She knew most of the others by name.

His cronies howled with laughter until another of them, Bob Clemens, round-faced and beefy, a stub of a stogie tucked in the corner of his mouth, caught sight of Marilyn. The *L.A. Times* reporter nearly swallowed what was left of his cigar, so surprised was he to see her arriving early.

"Hello, boys," she said innocently. She pretended to frown and shook a reprimanding finger. "I hope you aren't telling off-color stories again."

Pandemonium broke out as the men rushed her, flocking around, firing questions. For once she was prepared for the press—even glad to see them; she stood her ground and smiled radiantly, regally.

Clemens elbowed his way to the front of the pack, growling, "Hey, I saw her first!"

Marilyn had known Clemens since he covered her marriage to Joe DiMaggio in 1954, and the reporter had always treated her fairly—even after she'd divorced the baseball hero.

"Bob gets the first question," Marilyn said, with a solemn nod. She was like a teacher with a bunch of unruly boys—though in the sheer black dress, she made an unlikely schoolmarm.

"Marilyn, what's this about Khrushchev wanting to see you?" Clemens asked.

Publicist Rupert Allen must have called ahead, in spite of his misgivings about her attending. The dear man.

Marilyn slowly parted her lips. "I'm deeply honored that the premier of Russia would want to talk to me."

"Not everybody thinks old Nikita's worth meeting," Bob said.

She beamed and shrugged. "Well, I think it's just elegant!"

"What would Khrushchev possibly want to talk to you about?" the hawkish man asked snidely.

Marilyn studied the man's face for a moment, her smile turning brittle; she made a habit of remembering new enemies. "World peace, I hope," she responded.

The enemy snorted a laugh—several reporters around him winced, as they apparently understood what sort of special audience they were being granted—and he did not bother to write down her response.

"And where's your husband?" he followed up, with a smirk. "Didn't *he* want to meet the top commie?"

All eyes were on her, pen tips to pads, primed for her answer. This wasn't just show business, after all, but politics—her husband Arthur Miller was one of America's leading playwrights and had been a victim of what she considered a witch-hunt left over from the days of Joe McCarthy.

"Mr. Miller," she said pleasantly, "couldn't accompany me from New York because he's finishing up a screenplay. . . ." And now she turned the wattage up on her smile. "One that I'll be starring in."

In truth, Arthur could have made the trip, and had wanted to; he was as keenly interested in politics and world events as Marilyn was. But after much soul-searching and deliberation, he had decided—due to his past trouble with the House Un-American Activities Committee, regarding his refusal to name other writers sympathetic to the communist party—he had best not go.

"The press might make a meal of me," he'd said.

And—obviously—Arthur had been right.

Paul Hays, from the *Hollywood Reporter*, asked, "Is there any truth to the rumor that you and your husband are separating?"

"None whatsoever," Marilyn countered with a little laugh that she hoped didn't sound too forced. "The rumors that I'm leaving Arthur for Nikita Khrushchev are just so much *borscht*."

This made the boys laugh—even the hawkish enemy—and distracted them from digging deeper. For all intents and purposes, her marriage of three years to the brilliant playwright was over. She knew it; Arthur knew it. But the Millers had decided to keep up the pretense, through the filming of her next movie—and probably that of the following project, which he really was writing for her. Arthur believed she was ill-served by most of her scripts, and he still loved her enough to want to leave her with that gift, anyway.

Now other movie stars were arriving in through the commissary door, and when the attention of the newshounds turned their way, Marilyn slipped inside while the press swarmed new all-star victims, following them into the "Cafe de Paris," as well.

Bob Hope, natty in a light gray suit, was bantering with his on-screen cohort, Bing Crosby, attired causally in a beige banlon shirt and yellow cardigan, the ever-present pipe in one hand. Several reporters cornered them, and Hope made a loud nasal remark about maybe making *The Road to Moscow* with Bing.

Several other reporters honed in on Marilyn's nemesis, Elizabeth Taylor, those fat, bulgy bosoms of hers popping out of a low-cut emerald-green cocktail dress. Marilyn just knew that those were real emeralds around the munchkin's throat, watching as the woman made her entrance with lapdog Eddie Fisher on her arm, Fisher looking bewildered, nervous, uncomfortable.

Almost at once the press rushed past Taylor and the singer to another woman who had just stepped in through the door: Debbie Reynolds, looking cute as the teenage beauty queen she'd been not so long ago, petite and nicely shapely in a blue and white polka-dot dress.

Marilyn liked—and felt sorry for—the pretty, perky Reynolds, who had just lost her husband to Liz. Debbie had always been friendly to Marilyn, and there was no rivalry between them. Reynolds was no threat.

As the reporters converged on Reynolds, the spurned wife and mother held her head high, smiling, even laughing. If Debbie was acting, Marilyn thought, it was a damn fine job of it—Lee Strasberg would have approved. The press obviously adored Debbie, and were in her corner. And that pleased Marilyn, who hoped they would be as compassionate to her, the next time tragedy struck.

As the commissary began filling up—bobbing with more famous faces than the Hollywood wax museum, and alive with the chatter and laughter of dueling egos—Marilyn managed to catch Frank Sinatra's eye.

In a sharp gray suit, the singer—who had briefly been her lover, after the break-up with Joe—threw Marilyn a dazzling smile, his blue eyes twinkling, obviously happy to see her. She adored him, at least when he was in a good mood; depressed, he was no prize. But she considered him a genius in his way, and knew what kind of pressure he endured, and so cut him all the slack in the world.

The statuesque, flat-chested redhead on his arm, however,

was not happy to see her. Marilyn nodded at Juliet Prowse—who had a part in Frank's current movie, *Can-Can*—and bestowed the dancer her warmest smile. No sense in starting a feud.

Marilyn knew she could have Frankie, any time she wanted him. But even if she could have put up with his mood swings, she couldn't handle his hypocritically old-world view of matrimony. He'd told her that he only wanted a wife who wasn't in show-business . . . someone who would stay at home and take care of him and the kids.

And she had said to him, "Hmmm . . . didn't you already have that once?"

Sinatra hadn't talked to her for two months, after that; such a child. Nobody could pout like Frankie. But, also, nobody could sing like him. . . .

Anyway, for the moment at least, Sinatra served her best via her phonograph.

Relieved to be out of the clutches of the press—she hadn't always felt about them that way, there'd been a time when she longed for such media attention—Marilyn stopped occasionally for a chat with the likes of Judy Garland or Louis Jourdan, as she ambled her way to the front of the room, where a long banquet table was elevated on a small riser, setting itself apart from the tables on the floor.

While she was not to be seated at the head table with Khrushchev, the other dignitaries, and studio bosses, Marilyn had been carefully positioned at the round table nearest the premier.

As the only Hollywood star the premier had wished to meet, Marilyn had been told by Skouras that she would have the "best seat in the house."

"You bet I will," she'd said.

And Skouras had said, "No, no, not that kind of seat"; he had placed her thus, "so the Russian, he can gaze upon your beauty." The rest of the actors and actresses were scattered around, more stars than in any nighttime sky, but out of her immediate orbit. She had insisted that no other screen personalities, particularly female ones, be seated with her; the men at her table were writers and directors, including Walter Lang, whose *Can-Can* set would be visited later by the guests.

Marilyn noticed Henry Fonda, sloppily dressed, seated at a back table, facing the wall, legs spread lazily over the next chair, sullenly listening to a transistor radio, probably a ballgame. She had heard, through the studio grapevine, that Fonda had been required to come—even though he despised Khrushchev; this had surprised Marilyn, at first, since Fonda was openly left-leaning in a time when that was dangerous. She'd admired him for that, and maybe this bad behavior today came from Fonda feeling dictators like Khrushchev gave leftists a bad name.

Even so, Marilyn felt this was short-sighted, even immature. How was America supposed to thaw the cold war with bad manners like that?

After all, Hollywood stars were America's royalty. She believed that; she had aspired since childhood to such a throne. And with that came responsibility . . . from small things like being thoughtful to your fans, to bigger things like taking meaningful political stands, and improving yourself, your mind, your craft.

Marilyn stood quietly by her chair, feeling a tingle from the excitement in the air, drawing on it to sustain her movie-star persona. Five hundred people had been invited to the luncheon, honoring the premier of Russia. In this room were some of the most important, influential people in Hollywood—not just the royalty of stars, but the powers behind the thrones.

Suddenly the crowd hovering about the front door stirred . . . and made a pathway, like God parting the Red Sea (or anyway Cecil B. DeMille) as the most influential, important person in this room trumped all of the show business bigshots.

Nikita Khrushchev had entered.

He was a short, rotund man, bald, except for a silver fringe of hair rimming elf-like pointed ears. Round-faced, with an upturned nose and several chins, his eyes hard black marbles, the dictator seemed peeved, as if he'd been turned down for a job as a department store Santa. He was wearing a tan suit, well-tailored, a cream-colored shirt, silk chocolate-colored tie, and brown wing-tipped shoes.

Flanking Khrushchev, an entourage of perhaps twenty-five formed a protective, moving barrier: bureaucrats, agents from the FBI, CIA, and Russia's own uniformed KGB, and what appeared to Marilyn to be some of the premier's family members.

Finally, trailing behind the entourage came the mayor of Los Angeles—she couldn't recall his name, only that she hadn't voted for him—his lips a thin tight line, like a cut in his face that was refusing to heal. Frowning, Marilyn wondered if perhaps something had gone wrong at the airport, because Khrushchev was scowling back at His Honor, eyebrows knitted together, thick bottom lip protruding like a pouting child's.

Then—across the glittering panorama of jewels, furs, and suntans—Khrushchev spotted something; he froze, and his face exploded into a grin.

And at once she knew that she was the cause of his change of disposition. Standing in front of the dais, shoulders back, breasts out, Marilyn smiled at him with a fondness one might reserve for a favorite uncle. Still grinning, a strangely infectious grin at that, Nikita Khrushchev rolled toward her like a friendly tank.

With chest heaving, lips in her open smile aquiver, Marilyn extended one hand—not like a queen expecting a kiss and a bow, but one person ready to shake hands with another person. He grasped that small smooth hand with both of his, which were rough and callused and big.

A hush fell—no one breathed . . . even Hank Fonda had craned around to look.

In perfect Russian, Marilyn welcomed Nikita Khrushchev to the United States and to Hollywood, saying, "Even a cat and dog can live together in harmony, and our two nations must strive to do so, as well." He had nodded appreciatively when she paused; then she went on: "Meeting you is an honor I will never forget, Premier Khrushchev."

The premier beamed—in part, she would bet, because she had correctly pronounced his last name, Crew-*shove*—and two gold teeth winked at her as that infectious grin again split his face, which to Marilyn was a glorious face, at once homely and beautiful.

Then Khrushchev spoke to her in his native tongue, and Marilyn nodded at what he was saying. But she really didn't know what he was talking about, not exactly.

Oh, she knew some of the words; she and her former speech coach had often spoken the language—Natasha Lytess was famously Russian (even though really a German Jew), and they had been together for many years.

But they had since parted ways, and it was a current friend of Marilyn's, the great director and teacher Michael Chekhov—a student at the Stanislavski Moscow Art Theatre prior to his defection—who had helped her write, and then translated and taught her the little speech she'd just given, which she had practiced for hours on end.

Impulsively—for this part had not been planned—Marilyn leaned forward and kissed Khrushchev on one of his chubby cheeks.

The crowd hooted, and laughed, and burst into applause that rang through the commissary like gunfire.

The premier blushed, his smile disappearing . . .

. . . but Marilyn knew Nikita Khrushchev was pleased by her affectionate gesture. His eyes had twinkled at her, even when the grin was gone. And, anyway, he was a man, wasn't he?

Chair legs screeched as everyone began to take their seats at the tables. Khrushchev was escorted to the center of the long banquet table, placed between Erick Johnston, President of the Motion Pictures Association, and the head of Fox Studios, Marilyn's champion Spyros Skouras.

A quietly affable, heavy-set woman, two attractive girls, and a boy (the spitting image of Khrushchev) had trailed in after the premier; now they were shown seats at the end of the long table.

Marilyn overheard them being introduced as the premier's wife and family to those around them at the head table; from her catbird's seat, Marilyn could hear much of what was said there, even conversationally.

Mrs. Khrushchev, the pleasant-looking peasant-ish woman, reminded the star of her adored, now long gone, Aunt Ana Lower, who had saved Marilyn from the orphan's home and practically raised her.

Marilyn smiled at Mrs. Khrushchev—hoping that kiss she'd bestowed the woman's husband hadn't been a breach of etiquette—and, thankfully, the woman smiled shyly back. After a brief welcome by the mayor of Los Angeles—

Khrushchev again scowling . . . the enmity between the two men obvious—the luncheon was served: chicken Kiev, corn, and red roasted potatoes. Hardly Parisian cuisine—so much for the "Cafe de Paris." But when Marilyn looked up at Khrushchev, he seemed to be heartily enjoying the meal.

Above the clatter and chatter of the crowd at lunch, Marilyn could hear the Greek-born Spyros talking to Khrushchev, telling him—through an interpreter seated on the other side of Spyros—that he, too, had once been a poor shepherd boy, but had risen to great power under capitalism.

Khrushchev trained his bullet eyes on the president of Fox Studios, and spoke tersely in Russian. Said the interpreter to Spyros, "And *I* have risen to great power under communism!"

Marilyn found that a sharp reply, witty even, and she covered her smile with her napkin.

Spyros dropped the conversation.

A few moments slid by, and then an aide of Khrushchev's rushed up behind the premier, and handed him a note.

Careful not to stare, Marilyn nonetheless watched as Khrushchev accepted the piece of paper, put on a pair of wire-framed glasses, and read it. His face turned white, then crimson . . . with obvious fury. He pushed back his chair, nearly toppling it over as he stood, fists balled, body shaking, and he slammed those fists on the table, spilling drinks, making the china jump.

Everybody froze.

Another hush had fallen, but a different one, a deadly one.

Marilyn's gasp caught in her throat. *Something dreadful must have happened!*

As the interpreter translated, Khrushchev addressed those assembled in a quavering but strong voice, making no use of the dais microphone.

"I have come to this town where lives the cream of American art. And just imagine, I, a premier, a Soviet representative. . . ." He paused, shaking his head, his features tightening into a troll mask. "Just now I was told I could not go to Disneyland."

The room remained hushed, and yet a nervous undercurrent wondered: Is the premier joking? Is this Russian humor?

"Your government has said I cannot go," Khrushchev (and his translator) continued. "I ask, Why not? Do you have rocket-launching pads there? I do not know. Is there an epidemic of cholera there or something? Have gangsters taken hold of the place that can destroy me? Then what must I do? Commit suicide? This situation is inconceivable . . . I cannot find words to explain this to my people. . . ."

The premier bent down, removed one of his brown shoes, and, to the astonishment of everyone, proceeded to bang it on the table.

Making a hammer of the shoe, he emphasized each word: *"I . . . want . . . to . . . go . . . to . . . Dis . . . ney . . . land!"*

The room fell deadly silent, the guests looking on with amazement—unsure whether to laugh or cry or run screaming from the room into the nearest bomb shelter.

Studio chief Spyros—his expression consisting of equal parts embarrassment and apprehension—stood, bowing his head in a respectful, dignified manner.

"Mr. Khrushchev," he said solemnly, working hard to minimize his accent, "our first concern is your safety."

Khrushchev scowled.

"And," the studio head continued, placatingly, "the Secret Service could not guarantee that safety at Disneyland. Even your own *KGB* could not guarantee it. . . ."

Khrushchev said nothing.

"Now, we have lovely show for you next door on the sound stage . . . where we have been filming a delightful movie called *Can-Can*. We would please be honored if you would join us."

Ironically, Marilyn had been offered the female lead in the picture, which co-starred Frank Sinatra, who oddly enough she had never worked with; but, in spite of pleas from the Voice, she had turned down the lightweight part. It had gone to Shirley MacLaine—talented girl, but hardly in Marilyn's league.

Spyros Skouras turned to the audience and gestured graciously. "Everyone, please join us on the sound stage, where we will film an actual scene."

Relief flooded the banquet room, which soon began to buzz again, as the guests whispered, some snickering, over the spectacle they'd just witnessed. His shoe back on, Khrushchev, looking weary, was ushered from the head table, along with his entourage, and the crowd started to rise, and file out of the commissary.

Soon the room was empty but for the bus boys and other kitchen staff . . .

. . . and Marilyn, who hadn't moved from her seat.

A sadness cloaked her. She felt sorry for Khrushchev. He was a smart man but his background was unsophisticated, and the culture clash was surely jarring to him; his trip to the United States was just not going very well. The papers had reveled in plastering their front pages with his bellicose blusterings and outright threats. Didn't he know such behavior wouldn't go over with the American people?

But she also understood the man's frustration. She knew how the press could twist your words, and turn against you. . . .

Upset, preoccupied, Marilyn—getting in the way of the

staff now—finally rose from her chair, left the table, and wandered off to the bathroom.

Minutes later, she was straightening her dress in a stall, and about to flush the toilet when the door opened.

Male voices trailed in, in that echo-chamber way.

Mortified, she froze, wondering if she had—in her self-absorbed condition—gone into the wrong bathroom. Soon sounds of male urination confirmed this suspicion, and she could have just died. . . .

This wasn't even the first time this had happened to her. She had once asked her analyst, Dr. Marianne Kris, why she so often did this, blundering into men's restrooms; and the psychiatrist answered, "Perhaps you'd rather be in a man's world." And Marilyn had responded, "Only as long as I can be a woman in it!"

For now, Marilyn stood motionless, hoping no male eyes would glimpse her high heels under the edge of the stall.

Water ran in the sink.

One rough voice said: *"Sivodnya vyechiram."*

Another rough voice answered: *"Dva chisa."*

A hollow laugh preceded a chilling Russian remark from the first speaker: *"Da svidaniya, Khrushchev."*

Through the crack of the door hinge Marilyn could see the men—two of Khrushchev's people, in uniform . . . what was that spy agency called? The KGB—they were KGB agents! One wore thick wire-framed glasses and had a Kirk Douglas chin; the other had a pockmarked face and brown cow-eyes. The cow-eyed man with the ravaged face shut the water off, and they headed out, their boots slapping the tiled floor.

The bathroom door opened and whooshed shut.

Marilyn backed up into a corner of the stall. She had understood the words the two men spoke—that much she knew of the language—and those words sent fear rushing through her.

"Tonight."

"Two o'clock."

Laughter. *"Goodbye, Khrushchev."*

She stayed there for a long time, trembling, eyes wide, leaning a hand against the metal of the stall. She knew what she had heard.

Betrayal—unmistakable, in any language.

Chapter Six

CANNED CAN

"Ooo la la la," Frankie sang, with the burr in his voice that characterized the older Sinatra, the silky smoothness of the younger Voice replaced with something equally sexy, in the ears of many women and even a fair share of men. The singer usually left Jack Harrigan cold, however—he'd seen the mobster-friendly singer's FBI file, after all—even though the State Department agent's stomach growling provided a slightly off-key harmony.

Sinatra—now in costume, a black coat and vest and frilly cuffs and shirt and ribbon of a tie, an outfit that reminded Harrigan of Bret Maverick on TV, minus the cowboy hat—was swaying gently in the middle of the sound stage, performing a number he'd announced earlier as "C'est Magnifique," a romantic, lightly up-tempo ballad written especially for him by Cole Porter for the movie *Can-Can*, which featured many of the famous songwriter's standards.

Watching from the sidelines on the movie soundstage—which had been transformed into an eighteenth-century French dance hall—Harrigan had to admit that as much as he disliked Sinatra the man (whose file began in 1938 with an arrest for seduction of a minor), Sinatra in action was pretty goddamn impressive.

As he sang, Sinatra moved deftly along the glistening wooden dance floor, playing to the audience, as if each one of them was the specific person he was crooning to.

Providing the performer with a lavish backdrop, a wide staircase with ornate banisters opened onto the second-floor set—the red velvet-and-tasseled living quarters of the saloon's owner, played in the film by Shirley MacLaine.

Just as Sinatra finished his tune, Harrigan's stomach rumbled again, loud enough to be embarrassing, but fortunately got drowned out by thunderous applause from the hundred or so people who had come over from the commissary to see the show.

Marilyn Monroe didn't seem to be among those who'd accepted Skouras's invitation—visiting a set on a soundstage would be nothing special to her, and the blonde star had already had her moment in the spotlight, with Khrushchev. Harrigan was relieved she wasn't around—he'd been ducking her at the luncheon.

Too busy with security matters to have eaten anyway, Harrigan had denied himself the meal (except for testing the portions fed to the premier himself). So far, the State Department agent had lost fifteen pounds on this strenuous junket; if it weren't for his belt, he'd have his pants around his ankles. He'd stayed on the fringes, his Secret Service-trained eyes trained forward . . . in part to protect the premier, in part to avoid the famous sex bomb.

Harrigan had made a professional blunder where the actress was concerned, and he was embarrassed as hell about it . . . and afraid encountering her again might somehow—perhaps by way of something Monroe said or did—alert his superiors to what was at least borderline misconduct on his part.

About a month and a half ago, he'd been assigned the duty of approaching the actress, to request that she meet Khrushchev, who had seen her photos at some festival in

Moscow and wanted to be introduced to the famous movie star. Monroe was a potential security risk because of her leftist leanings—and those of her playwright husband—and there was also some residual embarrassment about unsuccessful efforts by the CIA to manipulate her into sexually compromising Sukarno of Indonesia, back in '56. That had fizzled, but the State Department wasn't sure how aware Monroe might be of the attempt to use her.

Harrigan had arranged to talk to her at the Millers's apartment on East 57th Street in Manhattan, on a very warm Thursday evening. He'd taken a cramped elevator up to the thirteenth floor, where he rang the bell at 13E. The door was answered by an attractive woman who at first he didn't recognize as Marilyn Monroe.

Her blonde hair—more yellow than platinum, at the time—was rather curly and pinned back in a bun. She wore no make-up other than a touch of lipstick; her white blouse was sleeveless, and she was in light gray short shorts with a black patent leather belt. Shoeless, the curvy, almost pudgy woman was shorter than he ever would have imagined Marilyn Monroe to be.

Of course, that might have been the memory of her looming, skirt-blowing-up billboard as it had hovered over Times Square for *Seven Year Itch* a few years ago.

Anyway, she had a girl-next-door quality that was at once endearing and a little disappointing.

"Yes?" Monroe seemed distracted, the famous eyes drowsy-looking. He sensed immediately an aura of sadness and vulnerability—and suspected she'd been drinking, though nothing about her suggested she was tipsy, much less drunk.

"Jack Harrigan," he said, and dug out his I.D. from the inside pocket of his lightweight tan summer suitcoat. "I was supposed to drop by—the Khrushchev matter?"

The eyes brightened. "Oh! Sure! I must have forgotten. . . . Come in."

As Harrigan took in the place, she told him she was by herself—her secretary, May, wasn't around, nor was her husband ("He's at the farmhouse, in Roxbury—you know, writing?")—and poured herself a martini from a pitcher, asking him if he wanted one.

He was on duty—he shouldn't have—but it was damned hot, even in the air-conditioned apartment. So he accepted her offer of a chilled martini.

The place overlooked the East River, and the living room was large, particularly for Manhattan, a rhapsody in white: white walls, white wall-to-wall carpet, white draperies, even white furniture . . . though the couch, where she sat, curling up under herself, was beige. Sipping her own martini, she patted the cushion next to her and he sat, too, with his own cool cocktail.

She was very unpretentious and relaxed, and smiled at him a lot while he filled her in about the Khrushchev visit, and the plans being made at the Fox Studios for a reception. For a long time she mostly listened, and then she asked him a lot of questions about himself, and she was particularly interested in his work with the Secret Service, asking about both Truman and Eisenhower.

He also told her—how they got to this, he couldn't quite recall—about his recent divorce, and she made him promise not to tell, but admitted her marriage was over, too.

They'd begun to kiss, shortly after that—three or four martinis were involved—and somewhere along the way the girl next door became Marilyn Monroe and she was as naked as her calendar, a dizzying dream of creamy female flesh, and they made love on the beige couch, twice. He would never forget it. He would never be able to make love to a woman again without thinking, "Yeah, but I had Marilyn Monroe. . . ."

When he woke up in Arthur Miller's bed the next morning, he was very hung over and embarrassed and more ashamed than he'd ever been in his life. Also, prouder.

She fixed him some eggs and at the kitchenette table, sat there in a man's white shirt, with no make-up whatsoever, not even lipstick, and said, "I'll have to see materials on him, of course."

His lips paused over the coffee cup. "Huh? On whom?"

"Khrushchev. Chairman Khrushchev. That's why you're here, right?"

"Uh, sure. Right. But I'm not sure I understand. . . ."

"Well, I want to know more about him, before I say yes. I don't want to shake somebody's hand who turns out to be Hitler, someday. Who would?"

"Right. Okay."

"And if I get in a situation where I have to talk to him, I want to do it intelligently. You know, I'm not just some blonde bimbo."

"Oh, I know."

"Everybody thinks I'm some round-heeled joke or something. And I'm not."

"I know you're not."

Her eyes tightened with thought. "Didn't he make a speech to the congress?"

"No—Khrushchev's never even been in America before—he . . ."

"Not our congress, silly. The one in Moscow—after he took over from Stalin."

"Uh, yes. He spoke for a long time . . . something like six hours."

She smiled, perkily. "Well, that's perfect, then."

"What is?"

"Send me over the transcript of that speech. The State Department has it, don't they?"

"Well, sure, but . . ."

"Send that, and anything else over that you think might be helpful. Do it right away, and I'll give you a quick decision. . . . More coffee?"

She had soon shooed him out the door—before anybody saw him, she said—and he left wondering who had fucked whom. . . .

Now, a month and a half later, as Harrigan wandered in and out of the standing guests, he was relieved that Monroe, like many of the movie stars, had skipped out on the after luncheon entertainment. Everyone here had security clearance, so he kept much of his attention on a balcony built to the right of the set, where the Russians were sequestered to watch the show.

Khrushchev seemed to be enjoying himself, beaming, clapping loudly, like a trained seal. His wife's plain, round face looked flushed . . . whether this was from the heat of the stage lights, or the well-documented effect Sinatra had on women, Harrigan wouldn't hazard a guess.

The premier seemed to be over his snit at being denied Disneyland, which relieved Harrigan, since the State Department man had, after all, been the one who'd pulled the plug on the excursion.

It had been an embarrassment, too, where Walt Disney himself was concerned. Harrigan's other dealings with the mouse mogul—arranging the details of the Khrushchev tour of the amusement park—had been pleasant, the famous animator businesslike but affable.

When Harrigan had called Disney earlier today, however, to inform him of the decision not to allow the premier to visit the park, the father of Mickey Mouse had exploded like Donald Duck.

"We're ready to go with this thing!" Disney's voice was gruff and not at all that of the kindly uncle of the television series that shared its name with the park. "Do you have any idea the trouble we've gone to? The expense?"

"I do. But we simply don't have the security, Mr. Disney. We'd been assured by Mayor Poulson that we would have the cooperation of the Los Angeles Police Department . . . but the mayor and the premier have rubbed each other the wrong way, and now Poulson's pulled his people."

"Well, hell, man," Disney said dismissively, "I have the Anaheim police in my pocket. They'll provide whatever you need."

"They just don't have the manpower, sir."

Disney roared back: "I've done my share of favors for the FBI, I'll have you know! I will call J. Edgar Hoover myself, personally, and your job will be on the line, Agent Harrigan!"

"Mr. Disney, with all due respect, I don't work for Mr. Hoover. And this decision is final."

Disney's response was the *click* of hanging up.

As the applause for the singer faded, Frank Sinatra—flashing a smile of impressive wattage—made a gracious bow toward the seated Soviet guests.

Then translator Oleg Troyanovsky stood in the balcony and said in a loud yet cordial voice, "Mr. Khrushchev would like to apologize for his earlier outburst; it was very hot in the dining room, and he was tired from our strenuous schedule . . . and while this is not Disneyland, he very much likes the show so far."

The room erupted into more applause.

Harrigan was still not sure if he had the premier figured out—was he really this willful child, subject to almost psychopathic mood swings? Or was he playing all these Americans like a five-cent kazoo?

After the clapping subsided, Sinatra, the studio's designated master of ceremonies, spoke. "Mr. Khrushchev," the singer said, with a sweeping gesture to the nearby set, "before we film an actual scene from the movie, *Can-Can*, I should explain what it's about." He grinned boyishly. "Frankly, it's about a bunch of pretty girls and some fellows who like pretty girls."

Oleg translated, and the premier smiled, nodding his recognition of a common human situation—you didn't have to be American, or Russian, or French for that matter, to understand this dynamic.

"In the picture," Sinatra continued, "we go into a saloon." He paused, then said with a straight face, "That's a place where you go for a drink."

Again Oleg spoke, and Khrushchev roared with laughter.

The room echoed this laughter; it reminded Harrigan of a gangster movie, where a Capone-type ganglord laughed and all his men, a step behind, laughed self-consciously with him.

"But before we film the dance number," Sinatra went on, "Maurice Chevalier and Louis Jourdan will perform their song from the picture. . . . It's called 'Live and Let Live.' " Sinatra looked directly at Khrushchev with a more restrained smile, now. "And I think that's a marvelous idea, don't you?"

On cue, trotting out from the back of the set came the legendary Grand Old Man of world show business, Chevalier, looking dapper in a black tuxedo with silver quilted lapels that complimented his silver hair; he was followed almost immediately by the much younger Jourdan, handsome, tanned and suave, wearing a gray suit with double-breasted vest and black Stetson bowler.

If either Frenchman had any qualms about following the likes of Frank Sinatra, he didn't show it, as they launched into their number.

In his famous French accent, Chevalier advised Jourdan to live and let live, and Jourdan—in an equally thick accent—countered with advice to be and let be. With a gesture to his ears, Chevalier suggested they should hear and let hear, and Jourdan pointed to his eyes to recommend they see and let see.

A cute number, and Harrigan noted that when the pair sang in unison—to the effect that the business of the one was the business of the other—a smiling Khrushchev sat forward and nodded in agreement.

Harrigan frowned—that was peculiar. How in hell could the premier have understood those last words? Troyanovsky hadn't had time to translate. . . .

Maybe Khrushchev was just nodding his approval of the performance.

As the Frenchmen continued their act, Harrigan walked the floor. He had paused among the technicians, when a hand settled firmly on his shoulder.

Harrigan about jumped out of his skin.

"Sorry Jack," a voice whispered in his ear, followed by a wry chuckle. "Should've known better than to come up behind a gunfighter like you."

Harrigan let out some air. Were his nerves *that* shot? He turned to Sam Krueger, his Los Angeles-based FBI contact, and admitted, "Jesus I'm jumpy."

"Who isn't?" Krueger smirked. The FBI man stood

several inches shorter than Harrigan, his sandy hair cut military short, his eyes hard and professional in the round, pleasant face. He curled a finger for Harrigan to follow him.

Harrigan did, whispering, "What the hell is it, Sam?"

Krueger shook his head: *not here.*

When Harrigan had first met the FBI agent at the Los Angeles Airport, just before the Russians landed, he'd been immediately impressed with Krueger's competence, and his friendly yet professional manner. Perhaps the agent had sensed—or seen the dark-circled eyes that gave it away—Harrigan's fatigue, and had stepped up to the plate, in this critical game, to play Roger Marris to his Mickey Mantle. It was Krueger's job to stay out in front of Harrigan, checking security at each of the sights Khrushchev would visit in the city.

Harrigan trailed Krueger over to the edge of the set, where beneath a fake gaslight lamppost, the FBI agent handed Harrigan a piece of paper.

Harrigan frowned as he read it. "Hell, Sam," he whispered, "I might've expected a bomb threat at the Ambassador Hotel tonight . . . but *three?*" He folded the paper and stuck it in his pocket. "We got a full fuckin' moon tonight, or what?"

"Are you surprised? Guy this famous, this hated, comes to town, all the kooks come out. Knock this guy off, you're famous *right now*—and half the country thinks you're a hero."

"The other half will be heading for bomb shelters. Do I need to—"

"My men are already on it," Krueger told him, shaking his head, keeping his voice low. "We're going over that hotel from top to bottom—broom closets to the honeymoon suite."

"Good idea—you need to check every screw." Harrigan looked at his watch. In four hours Khrushchev was scheduled to speak at the Ambassador at a banquet for a large civic group. Would there be enough time for a thorough check of the facility?

Krueger answered the unspoken question. "If there *is* a bomb," Krueger said confidently, "we'll find it. . . . Probably just cranks. Typical hollow threats."

"But we have to assume they're not," Harrigan said.

"Roger that. . . . I'm heading back to the Ambassador, now."

Harrigan nodded. "Understood. I'll be there as soon as I can."

He watched the FBI agent disappear into the shadows of the soundstage, then turned his attention back to the set where Chevalier and Jourdan had finished their routine. Bowing, they graciously received the enthusiastic applause, which rang through the massive chamber. Sinatra once again took center stage.

"And now," the singer announced, "we're going to film a real scene that will be used in the movie. Mr. Walter Lang, the director, will explain the procedure. . . . Mr. Lang, I turn the show over to you."

From his director's chair at the front of the stage rose Walter Lang, who even at sixty was tall, dark, and handsome enough to be his own leading man, a beefier George Raft with similar slicked-back black hair, straight nose, and prominent chin. Lang strode onto the set with typical confidence, turning to face the audience, speaking in the strong, authoritative manner that was needed to keep the volatile likes of Sinatra and MacLaine in line.

"Ladies and gentlemen," he said, his voice only slightly touched by his Memphis, Tennessee, upbringing, "I must have complete silence on the set. We are going to film the big dance number that comes at the end of the movie."

Harrigan, of course, knew this was a lie . . . call it a fib. The camera had been checked earlier for security reasons—along with the other equipment—and contained no film. The sham was designed simply to show their V.I.P. guest a good time.

Lang returned to his director's chair.

He called out, "Are you ready, girls?" Then, "Cue the music!"

A pre-recorded tape began to play a lively, orchestrated number.

"And . . . *Action!*"

Flowing from the wings of the second-story set, from both the right and the left, came a bevy of beautiful girls, twelve in all, slender red-haired Juliet Prowse among them. Wearing colorful velvet dresses, the women shrieked and squealed as they descended the staircase, lifting the hems of their petticoats in *Moulin Rouge* style to revel shapely, long legs encased in provocative black stockings.

When the last of the dancers reached the floor, a thirteenth appeared—Shirley MacLaine, similarly clad.

As she came dancing down the stairs, Lang stood from his chair and shouted, "Cut!"

The music stopped. The girls on the floor stopped mid-twirl.

"Shirley, darling," the director said to the actress, "your entrance needs to be a little quicker."

"All right, Mr. Lang," she responded sweetly.

The director returned to his chair. "Places everyone! This will be take number two. . . . Quiet, please!"

The soundstage fell silent.

"Cue the music!" Lang repeated. Then, "Action!"

The scene began again, this time continuing through

MacLaine's entrance as she joined in on the zestful choreography.

Amused by the harmless deception, Harrigan watched Khrushchev watching the dancers. The premier seemed to be a normal enough male, red blood running in the Red's veins—he was smiling as the chorines jumped in the air, then fell to the floor in the splits, got up and whirled some more, shaking their legs before finally kicking them in the air.

But when the dancers bent over in unison, showing their lacy-pantied posteriors in a flirtatious flip to the Russian delegation, Khrushchev's smile disappeared, and he turned a whiter shade of pale, bolting to his feet.

His smile had become a scowl, and he spoke tersely in Russian, his face growing redder than his politics, as his wife tried to calm him, with pacifying but ultimately unavailing gestures.

The commotion in the balcony brought the dancers and the music to a halt—no need for Lang to pretend to end the scene with a shouted "Cut." And certainly no one needed to cry, "Quiet on the set"—the silence was ominous, nerve-racking, as all heads turned toward Khrushchev.

The interpreter, standing beside the fuming premier, spoke solemnly . . . patronizingly.

"Mr. Khrushchev," Oleg said loudly enough for all to hear, despite the lack of a microphone, "considers this dance immoral—and says in Russia, we find faces prettier than backsides." Then he announced, "We are leaving."

A concerned murmur spread through the crowd, as a stunned Shirley MacLaine covered her open mouth with a hand, her choking sob audible as she fled the dance floor in tears.

Harrigan sighed and shook his head in disbelief. Again, he couldn't be sure—had Khrushchev really been offended?

Or was Twentieth Century Fox being outsmarted by that Russian-style twentieth-century fox?

In the parking lot outside the sound stage, Harrigan had just helped Mrs. Khrushchev into the back seat of their limousine when Spyros Skouras motioned to him from a soundstage doorway.

Skouras looked understandably distressed; an enormous amount of money had been spent for the catastrophic luncheon. But this was the kind of bad publicity money couldn't buy. . . .

Harrigan approached the studio boss.

Skouras raised an eyebrow as he said, "Miss Monroe . . ."

Harrigan felt a sudden chill, despite the warmth of the day. "Yes—what about her?"

"She wants to see you."

"What? Well, where is she?"

"At her bungalow at the Beverly Hills Hotel."

Harrigan frowned. "She's back there already?"

Skouras nodded.

"And . . . she asked for me?"

"Specifically. By name. She seems to know you are in charge of Khrushchev." He shook his head. "How does she know these things?"

Harrigan ducked the question with one of his own: "What does she want? I don't mean any offense, sir, but I have bigger fish to fry."

"She is one of the biggest fish in town."

But Harrigan had no time to placate any movie star, even Marilyn Monroe. Particularly Marilyn Monroe. . . .

The president of Fox was saying, "She says it is matter of life or death. . . . That's what she said, in those words. Life. And death."

"Whose?"

Skouras looked past him, toward the limousine where a glaring Khrushchev, accompanied by his uniformed KGB guards, was getting in. "That Russian son of a bitch." The studio boss shrugged. "So don't talk to her. I don't give a damn what happens to that fat bastard."

And Skouras disappeared back into the soundstage, closing the door, making as effective an exit as any of his stars might have mustered . . .

. . . leaving Jack Harrigan feeling like a bit player in his own life.

And now he had no choice but to once again go calling on Marilyn Monroe.

The State Department agent tightened his belt—hoping to keep his pants from landing down around his ankles . . . again.

Chapter Seven

GOODBYE, KHRUSHCHEV

Marilyn Monroe—having traded the little black dress for her comfy white robe, but still wearing her black high-heeled shoes—paced nervously in the living room of her Beverly Hills Hotel bungalow, the spiked heels leaving a trail of little bullet holes in the plush white carpet behind her.

For the past hour, ever since returning from the Fox luncheon, the actress had been chain-smoking, adding more and more cigarette butts to an already overflowing ashtray.

Normally, Marilyn didn't smoke—any camera, professional or amateur, catching the movie star with a cigarette drooping from her famous lips made for bad publicity. It wasn't a health concern; she simply didn't look her best. And of course cigarettes made the likes of Bogart or John Wayne seem like men; but for a woman, in this world of double standards, smoking remained a filthy habit. Furthermore, tobacco stained Marilyn's teeth, gave her bad breath, and—over time—would encourage tiny wrinkle lines around her mouth. Besides, she had far more serious cravings than nicotine.

But once in a while, now and then, here and there . . . when she was *really* tense . . . Marilyn did light one up. And her anxiety at the moment outdistanced attending an important Hollywood party, or going before the camera on a soundstage, either of which could paralyze her. She was a woman of enormous self-confidence, which happened to be undermined, somewhat, by cataclysmic self-doubt.

Sighing smoke, pausing in her pacing, she turned to her secretary in building despair. "May—what if he doesn't come?"

In the limousine on the way back from Fox Studios, Marilyn had, in hushed tones, told May what she'd overheard in the bathroom at the commissary . . . and why she was convinced that Nikita Khrushchev was marked for assassination—*tonight.*

And the secretary—who knew how to sort through the frivolities and the serious concerns that equally characterized her charge—had also been alarmed, and suggested that Marilyn contact Spyros Skouras immediately on returning to the bungalow.

"Have him paged on the soundstage," May advised, not in the least humoring her. "You're right—this could be very serious indeed."

At the moment a somber May, in the same prim navy suit she'd had on since morning, was seated at a small white secretariat near the entrance to the master bedroom. Always pragmatic, even in a crisis, she was attending to Marilyn's mail that had been forwarded from New York.

The secretary looked up from her work. "Mr. Skouras told you he'd contact your Mr. Harrigan, didn't he?"

"Yes . . . but what if . . . Agent Harrigan doesn't come?"

May seemed to frown and smile simultaneously; she knew nothing of the brief tryst between Marilyn and the State Department man last summer. Some things Marilyn did not trust even to May . . . who, after all, still had certain loyalties to Arthur.

"Then I'm sure," May said gently, "he'll send someone else who's involved with the premier's safety and security."

"But I want to talk to Mr. Harrigan." Even Marilyn herself, finished with the cigarette and now biting her platinum colored nails, could hear the pouty little girl in her voice. "Mr. Skouras said he'd make sure it was Mr. Harrigan."

"Why does it matter? Do you know Mr. Harrigan?"

"A little. He's the one who contacted me, and gave me those materials on Mr. Khrushchev. I'm just . . . used to talking to him, is all."

May shrugged, smiled reassuringly. "Then I'm certain he's the one who'll come around. Agent Harrigan'll probably want to talk to you about your meeting with Khrushchev, anyway. I understand these agents like to debrief civilians they recruit."

I'll say, Marilyn thought.

"Anyway, Spyros won't let you down," May said to her, calming yet firm. "I'm sure he could tell how urgent you consider this, and how upset you were."

"*I* wasn't upset," Marilyn said, lighting up a fresh Chesterfield, "*he* was upset! With *me!*"

May looked up from her work. "Why?"

Marilyn shrugged and began to pace again. "For skipping the show. He said the premier asked about me. I guess I was supposed to sit next to Mr. Khrushchev . . . but I just couldn't, *knowing* what I know. Y'know?"

"I know."

Abruptly she stopped again, eyes popping. "Was I a fool *not* to go? Not to sit next to the premier, and warn him? But I would have had to use a translator, and who *knows* who might have heard me? One of the conspirators might have! How do we know the translator himself isn't in on it?"

May was patting the air with both hands. "Now, dear . . . calm yourself . . . you have a genuine concern, but you're starting to make a movie out of this."

"If this were a movie," the actress said, irritably, "I'd know what to do!"

And if this were a movie, a leading man would enter, and believe her, and solve all her problems.

Marilyn started back in pacing, puffing the cigarette, wobbling in the heels. The shoes hurt her toes, but she didn't dare kick them off; her feet were swollen and she'd never get the fucking heels back on again.

"It's so goddamn *hot* in here," Marilyn said irritably. "Is the air conditioning working?"

"I think so."

The actress untied the robe, letting it fall open over her otherwise naked form.

May started to rise from the desk. "I can open some windows. . . ."

"No!" The whole business with the KGB guards in the bathroom had fueled Marilyn's paranoia. What if they somehow knew she'd been there? What if someone had seen her leave the restroom after the guards had? "Please, May . . . let's keep the curtains closed."

May shrugged and nodded, and returned to the letters.

Marilyn sank down on the couch. "Maybe I should call the White House . . . ," she wondered aloud.

May's eyes tightened as the woman formed a response—a public figure like Marilyn Monroe calling the White House was no wild fancy, and definitely a possibility . . . MM might even be put through to Ike himself—but Marilyn discounted the notion herself.

"No," she said, shaking her head, Guilaroff's pageboy 'do bouncing. "They'd think I'm just a dumb blonde, well-meaning but nuttier than a Baby Ruth."

"I don't know. . . ."

"I do. Hell, May—I don't have any *real* proof. . . . Just a few Russian words and a . . . a *feeling.*"

"Your fleeting 'feelings' are worth more than most people's well-considered thoughts," May said, sincerely if placatingly.

But Marilyn was not mollified. She looked helplessly over the back of the couch at her secretary. "What if no one believes me?" she asked.

"Why shouldn't they, dear?"

How could Marilyn explain to this refined, intelligent woman, who could be as naive as she was wise? How could May understand this the way Marilyn did? That you could tell your foster mother how the father of the house was molesting you, and be ignored? Or even vilified?

Then came a sharp gunshot of a knock.

Marilyn jumped up from the sofa and dashed toward the bungalow door; but a spiked heel caught in the hem of her robe, and just as Marilyn opened the door the robe fell from her shoulders, puddling at her feet, leaving her naked as *September Morn.*

The rangy, hazel-eyed man standing on the bungalow stoop wore a dark suit, blue shirt, gray tie, and stunned expression.

Marilyn herself was mortified—she'd suddenly realized her perfectly manicured and polished nails were now ragged and chipped. She hoped Harrigan—was it Jack, or Frank?—wouldn't notice.

May, coming to her employer's rescue, retrieved the robe and snugged it up and over Marilyn's shoulders.

Marilyn had a sensitivity that often allowed her to read people unerringly; but she did not understand the odd look of relief in Harrigan's eyes when May appeared, to return the robe to her. The actress had no self-consciousness about her body, and was particularly proud of it at the moment, because she had lost just enough weight to get the chubbiness off her belly and return the sleekness to her legs while still retaining the bustiness she was famous for (few knew that, when her weight was down, her bosom was a rather average B-cup affair).

Marilyn, tying the robe's belt in a secure knot, beamed at him. "I'm so glad to see you, Agent Harrigan. Please come in . . . what's your first name again? I'm afraid I've forgotten."

Like May had earlier, the man seemed to frown and smile at the same time; he said, "It's, uh . . . Jack, Miss Monroe. Or do you prefer Mrs. Miller?"

"Marilyn's fine. Jack, come in . . . make yourself at home. This is my secretary—May. I'd trust her with my life. You can speak freely in front of her. . . ."

May—who had already returned to her desk—smiled and nodded at the agent.

Marilyn, her back to May, whispered to Harrigan, "Except for . . . you know."

His eyes flared, then narrowed, and he nodded. "Of course," he whispered.

She took the agent by the arm and led him to the white couch by the stone fireplace, saying, "You spoke to Mr. Skouras . . . Spyros. He sent you."

"Yes."

"Did he tell you anything?"

"No . . . just that you had something important to report, about the premier. Concerning his safety?"

Marilyn felt a wave a relief. Agent Harrigan . . . Jack . . . was taking her seriously. The State Department was listening to her . . . something could be done, something *would* be done. . . .

"I was afraid maybe you were no longer in charge of Mr. Khrushchev's security," she said. "I didn't see you at the luncheon."

He smiled a little. "Oh, I was there. Sort of on the fringes . . . running around like a crazy man."

She shrugged. "It's like Hollywood. All the really important people are behind the cameras and lights."

"I guess that's right, Miss Monroe."

"Marilyn."

"Maybe we should make it 'Miss Monroe.' "

"*Marilyn* . . . you're mad at me."

"I am? I mean, no, of course not. Why would I be mad?"

"Because I forgot your name. It's just . . . you look more like a Frank to me than a Jack. I won't forget again . . . I promise."

He swallowed. "Miss Monroe . . . Marilyn . . . I don't mean to be rude, but I have a lot on my plate."

"Oh! Did I interrupt your lunch?"

"No, I just . . ."

"How thoughtless of me! You couldn't have lunch until after the festivities . . . and now I've—"

"No. I just meant, I'm very busy. Looking after the premier's security and such. Much as I'd like to socialize . . ."

The relief faded. "This isn't a social call, Jack. Agent Harrigan. This is serious. Very, very serious."

"I apologize, Miss Monroe. What is this about?"

She took a long, hard look at him. His hair could use some Brillcream, she thought, and his face could stand a shave—that five o'clock shadow made his cheeks look dirty, and the pouchy darkness under his eyes said he'd suffered a lack of sleep. Poor baby.

And this was her leading man? The hero who would ride in to save the world from destruction? He might look a little like Bob Mitchum, but she would have preferred the real, fake thing.

"You look like hell," Marilyn blurted.

His eyebrows climbed. "Thanks a bunch."

She placed a hand on his knee, which twitched at her touch. "No—you're a beautiful man. I only meant that it's obvious your job's been a terrible strain."

He chuckled, leaned back on the couch, admitting, "It has been one hell of a bad day."

"Well," she said, leaning in close enough to kiss him (but didn't), "it's going to get a lot worse. . . ."

"It is?"

She nodded. "It is if somebody doesn't do something about . . . something."

His brown tightened. "Do you think you could be just a little more specific, Miss Monroe?"

"Marilyn."

"Marilyn."

She nodded gravely. "I have to whisper."

"You do?"

"Yes—one time I was with Sukarno . . . the President of Indonesia?"

"Really."

"Yes, and somebody in the government monitored our conversation. So I can't take any chances."

"Oh. Well, of course. I understand."

She looked around, even though she knew it was silly—what, did she expect to see one of those KGB guards peeking out from around a potted plant?

Sotto voce, she said, "Unless you stop it, Jack . . . Mr. K is going to be killed tonight."

He frowned, as if hard of hearing. "Mr. who?"

Silently she mouthed the name, *Khrushchev*.

"Oh." And right out loud, he said, "Khrushchev."

She glared at him and slapped his arm, as if he'd said a bad word. Wasn't he at all concerned about bugging?

Harrigan ignored the slap and asked her, “What makes you think that?”

Marilyn sighed and returned to her normal voice; if the State Department wasn’t taking any precautions, why should she? “*Because* . . . I overheard them plotting.”

“Overheard who?”

“The ones doing it. Plotting it. The conspirators. His own people!”

“Oh, really.”

Marilyn shifted on the couch, suddenly feeling insecure—she might have been back at Hollywood High, in class . . . under-prepared.

She tried to start over, and stay calm, and be clear. “I was in the men’s bathroom, at the commissary, when—”

“Excuse me?”

She blinked at him. “Excuse you for what?”

“You were where?”

“In the commissary.”

“No . . . before that.”

She shrugged. “Well, before that I was here . . . getting ready. Why?”

He put a hand on his forehead, as if trying to take his own temperature. “No . . . I meant, what did you say *before* you said . . .” He swallowed; he sighed. Maybe he *had* been trying to take his temperature, Marilyn thought; he looked like he didn’t feel so good, at that.

“Never mind,” he said. “Marilyn, could you just start over . . . from the beginning?”

Marilyn took a deep breath. “Well, my masseur, Robert, came around at eight-thirty . . . a.m. He must have worked on me until about—”

“Not that beginning. The other beginning.”

"Oh! Oh. Well. Like I said, I was in the men's bathroom . . ."

"There! That beginning! What were you doing in the men's bathroom?"

"Oh. I go in there, sometimes."

Again Harrigan's eyebrows shot up—Groucho Marx minus the punchlines, mustache, and cigar.

"Just *some* times," Marilyn quickly went on. "You know . . . by mistake. Or sort of by mistake, but sort of on purpose."

Harrigan looked like he was just realizing someone had slipped him a mickey.

She hurried on to explain. "My analyst in New York . . . Dr. Kris? . . . says I do that, sometimes, because I have a Penis Envy Complex." Marilyn shook her head. "But I don't agree! What would I do with a penis?"

Harrigan just looked at her.

"I mean, do I look like I would know what to do with a penis?"

The agent's head lowered; he seemed to be staring at his lap.

Marilyn leaned toward him. "Do you need an aspirin, or maybe a Tums? . . . Or anything else, really. If you need some kind of pill, believe me, I can get you one." The State Department must have really been overworking this poor man.

"No," he said, "I'm fine . . . really," then, "let's pick this up again. . . . You were in the men's room in the commissary . . . now what was it that you overheard?"

In a businesslike manner, she said, "I heard two of Mr. K's men talking—the uniformed ones. What is it, KGB?"

"KGB, yes."

"Anyway, one had really bad skin, and the other had thick glasses. Coke bottles."

Harrigan was nodding. "Titov and Yepishev."

She breathed a sigh of relief. "Oh, you know who I mean!"

"Of course," he said, nodding again. "They're two of Khrushchev's top guards." His eyes narrowed, his voice deepened, as he said, "Can you tell me, Miss Monroe . . . Marilyn . . . what did they say, exactly?"

Marilyn drew herself up on the couch, and her face was as expressionless as a bisque baby's as she recited dramatically, " *'Sivodnya vyechiram,'* one said. *'Dva chisa,'* the other said. And the first one said, *'Da svidaniay, Khrushchev.'* "

Harrigan seemed shocked, but not by the content of what she'd said . . . rather by her ability to say it at all. "You speak Russian? You understand the language?"

"Some," she said, and quickly explained about her Russian drama coach.

"Well, I don't speak it and I don't understand it," he said. "Can you translate for me?"

Again Marilyn reported what she'd heard by playing the scene with all its melodrama: "The words mean: 'Tonight.' . . . 'Two o'clock.' . . . 'Goodbye, Khrushchev.' "

It was a moment before Harrigan, eyes wide, face blank, asked, "That . . . that's it?"

Marilyn nodded somberly.

"And from this you think there's a plot to assassinate Nikita Khrushchev?"

Again she nodded.

Harrigan's next reaction alarmed Marilyn: he broke into a grin, and chuckled softly.

"Don't laugh at me," she snapped.

"Oh, oh . . . I'm not." And he forced his smile from his face, and the chuckling ceased.

Hurt, angry, she touched the terrycloth over her heart.

"I'm just trying to prevent World War III!"

He covered his mouth with a hand, and, a few seconds later, removed it; any lingering amusement had left the agent's face. "I apologize," he said.

"If you're writing me off as just some . . . some dumb blonde," she said, "you're making a big mistake . . . a mistake a lot of Americans will have to pay for."

"Miss Monroe, please settle down. . . ."

With a frustrated squeal, she jumped up from the couch and, lips trembling, spread her hands, palms up, fingers apart, like she was trying to grab onto something. "It was the *way* they said it—those two men spoke with such contempt . . . even *hatred!*"

Harrigan rose and faced her.

His smile was slight, not mocking, rather serious and conciliatory. "Miss Monroe . . . Marilyn. I'm not laughing at you . . . truly. Please understand—it's just that I'm relieved that there's nothing more to your story."

"Nothing *more* . . . ?" she repeated. She looked at him with wide eyes, as if trying desperately to bring this man into some kind of focus.

The agent took one of her hands in his. "Look," he said gently, "this Russian visit has got all of us jumpy. Right now I've got several real, credible threats on the premier's life that we're investigating . . . bomb threats, that kind of thing. Believe me, what you overheard was nothing."

Marilyn pulled her hand from his grasp. She turned to look at her secretary, who had been quietly listening at the desk.

"May," the actress said tensely, "he's not going to do anything."

The secretary got up from the desk and approached the agent.

"Mr. Harrigan," May said, coming to her employer's defense, "I've been with Marilyn a good number of years . . . and I've learned one thing: her instincts are seldom wrong."

Harrigan put both hands in the air, surrendering. "Please! If you both will just take a deep breath, I'll explain to you why I'm not concerned. . . ."

He gestured for the women to sit. Marilyn returned to her previous spot on the couch, while May perched on the armrest. Harrigan remained standing.

"First of all," he told them, "the two men Marilyn overheard are trusted KGB agents—*Okhrana*—special guards sworn to protect the premier, hand-picked by Khrushchev himself." He paused, then continued. "And second . . . and critically . . . there's a regular changing of Khrushchev's personal bodyguards at two o'clock in the morning."

Harrigan shifted his gaze to Marilyn. "That's what the exchange you heard meant. 'Two o'clock. Goodbye, Khrushchev.' " The agent spread his arms wide, like Al Jolson singing "Mammy." "Now . . . do you see? Perfectly innocent."

May was nodding; she seemed to accept Harrigan's explanation. But Marilyn could not.

"I don't care if those men *are* okra—or whatever you call them," Marilyn said firmly. "I didn't just hear *what* they said—I heard *how* they said it. And Agent Harrigan . . . they intend to kill Mr. K tonight."

Harrigan sat next to the actress. "Okay," he conceded, nodding, "let's assume you're right. Let's say there's a conspiracy among several of the premier's key, most trusted guards, to assassinate him . . . political assassination is a way of life in Russia, after all."

"Thank you," Marilyn said.

Harrigan went on: "Then why wait until Los Angeles to

do it? They could have just as easily assassinated Chairman Khrushchev in Washington, or New York."

"But they didn't," Marilyn said, unconvinced. "They waited—knowing you would think exactly what you're thinking, that you'd let your guard down. By waiting until the end of the trip, they have their best opportunity . . . because you and your men are all worn out."

The agent seemed almost startled by this analysis. And her words clearly had struck a chord, because the agent gave her a sharp, respectful look.

"If you don't mind hearing a dumb blonde's opinion," she added.

Harrigan nodded and smiled a little. "Very well reasoned," he said, genuinely impressed.

"Thanks."

Then he sighed and again got to his feet and looked down at her with a wry yet peace-making grin. "What if I promise you that I'll be on hand . . . personally present . . . at the changing of Khrushchev's guards, at two a.m. tonight?"

Marilyn gazed up at him. "Would you do that for me?"

"I'd do it for any concerned citizen," he said, "reporting suspicious activity of such a vital nature . . . and I hope that will put your fears of an assassination attempt to rest."

Marilyn rose and extended her hand, which Harrigan took, in a gesture that was half-handshake, half something else. "Thank you, Jack," she whispered.

May patted Marilyn's arm. "There now, dear—don't you feel better?"

Marilyn nodded.

But after the State Department agent had gone, and May had disappeared into the bungalow's kitchenette to fix them a salad for supper, Marilyn remained on the couch, fretting.

Would Jack Harrigan be able to rouse himself in the wee

hours of the morning, exhausted as he seemed? Or would he sleep right through the execution of the conspirators' plot?

Marilyn believed he'd been sincere; his promise to supervise the changing of the guards had seemed more than just giving her the bum's rush . . . but Harrigan was a harried man, getting hit from all fronts and on every side. So she couldn't take that chance. She had to do something, and fast.

Marilyn Monroe believed, however, that one should always make haste slowly. . . .

So it took her a few hours to devise her own scenario . . . one that did not include a leading man, unless you counted Nikita Khrushchev himself.

Chapter Eight

THE HUNGARIAN AMBASSADOR

On Wilshire Boulevard, between Seventh and Eighth Streets—set back on an expansive, immaculately manicured lawn, as if a palace had dropped from the sky into the midst of so unlikely a place as Hollywood, California—the Ambassador had been a mainstay in downtown Los Angeles ever since its grand opening on New Year's Day in 1921.

The construction and decoration of the stately hotel had racked up the then-outrageous cost of five million dollars. Built on twenty-three acres of former dairy land, the H-shaped structure ("H" for hotel) boasted 1,200 rooms and suites; on the first floor, a guest could stand on the grand ballroom's stage and gaze all the way through the elaborate fern-adorned lobby and into the immense dining room at the other end.

Anybody who was anybody stayed at the Ambassador—from movie stars to captains of industry, from statesmen to sports figures—but they came not merely for the prestige of the place, or even the elegant rooms and five-star service. Rather, the elite lodged here because of an added attraction that offset the otherwise somewhat stodgy air of the hotel: the renowned Coconut Grove nightclub.

Originally ensconced on the Ambassador's lower level, the club had become so popular—after only four months!—that the management was sent scurrying to relocate the nightspot in the hotel's grand ballroom, renovating it in keeping with the original's tropical decor. Coconut palms (left over from the set of Valentino's *The Sheik*) rose to a twinkling, azure sky, high above rococo Moorish furnishings in Deco-ish red, gold, and black. Simple cane chairs accommodated the ever-changing procession of famous backs and backsides, while a mural of island mountains and waterfalls added to the aura of a movie-set Pacific paradise.

No desert under a real starry purple sky could boast an oasis more dazzling, nor decadent. In the 1920s, Joan Crawford had won Charleston contests here, and John Barrymore brought his pet monkey to swing from the trees. In the 1930s Rudy Vallee headlined, Jean Harlow frolicked, and volatile lovers Lupe Velez and Johnny Weissmuller slugged it out; and until '36, the prestigious place even hosted the Academy Awards. Throughout the 1940s—even after the war when nightclubbing waned—the Ambassador thrived, and remained Hollywood's acknowledged "Playground of the Stars."

As the 1950s wound down, however, the Ambassador Hotel and its famed Coconut Grove were beginning to lose their luster. . . . If the grand old lady of Los Angeles wanted to continue to attract the ever-fickle Hollywood set, she would need a facelift at least as good as those of the older stars who still frequented the place. So in 1957 a $750,000 renovation toned down the palm-flung, Moorish ambience, a modernization appropriate to the likes of Jayne Mansfield, Jack Lemmon, Sophia Loren, and other modern stars.

In the fall of 1959—even as Los Angeles pushed itself west toward the ocean, threatening to leave the Ambassador straggling behind—the hotel remained the choice of many of the elite of show business and beyond.

It was not, however, the hotel that Jack Harrigan had chosen to house Nikita Khrushchev and crew—although the press had been told the premier was staying there, to throw the bloodhounds off the scent. Keeping tabs on the Russians at the Ambassador, along with all the other guests at the sprawling facility—not to mention the nightclub patrons—would have been a logistical nightmare . . . especially with the relatively small security team Harrigan had at his disposal.

Which was why the Soviet guests were staying at the more secluded Beverly Hills Hotel, where the main building was smaller than the Ambassador's, and the landscaped grounds more friendly to Harrigan's prowling security force.

But the dinner tonight would be held at the Ambassador, a fact that Harrigan deplored; this aspect of the dictator's itinerary had not been his call.

After the State Department man had left Marilyn Monroe's bungalow at the Beverly Hills Hotel, he'd returned to his own room, just down the hall from the Presidential Suite where the premier was billeted; the fat little man should be resting, at the moment, after a hard day of stirring the local shit. Khrushchev's family was in a separate suite, away from the snorting snoring of their paterfamilias. The agent took a quick shower, and changed into another wrinkled suit—straight from his suitcase, there'd been no time to send the threads out for a pressing—and within minutes was striding through the Beverly Hills Hotel's lavish lobby and out into the parking lot.

Soon Harrigan was driving along Sunset Boulevard in a government sedan, the California sun just beginning to set, casting soothing unreal shadows on the shabby reality of Hollywood. Traffic was on the slow side, giving Harrigan time to reflect on his meeting with the movie star.

He knew, from his first encounter with the woman, that Marilyn Monroe was no dummy—she had her scatterbrained side, yes, but that brain often scattered itself in most impressive and surprising ways. And certainly she had appeared sincere in her concern for the premier's safety, and afraid of the ramifications his assassination might bring—she'd had tears in her eyes, for Christ's sake!

But then, she *was* an actress, and like all of her ilk, prone to the over-dramatic.

One thing was for sure, though: her story, her concern, was no publicity stunt. After all, the woman had been cleared to sit in the balcony next to Khrushchev during the floor show at Fox Studios, and by her not being there, Marilyn had given up extraordinary media coverage, the kind any actress, or actor, would just about kill for.

Still, it seemed obvious to Harrigan that Marilyn Monroe was not exactly dealing with a full deck—not that he felt any guilt for taking advantage of her back in New York . . . she had manipulated *him,* hadn't she? Any shame he felt was for the unprofessionalism of it. Not that he had minded her answering the door naked today—even now his trousers were tented with the memory.

By her own casual admission, the actress was under psychiatric care, and she'd even offered to play pharmacist for Harrigan. Not that any of this was news to the State Department man: extensive FBI files had been made available to him on everyone coming into direct contact with Khrushchev, including Marilyn, whose file mentioned the movie star's daily trips to a shrink . . . and her heavy use of (and even possible addiction to) barbiturates and alcohol, which would naturally distort her perception. . . .

The lovely actress had been correct about one thing, however, which had made the back of Harrigan's neck tingle; in fact, the skin back there was tingling right now, as he tooled along Sunset. The agents guarding Khrushchev—

besides being far too few—were burned-out cases about now, weary, bleary, not at the top of their game . . . himself included. Even if his boss Bill Larsen could arrange for more men tonight, they would be arriving pretty much after the fact: Khrushchev and his entourage were flying out of Los Angeles in the morning.

So.

Harrigan and his people only needed to make it through one more night. . . .

On the third floor, just outside the banquet room doors, Harrigan found Sam Krueger, gazing in on where the civic dinner honoring Khrushchev was to be held in just a few short hours.

The round-faced, sandy-haired FBI man waved him over. "The hotel has been combed," he reported. "Looks like we won't be bothering the bomb squad. As we suspected."

"Good."

Krueger nodded to the nearby bank of elevators. "Only the one on the far right stops here," he told Harrigan. "We have our own men acting as elevator operators on all three. And the other two cars will bypass this floor . . ."

Nothing of this was a surprise to Harrigan, who said, "Fine."

". . . and we have men positioned on the stairs to check everyone coming up." Krueger gestured to the two wide carpeted staircases on either side of the elevators.

"Okay."

"Wish we could have talked the hotel into closing down the Coconut Grove tonight. Those extra people make security all the tougher."

"Yeah."

Krueger grinned at him. "You're a card, today, aren't

you? Are the rumors true, you dropped by Marilyn Monroe's bungalow this afternoon?"

"Yes."

"Well? . . . Get any?"

"Not this time."

"Not this time. . . . You *are* a card." Krueger nodded toward the banquet doors. "Come on inside."

Harrigan followed the shorter agent into the dining room where massive chandeliers glimmered like icicles high above linen-covered tables set with gleaming sterling silver and sparkling crystal goblets . . . and where prominent businessmen and businesswomen of Los Angeles would soon have the honor of supping with the premier of Russia, and hear him speak in his less-than-dulcet tones.

Harrigan wondered what these poor bastards had in store for them tonight—raving, ranting, the pounding of a fist on linen-covered table, most likely. He could hardly wait . . . for it all to be over.

"There won't be reporters at any of the tables," Krueger was saying, gesturing around with a pointing finger. "They'll be divided along the walls . . . here and here." He indicated the right and left of the dais.

"I don't want them crowding the platform," Harrigan said.

"They'll be told not to go beyond the first row of tables. . . . So what did the blonde bombshell want? To hold your service revolver?"

"She thinks somebody's going to try to kill Khrushchev tonight."

Krueger's eyebrows climbed. "Really? Did she show you her Junior G-man badge pinned to her brassiere?"

"I don't think she wears a bra."

"You don't think she . . . you're a card, I tell ya."

A swinging door to the kitchen opened and a man in his late fifties, wearing a black tuxedo, emerged carrying a pitcher of water that was a silver closely matching the color of his hair.

"Headwaiter of the Coconut Grove," Krueger said. "Of course, you know that, from all the times you and Marilyn have been here."

"We don't usually go out," Harrigan said.

"Just stay at home, huh? Quiet evenings."

"That's right."

"Card."

Following the headwaiter out through the swinging kitchen doors came a dozen or so other men, all younger, wearing black tuxedo slacks, white shirts, and stiff white aprons. They gathered around the older man, who began instructing them on the proper way to fill water glasses and serve dinner plates.

These were not ordinary bus boys, however, rather FBI men under Krueger's command, whose eyes would be searching the seated guests for anything suspicious, as they waited on the tables.

Harrigan and Krueger returned to the hallway where other security men had taken their posts by the banquet doors and elevators, in anticipation of the soon-to-begin arriving crowd. A few reporters were already there, including William H. Lawrence from the *New York Times*—and Harrigan groaned when he saw him.

"Christ, Sam," Harrigan whispered to Krueger, "who let that son of a bitch in?"

In New York, Lawrence had infuriated Khrushchev at a National Press Club conference, by demanding an explanation of the premier's earlier statement, "We shall bury you." It was safe to assume the reporter wouldn't make life any easier on Khrushchev tonight—or Harrigan and his men.

"I did." Krueger shrugged. "He had a press badge."

"Is that all it takes to get in here?"

Lawrence was by the elevators, bending over a squat ashtray stand, extinguishing a cigarette, when Harrigan approached him.

"Lawrence," Harrigan said.

Lawrence looked up, smiled unpleasantly, as he stubbed out the smoke. "Agent Harrison."

"Harrigan. Get your facts straight."

The reporter straightened. "I always do."

"I hope you plan to behave yourself tonight."

Lawrence gave him a mock-innocent smile. "Who, little old me?"

"Yeah. Little old you." Harrigan thumped the man's chest with a finger. "You cause any trouble tonight, I'm going to throw your ass out of here, personally."

Lawrence's expression turned lip-curl defiant. "Hey, pal, ever hear of freedom of the press? I can ask that commie bastard whatever I damn well please."

"Of course you can." Harrigan latched onto the reporter's lapels and shoved him against the wall and went nose to nose. " 'Course, you know what they say—freedom isn't free."

"Hey!" Lawrence bleated, wide-eyed. "You can't do that!"

Harrigan let loose of the man and stepped away. "I must be imagining things, then—'cause I thought I just did."

Krueger's hand settled on Harrigan's shoulder. "Jack," the FBI agent whispered, "take it easy."

Lawrence was smoothing out his suitcoat, trying to regain his dignity, sputtering, "Somebody's gonna hear about this! You don't fuck with the press."

"After foreplay I do," Harrigan grinned and stepped forward, and the reporter jumped back and scurried off toward the banquet room doors.

Krueger was looking at Harrigan, who said, "What?"

"He might file a complaint."

Harrigan shrugged. "His word against ours, buddy."

"Suddenly you're too much of a card."

"S.O.B.'ll think twice before causing trouble tonight."

"Maybe. Or maybe you've goaded him into bein' a bigger bastard than he was planning on."

Harrigan sighed. "Yeah. Well."

Krueger patted Harrigan's shoulder. "Jack, why don't you go cool off somewhere? I got this covered."

Harrigan grunted a laugh and gave Krueger a rueful grin. "Sorry, Sam. That guy gets under my skin."

"Which seems to be pretty thin, right now."

"Maybe so," Harrigan admitted.

"A guy with Marilyn Monroe in his pocket oughta be in a better mood."

"I suppose so . . ." He checked his watch. ". . . I guess I'll go on down to the service entrance. . . . K should be arriving soon. You seem to have everything under control up here."

"I did till you showed." Krueger smirked. "Go!" He gestured to the small walkie-talkie attached to his belt. "I'll call, if I need you to shake somebody down or something."

"Okay."

Taking one of the curving staircases next to the elevators, Harrigan trotted down to the second floor. As he neared the bottom, a beefy FBI agent with a blond crew cut was in the middle of his own argument with a journalist.

Harrigan knew the reporter, John Davis from *Newsweek*, a guy about as mild-mannered as Clark Kent but with absolutely no possibility of turning into a man of steel; Davis was also one of the few in the press who'd been giving Khrushchev a fair shake.

The slight *Newsweek* reporter spotted Harrigan. "Hey! *He* knows me. Ask him!"

"What's this about?" Harrigan asked the brawny FBI agent.

"Guy doesn't have a badge," the agent said, frowning, jerking a thumb at Davis. "And he's trying to talk his way in. I've told him ten times that's not a possibility."

The reporter spread both hands, palms out. "And I've told him ten times I must have lost the darn thing." He looked pleadingly at Harrigan. "You've cleared me before . . . John Davis, *Newsweek* . . . remember? You're agent Hannigan, right?"

"Harrigan. Yes, I remember." To the FBI agent he said, "This one's okay. Pass him through."

But the agent shook his head. "Sorry, sir. No badge, no entrance—those are my orders."

Normally, Harrigan would have agreed. But his recent altercation with Lawrence had left a sour taste in his mouth; he didn't need any more bad press with the press.

"I'm the one who sent down those orders," Harrigan told the agent. "Let him in. I'll call Sam Krueger by walkie and Sam'll meet him upstairs, and clear him."

The FBI agent raised his eyebrows at this breech, but reluctantly stepped aside.

"Thanks," Davis said to Harrigan, "I owe you one. . . ."

"Then do me a favor," Harrigan responded. "Take it easy on Khrushchev with the questions, will you?"

"Haven't I always?" Davis replied, and hurried up the stairs.

Harrigan stepped away from the beefy FBI agent and got

Krueger on the walkie-talkie, informing him of the *Newsweek* reporter coming up the stairs.

"And spread the word we may have an interloper," Harrigan said.

"What?" Krueger's voice crackled back. "What do you mean?"

"We may have an extra badge floating around."

The first segment of the evening, the dinner, went smoothly, and for that, Harrigan was grateful and relieved. The three hundred or so businessmen and businesswomen of Los Angeles—much more conservatively dressed than their Hollywood counterparts—behaved respectfully toward the premier of Russia, giving him an enthusiastic round of applause when he suddenly appeared from an entrance behind the dais. The clapping continued until the beaming Khrushchev took his seat at the long banquet table.

The atmosphere of the room, while certainly not festive, did seem upbeat to Harrigan, even optimistic, as people chatted at their tables while the meal was served, even light laughter occasionally sprinkling itself in.

Absent this evening were Nina Khrushchev and the grown children, who were being shown some of the local sights, an approved, highly controlled list that included Grauman's Chinese Theater, the Santa Monica Pier, and one of those new outdoor shopping centers.

As Krueger had indicated, two groups of reporters were corralled at the left and right side of the dais—Harrigan noted, among those at left, the notorious William Lawrence of the *New York Times*, and on the right, *Newsweek*'s benign John Davis. Not that Harrigan was familiar with every reporter covering the evening's event; some were new faces . . . others, members of the foreign press, possibly including a dark-haired, dark-complexioned fellow who seemed to be working hard to jockey his way toward the front of the pack, a camera in hand—though unlike his brethren, he hadn't bothered snapping any shots yet.

Looking refreshed after his afternoon nap, Khrushchev—seated next to Henry Cabot Lodge—seemed to be enjoying himself. During the meal of garden salad, rare prime rib, and a large baked potato, the premier traded stories (through translator Troyanovsky, seated on Khrushchev's other side) with the handsome, urbane U.N. ambassador.

As Harrigan made another slow pass in front of the dais, he picked up on Khrushchev saying to Ambassador Lodge, "You know, we had to force the people of Russia to plant potatoes—they were suspicious of them—and now we eat them all the time!"

Lodge leaned toward the premier. "Are they as big as this in Russia?" he asked with a smile, pointing to the huge potato on his plate.

"No," Khrushchev chuckled. "Where I come from, we call that a Sputnik."

Lodge's laughter in response was genuine.

This was going so well that Harrigan was getting nervous.

As FBI waiters were clearing away the dishes, Norris Poulson rose from his chair down at the far end of the dais and approached the podium. Through narrow eyes, the State Department man watched the mayor of Los Angeles as if he were a suspect under surveillance. Harrigan had heard from Sam Krueger that Henry Cabot Lodge—in the lobby of the Ambassador—had given Poulson a dressing-down, over the mayor's ill-advised, undiplomatic behavior at the airport.

Poulson was scheduled to give a short introductory speech after the dinner.

But something in the mayor's eyes said otherwise.

Harrigan tensed as Poulson, at the podium, chin high, looked sideways at Khrushchev and patronizingly pronounced, "You shall not bury us, and we shall not bury you. But if challenged, we shall fight to the death to preserve our way of life."

Poulson's delivery was worthy of a high school kid playing Patrick Henry in a Fourth of July pageant . . . but perhaps a little more pompous, and a bit less skillful.

Lodge lurched forward in his seat and glared at Poulson, looking like he wanted to strangle His Honor.

Khrushchev's previously cheerful face turned purple, and the premier launched from his seat like a rocket. Clutched in the Russian's hands was the speech he'd intended to deliver after receiving yet another "introduction" from the mayor; but Khrushchev ripped the pages into little pieces and threw them in Poulson's face.

The audience gasped, while the reporters grinned and flashbulbs popped and pencils flew on pads; that swarthy unfamiliar journalist was still working to get a better view of the premier.

Khrushchev pointed a thick finger at Poulson. "Why would you mention that?" he shouted, as his translator quickly gave the English version. "Is it your tradition to invite people to a banquet to insult them? Already in the U.S. press I have clarified this 'We will bury you'—I only meant that communism will *outlive* capitalism. . . . I trust that even minor officials in your country learn to read."

There was a smattering of applause from the crowd.

"In our country," Khrushchev continued, eyes wide, nostrils flared, his whole body shaking, "chairmen of councils who do *not* read what is in the papers are at risk of *not* being re-elected."

Now the entire audience clapped its approval.

Harrigan couldn't help smiling; the mayor, soon to be up for re-election, had shot himself in the foot . . . or perhaps higher up.

"And I promise if your president comes to Russia," the premier said with acid sweetness, "the mayor of Moscow will not dare to insult him."

This invoked a few smiles.

Poulson's face turned crimson, and—trembling, obviously as afraid as he was embarrassed—returned to his chair and sat.

Khrushchev took the podium.

"Ladies and gentlemen," the premier said loudly, Troyanovsky interpreting at his side, "you want to get up on this favorite horse of yours and proceed in the same old direction. Fine—if you want a continuation of the arms race, then, very well, we accept that challenge. And as for the output of our missiles, those are on the assembly line."

A hush fell over the room.

"I am talking seriously because I have come here with serious intentions," Khrushchev went on, the interpreter struggling to keep up, "and yet you try to reduce the matter to simply a joke. It is a question of war or peace between our countries, a question of life or death of the people."

Silence draped the room like a shroud, a silence that the premier shattered by pounding the podium with a fat fist.

"I have never before in any of my addresses in your country spoken of or mentioned any missiles . . . but I did so just now, because I had no other way out—because it would seem that we have come here to *beg* you to eliminate the cold war. Perhaps you think we are afraid. If so, and if you think the cold war is profitable to you, then go ahead. Let us compete in the cold war . . . but in my country we have a saying: it is much better to live in peace than to live with loaded pistols."

The audience broke out in applause to show the Soviet leader some much-needed support. But Khrushchev was not to be pacified by their gesture.

"The thought sometimes," he went on angrily, "the unpleasant thought, creeps up on me as to whether I was not invited here to enable you to sort of rub my face in the might and strength of the U.S., so as to make me shake in my shoes. . . ."

Khrushchev bent and removed one of his brown leather shoes, which he brought up and banged on the table, startling everyone in the room, making those seated on the dais jump, spilling drinks and rattling dishes.

"If that is so," the premier growled, "then if it took me about twelve hours to get here, I guess it will take me no more than that to fly home!"

The banquet hall fell deadly silent again, at the implication of his words.

"I am going to close," Khrushchev said, more restrained now. "I believe you have suffered through my speech . . . and I would apologize for that, but so was I made to suffer. You see, I have such a nature that I do not want to remain in debt . . . nor do I not want to be misunderstood."

Khrushchev was turning away from the podium when William Lawrence called out from the cluster of reporters on the left.

"Where were *you* when Stalin was killing innocent people?" the *New York Times* reporter shouted.

Instantaneously, the audience reacted. Fearful of antagonizing Khrushchev further, they rushed to their guest's defense and jumped the journalist, some booing him, others yelling, "Shut up!" and "Leave him alone!"

Fire returned to Khrushchev's eyes. "I will not answer such a stupid question!" the premier snapped. "You are a silly, ignorant man. . . ."

Then, from that same pack as Lawrence, that dark reporter shouted in a thick Middle European accent, "What about the people you murdered in Hungary?"

On the right side of the dais with the other journalist, Harrigan—who had stayed aware of the reporter as he'd kept inching forward—wondered who this fellow was, this reporter with no pad or pencil for notes, and a camera that, so far, had not taken any pictures.

Hadn't he seen this man before . . . ?

But where?

From his position across the room, Harrigan could not read the man's badge . . . and a chill went through him as he wondered if that might be a badge lifted from John Davis. . . .

Harrigan moved through the throng of reporters that had closed in around the front of the dais, squeezing by Davis, whose own makeshift badge was pinned to his shirt.

"Well, you see," Khrushchev responded from the podium, "the question of Hungary sticks in some people's throats like a dead rat."

Harrigan ducked behind the dais, picking up his pace.

Khrushchev was saying, "He feels that it is unpleasant, and yet he cannot pull the dead rat out. . . . We, for our part, could think of quite a few dead rats we could throw at you!"

Harrigan reappeared on the other side of the dais, now able to see the questioning reporter's badge . . .

. . . *John Davis, Newsweek*!

The swarthy "reporter" was fumbling with his camera, trying to open its back, saying defiantly, "No, no—it is *you* who are the dead rat."

There was no time to raise Krueger on the walkie-talkie, or even signal him; the FBI agent was at the back of the room, stationed by the banquet doors.

So Harrigan rushed the dark-haired man, coming between him and Khrushchev.

"That's enough of you," Harrigan said, grabbing onto the camera—which the man would not let go of—while forcibly pushing him back. Harrigan kept shoving, the two doing an awkward little dance, until the agent bodily forced them both through the swinging kitchen doors.

The "reporter" was slender but strong, and he would not let go of that camera, even after Harrigan slammed a forearm into the man's chest, sending him to the hard kitchen floor. As the kitchen staff reacted by rushing the hell out of there, Harrigan jumped on the son of a bitch, whose eyes were wild, body thrashing . . . but that camera still locked in his hands.

They were still scuffling over the camera, Harrigan on top of the man, when Sam Krueger burst into the kitchen.

"Jesus Christ, Jack!" Krueger blurted. "How many times I gotta tell ya—you can't treat the press that way!"

With a final yank, Harrigan wrenched the camera out of the man's fingers, but with such momentum that the thing flew out of his own hands, hitting the floor with a crack, spilling its deadly contents: a small black revolver. The gun skittered across the linoleum, spinning to a stop under a utility cart laden with dirty dishes.

Harrigan figured the assassin would dive for the weapon, but instead the man scrambled to that cart and shoved it, sending it careening toward the agent, who dove out of the way, leaving the cart to narrowly miss a startled Krueger, and slam into a wall, sending dishes flying and crashing and cracking. In the meantime, the would-be assailant took advantage of the upheaval to make a dash for a door at the rear of the kitchen.

Yanking the .38 from its holster under his shoulder, Harrigan took pursuit, as Krueger yelled behind him, "I'll take the service elevator!"

Shouldering through the door, revolver clutched in both hands, thrust forward, poised to shoot, Harrigan found himself on the landing of a stairwell; above him the stairs led to little landings where the doors were locked—these stairs were for room service pick-up and delivery, the agent knew, accessible only by a kitchen-staff keys.

Of course maybe the would-be assailant had pilfered one of those, too.

Shoes above him echoed like gunshots off the metal steps, and Harrigan peered up, gun poised as he leaned out the stairwell; he could see above him the would-be assassin's hand on the railing.

If the guy didn't have a key, they had him: Harrigan raced up the stairs, knowing that any moment Sam would come barreling down, squeezing their man between them.

Then he heard Krueger's voice: *"Stop! Freeze! Hands up!"*

But Harrigan kept running anyway, in case the guy came back down . . .

. . . which he did, but not in the way Harrigan expected.

The would-be assassin came flying past him, down the stairwell, like an Olympic diver heading for the water, filling the space between the railings, and Harrigan barely saw him, catching just a flash of the whites of wide eyes in the dark, tortured face.

The man was screaming something, and at first Harrigan thought it was just a cry of terror: *"EEEEeeee . . ."*

But it turned into something else, a word . . . a name?

Eva?

Then came a dull thud below, punctuated by the

twig-like snapping of bones.

Harrigan looked down at the twisted form, then glanced up at Krueger, leaning over the railing several floors above, arms spread wide (revolver in one hand), as if to say, *Hey, I didn't* touch *him.*

By the time Krueger joined him, Harrigan was bending over the limp body of the young man, searching for a pulse he knew wouldn't be there. The poor bastard had landed on the side of his head and half of his face was smashed in, one shoulder crunched under him unnaturally.

"The guy just fucking jumped," Krueger said, out of breath.

Harrigan checked for I.D. and—other than the pilfered press badge—found nothing. He stood.

Holstering his revolver, Krueger asked, "Who the hell is he?"

"Well," Harrigan said, putting his own weapon away, "he sure as hell's not from *Newsweek.*"

"Shit—Davis's badge. . . . I screwed the pooch on this one, Jack."

"No. We stopped him, Sam—that's all that counts. Anyway, I had my chance earlier and blew it."

"What do you mean?"

"I saw him at the airport this morning, when he was heckling Khrushchev. . . . That's no doubt where he lifted the badge. . . ."

Krueger stared down at the twisted body. "I wonder what ol' Nikita did to piss him off."

"I think we're looking at a serving of Hungarian goulash," Harrigan said dryly, nodding at the corpse. "We have to keep a lid on this, Sam—full lockdown."

"The kitchen's already sealed off," Krueger said, patting his walkie-talkie. He looked up the stairwell. "All those doors, too."

"Well, aren't you right on top of things tonight?"

"Don't rub it in. Jack. . . ."

Harrigan frowned, taking in the FBI man's quizzical expression. "What, Sam?"

Krueger shook his head. "You know what those goddamn Russians did in Hungary—those kids they mowed down. You know this pitiful slob was just trying to strike back, most likely."

"Yeah. Your point being?"

"My point being—how in the hell can you stand it?"

"Stand what?"

Krueger made a distasteful face. "Putting your life on the line for that commie prick. . . . It's not like when you were Secret Service, guarding Ike. . . ."

Harrigan shrugged. "Khrushchev's just a guy I'm sworn to protect. I leave it to the world to decide if he's good or evil . . . or something in between."

Krueger sighed, then gestured to the body. "We'll get him out of here—without the press knowing. That's what you want, isn't it?"

"That's what I want," Harrigan said, smiled, and patted the agent on the back.

"Anything for you, buddy," Krueger said. "You and ol' Nikita."

"*Now* who's the card?" Harrigan asked, and left the FBI man to his corpse.

Chapter Nine

RESCUE MISSION

In the Presidential Suite at the Beverly Hills Hotel, Nikita Khrushchev lay on his back in bed like a beached sea beast, arms and legs spread wide, in an X-formation. Darkness enveloped the room and he could not see the ceiling at which he stared. The most powerful man in Russia felt like the most impotent man in America, and he did not like it one bit.

In the suite next door, his wife Nina and their older daughter Julia (Rada and her husband Alexei had their own room), would be slumbering soundly, not a care in the world, visions of capitalist sightseeing dancing in their untroubled minds. Nina had not shared a bed with her husband for some years, because (she said) of his thrashing about, when he couldn't sleep, and his night-rending snoring, when he could. Tonight was one of the "couldn't" ones; though it was well after midnight, and he was thoroughly exhausted—both mentally and physically—Nikita had not yet even *tried* to court slumber. His mind danced furiously, racing from one outrage to another, from assaults by the press to poor security from the American government, the premier incensed over the generally boorish, disrespectful treatment he had received during his short stay in Los Angeles, especially from that *vyesh brakovanaya* mayor, Poulson.

Beyond that, the premier was disheartened, feeling more

depressed than he had in years. The stakes were so high now: these Americans, in their arrogance, could not seem to fathom the reality of potential Armageddon. He had not felt such despondence since World War II, when he was left at the front to fight the overpowering Germans, while Stalin hid under the bed back at his dacha, having his latest nervous breakdown.

Nikita's trip to America had not gone at all well. He could not fault himself—hadn't he been on his best behavior, throughout? He realized his occasional so-called "outbursts" had brought criticism and not just in the American press; but Nikita could not have looked the other way when he was insulted, because to insult him was to insult Russia; it was not a matter of pride, rather the projection of strength.

But so much, so very much might have been accomplished by a successful visit, affecting positively the future of Soviet Russia, the United States, the very world itself.

Didn't the egotistical Americans realize they were playing with atomic fire? That when you got burned in such a game, the result was more than just blisters . . . or had they forgotten Hiroshima? Maybe so, since it had been the enemy on the receiving end. Well, if the Americans weren't concerned about disarmament, then so be it! The Russians already had nuclear rockets aimed at every one of the USA's major cities . . . and there could easily be more Russian rockets to aim at more American cities. . . .

Nikita rolled onto his right side, and the bedsprings seemed to cry in agony.

Rage gave birth to frustration. The problem with this arms race was that all these missiles cost money . . . money that was necessary for seed to feed the Russian people. And the people needed to be working the farms, not making rockets, or out fighting wars. When farmers traded wheat fields for battlefields, where were the crops?

Why, in this modern world, must men still harvest death?

The Soviet Union was not like the affluent, decadent United States, where waging war turned a profit, benefiting big business; even Eisenhower had warned of the power of the U.S. military industrial complex, had he not?

But for Russia, another war would only bring starvation and further suffering . . . and the Russian people had suffered enough! And so, when the Americans challenged him, he blustered and threatened. They might think him a bully or a thug, but what else could he do? He had to show America his . . . his *country's* . . . might.

After all, if they ever came to his country, and had a good look around . . . they would see just how poor Russia really was.

Nikita rolled onto his back again and the bedsprings whined and he put his hands behind his head, elbows splayed out on the pillow, his eyes searching unsuccessfully for the ceiling. His insomniac's mind leapt to another indignity, one that seemed especially galling to him.

Why couldn't he go to Disneyland?

The State Department had promised he could! He had made so few specific requests that by denying him, the Americans had served up yet another insult. And he had so been looking forward to it. After his journalist son-in-law had visited America several years ago, Mikhail had enthusiastically described the park's magnificent "rides" and "attractions," as the Americans called them.

But whenever he'd brought up the subject to his hosts, Nikita had been treated like a child denied his fun, when he knew full and well the Americans were protecting the park from prying eyes, treating it like another state secret.

And they were right: if he could have even the most cursory tour of the site, he could copy the idea for his country. After all, he built the Moscow subway by patterning it upon the New York one; he could certainly make the plans for a similar amusement park.

Russia's amusement park would not be named after one man—the California park was named for this "Walt Disney," in a debauched deification of a capitalist entertainer—and he would resist any effort to have it called Khrushchevland. After the abuses of Stalin, who had changed the name of Leningrad to Stalingrad, Nikita had forbidden anything—city, building, or otherwise—to be named after a politician . . . even himself . . . because it might elevate that person to a "cult personality," a concept that flew in the face of true Lenin doctrine.

And if he did build this "amusement" park, there would certainly not be anything as insignificant as a tiny field mouse appointed as its chief emissary! Anyway, Nikita failed to see what was so funny about this Mickey Mouse, a cartoon that talked and sang in a squeaky little voice. . . . No, Russia would have something big as its envoy—what else but a bear! . . . a dancing, growling bear that could, if it so desired, *step* on and squash such a squeaky little mouse.

Now *that* would be amusing!

Smiling, Nikita rolled onto his left side, then sighed. Just about the only bright spot in the otherwise bleak day had been his encounter with the lovely actress, this Marilyn Monroe. She was even more beautiful in person than in the glamorous photos he'd seen of her on display at the American National Exhibition in Moscow. That's where he got the idea of meeting her during his trip to the United States.

In the privacy of his mind, he allowed himself to wonder if the heavy, garish make-up the woman had worn had added to, or detracted from, her beauty. Had his own conception of beauty been corrupted by Hollywood customs? He wished he could see her stripped of that paint, those pretty features free of Western decadence, that wonderful smile shining bright without the crimson frame. . . .

He frowned. But why hadn't she been at the show at Fox Studios? She just disappeared after the meal—which had been yet another American insult. Red potatoes and corn! He well understood the disparaging symbolism of that menu—that he was an unsophisticated "red" (and Mikhail had explained the slang term "corny" to him). Did they think the premier of Russia would be so unworldly as think it appropriate that a "French cafe" would serve such a farmhand's meal?

Shifting to his right side, Nikita sighed again, chest deep. The goddess Marilyn Monroe, he thought, had probably been too repulsed by him, by his many chins and warts and his corpulence, to sit at his side during the filming of that bawdy picture, what was it called? *Can-Can*! More pseudo-Parisian tripe.

Ha! What stupid, silly trash! Russia, East Germany, even Romania, all made much better musicals than this gaudy Hollywood nonsense. What could Twentieth Century Fox come up with to compete with the likes of *The Bright Path*, or *My Wife Wants to Sing*, or *Volga Volga*?

The latter film, admittedly, had worn its welcome out with Nikita—an epic agricultural operetta, *Volga Volga* had been shown so many times by Stalin at his private dinners that Khrushchev had for a time hoped to never hear another song or, for that matter, see another tractor.

Even so, the musicals the Soviets made had real meaning, designed to stir the masses and give them hope and inspire them to become better communists. The

Eastern Bloc films weren't about a bunch of trollops twirling around and flashing their undergarments and showing off their legs and exhibiting their backsides—although, he had to admit, in the secrecy of his insomnia, that those *were* shapely backsides, and in fact were preferable to the face of Mayor Poulson. Still, what idiocy, those girls prancing in front of a camera that clearly didn't have any film in it.

That might have been what had wounded Nikita the most, the worst of all the insults: the Americans considered him nothing more than a country bumpkin they could fool and trick. Did they suppose he'd never been in a movie studio before?

Well, they could go to this hell they claimed to believe in.

Back on his back, he stared up at the blackness, his chin crinkling, lips trembling. Could a country bumpkin have outwitted Stalin, the most evil, treacherous man in the world? A world that had included Adolph Hitler—who had been a piker in the genocide business, compared to old Joe. And could a country bumpkin have been the only man in Stalin's inner circle to survive his perfidious purges?

And yet some uneducated fool from the American press could have the gall to ask Nikita where *he* was when Stalin was murdering innocent people. . . .

The Ukraine—that was where Nikita Khrushchev was! . . . Saving thousands of people from starvation . . . unaware of Stalin's atrocities!

Afterward, his translator Troyanovsky had asked him, respectfully, why Nikita had not responded with the truth of it.

"Because," Nikita had snapped, "there is no good answer to a stupid question!"

Of *course* Nikita had supported Stalin, even worked for him—as the saying went, "If you ride in another man's cart, you must join in his song!" To oppose Stalin would have meant certain death. And the dead cannot help the living.

How else, but by such compromise, could Nikita have survived the dangerous years to reach the pinnacle of power, where he was finally in a position to change bad conditions for the better? Hadn't he then thrown out all of Stalin's men after the dictator's death?

Hadn't he then denounced Stalin and everything that butcher stood for?

Hadn't he released tens of millions of innocent people from the prisons, given them back their homes and jobs and reputations?

Hadn't he relaxed the Lenin doctrine by allowing for a few western ideas, even at the expense of angering hard-line party members, including the Republic of China?

Hadn't he improved agriculture, education, technology, and the human spirit of the Russian people?

Could a country bumpkin do all that?

Worked up, sweating despite the air conditioning in the suite, Nikita rolled over on his left side, mind racing.

And that mayor, that stupid mayor, digging up Nikita's statement about "burying" capitalism . . . it was a proven fact, throughout history, that first comes feudalism, then capitalism, then communism. So why didn't these Americans (if they were so smart) learn from history and just skip a step and adopt communism, and save themselves and everybody else a whole world of trouble?

After all, communism was the only true and fair government—the only system that put the people first. It was just an unfortunate accident of history that a murderous snake called Joe Stalin had been in charge of that system for twenty-five years. . . .

Another thought would no doubt have formed—Nikita

was hours away from sleep—but a sound interrupted, something small but insistent, coming from across the room. Nikita's eyes tightened, his ears perked—he turned his head and listened close.

Nothing.

Had he imagined it? With a sigh, he flopped onto his back, the bedsprings protesting, and then, after a moment of silence, the noise started up again: a tapping.

A tiny tap, tap, tapping . . .

Nikita leaned on an elbow in the bed, and reached for the Tokarev Model TT-30 that he always kept under the pillow on his absent wife's side of the bed.

But the pistol wasn't there.

Wide awake now, sitting up, knowing that the only way the gun (which he'd tucked under that pillow personally) could be gone was if someone had stolen it . . . and he doubted a maid had done so . . . Nikita Khrushchev listened as the tapping persisted.

Nikita crawled out of bed, as quietly as possible—which wasn't quiet at all, the bedsprings screeching—and padded in his bare feet and silk burgundy pajamas across to the bathroom, where he did not turn on the light. In his shaving kit he found his straight razor; he flipped open the blade and a sliver of light from somewhere in the room winked off its deadly steel.

The tapping continued . . . picking up in pace, a frantic edge to its unspecified message.

Peering through the darkness, Nikita—razor at the ready—moved slowly toward the sound, which revealed itself as coming from one of the velvet-curtained windows. A guard was stationed on the fire escape beyond . . . was he signaling Nikita?

Was something wrong?

Cautiously, at one side, he touched the heavy, drawn drapes and peeked around their edge.

Out on the black wrought-iron balcony of the fire escape, the guard was nowhere to be seen—but a young woman was, crouching on the other side of the window. The fingers of one of her hands were tapping on the glass, and her eyes were wide in the moonlight.

Could it be . . . ?

No, his eyes must be betraying him. Was he dreaming? Yet the sharp-edged blade in his hand was real. Still, he closed his eyes, and opened them again.

Yes, it was her!

Marilyn Monroe . . . outside his bedroom window. . . .

Nikita Khrushchev had no idea what the actress wanted; he was a faithful husband and a good communist, but he was also a man whose blood was at least as red as his politics, and he was not about to take lightly such a visitor. He moved around and drew the curtains wide. Quickly he unlatched the window, raising it up high.

She gasped.

Then she said, "Hello. Remember me?"

He just stared at her.

She was wearing American blue jeans with sandals, a red-and-blue plaid blouse knotted at her waist. Her hair was tousled, a tangle of blond curls, her face free of any make-up.

In the moonlight, she was even more beautiful than she had been at the luncheon. It was as he'd mused: without the Hollywood paint, she was radiant, like a young, fresh-faced, well-scrubbed Russian peasant girl. To gaze on such beauty made his heart ache.

"You have to get out of here!" she whispered. The woman's forehead was taut with terror.

Her distress took him aback; the missing pistol gave the woman credibility, but how was she part of anything that might concern him . . . ?

She narrowed her eyes and shook her head, clearly frustrated, obviously distraught. "How can I make you understand? . . . I only know a little Russian. . . . I don't know how to tell you in your language. . . ."

"I understand you perfectly," Nikita said in English.

Her eyes became large. "You . . . you do?"

He nodded.

"But . . . but . . . your interpreter . . . ?"

Nikita shrugged. "Letting others think I speak no English gives me advantage."

"Oh," the movie star said, impressed, "I see . . . how clever of you!"

Her reaction pleased him, and he was wondering if he should invite her into his bedroom; but he was a married man, a husband, a father, and the woman was young and beautiful . . . and they were both what Americans called a "V.I.P.," and the danger presented by the missing pistol was matched by the scent of scandal.

These thoughts passed through Nikita's mind in a moment.

"Why have you come?" he asked, leaning a hand on the sill, playing portly Juliet to her comely Romeo.

The terror returned to her eyes. "I'm afraid something bad is going to happen to you," she said, "if we don't leave here at once."

Holding the razor behind him—he did not suspect her, he instinctively trusted the woman, but he did not want to frighten her—Nikita smiled. He was flattered that the famous Hollywood actress was concerned for him, and it affirmed his belief that the American people and its government were not necessarily of the same mind.

"What could happen to me here?" he said with a chuckle and a shrug. "Over one hundred people are on this floor and around hotel ground, to guard and protect me."

"Well, if that's true," she said, eyes big and seemingly innocent, "then how come *I* made it up this fire escape and nobody stopped me?"

Nikita felt his smile fade. The woman had made a valid point. Where *was* the guard supposedly stationed on the fire escape? Had the guard gone to that same place as the pistol under his pillow?

Nikita crouched down, face to face with Marilyn now, the windowsill between them, his eyes locking onto hers. "Why is it you think I am in danger?" he asked.

He listened intently as she told him of overhearing a troubling conversation today in a men's room between two of his trusted KGB guards; she suspected a conspiracy to assassinate him among his own people.

In these circumstances—in this unfriendly town, in a hotel room where his personal pistol and the guard guarding his window had both vanished—the woman's words rang all too true.

"Please," she pleaded as he pondered, "it's almost two o'clock! That's the *time* they say 'goodbye' to you! You *must* come with me. . . ."

He frowned, confused. "Come with you . . . ?"

"I rented a car for us—hurry up!" She reached out with both hands, grabbed onto his pajama top, and tugged, trying to pull him out onto the fire-escape balcony.

"Please," he said, pulling away with dignity, holding up one hand. "You must allow me to get pants."

"All right—but shake a leg!"

Having no idea how shaking a leg would quicken the act of putting on pants, Nikita rose from the window. *Should he believe her?* He gazed down at her sweet, earnest face. *Yes—of course he should.*

This instinctive belief in Marilyn—along with other gut instincts that had saved his life more than once over many a harrowing year—now urged him to flee.

He snatched his tan trousers from a nearby chair, pulled them quickly over his pajama bottoms, then plucked up his brown shoes. He closed the straight razor and slipped it in his pants pocket.

"Hurry, hurry!" Marilyn cried from the window.

No time for socks, and for a shirt the pajama top would have to do. Shoes in hand, Nikita climbed through the window, and swiftly, agilely, followed Marilyn down the fire escape, even as behind him he heard the splintering of the door to his locked room . . .

. . . then the unmistakable *snick, snick, snick* of a sound-suppressed automatic pistol, as bullets chewed up the bed where fortunately—thanks to Marilyn Monroe—he was no longer at rest . . . though had she not, sleep would finally have come to him.

Nikita and Marilyn were halfway down the fire escape when a bullet zinged off the railing just behind them, barely missing the premier.

Marilyn shrieked and froze.

Nikita grabbed her hand and pulled the trembling woman along, and they raced down the fire escape, feet clattering and clanging on the metal, and above them other feet were doing the same; then they jumped the last few steps as another bullet from the silenced gun smacked into the hotel's wall with a *poof!*, spraying them with pink plaster.

Together they ran around the back of the building, and along the deserted swimming pool, the moon placid and unimpressed as it shimmered off the still water. Then the couple burst through the foliage at the pool's end.

"This way!" Marilyn cried, taking the lead, pulling Nikita across the hotel grounds by one hand, his shoes clutched in his other, as the two went winding around and through the lavishly flower-arrayed and shrub-flung landscape. They did not hear anyone in pursuit, and maybe they'd eluded the assassin . . . Nikita sensed it was only one person. . . .

As they rounded a bush, Marilyn stumbled, nearly falling over a body sprawled on the grass. She stifled a scream with her hands.

Nikita, breathing heavily, looked down at one of his *Okhrana* guards, lying face up, a small black hole in the forehead of his pockmarked face.

"This is guard on fire escape," he said flatly.

Her voice was breathy, an out-of-wind whisper. "But . . . *he* was one of the men in the bathroom!"

"A traitor betrayed. Forget him." Nikita looked at her urgently. "Where is car?"

"Over there!" Marilyn pointed to a blue vehicle parked in front of one of the hotel's little houses. Then she dug in a pocket of her jeans and pulled out some keys.

"I'll drive," she said.

"It is your city," he said.

Hand in hand, they ran to the car and climbed in, Marilyn behind the wheel, Nikita next to her.

She started the engine and drove quickly out of the hotel grounds. At the street, she turned left, the car making a protesting squeal, and sped away down a wide, all-but-deserted street bordered by palms. The famous Sunset Boulevard, a street sign told him.

"Where are we going?" Nikita asked Marilyn, as the city streaked by. "Police?"

"No! I don't trust anybody right now . . . except you."

Bright lights in the darkness flashed around them, as he managed a smile; he began to put on his shoes. "You are smart woman."

"I thought of somewhere safe," she said, her face wet with tears; but she was smiling—she seemed proud of herself. "The one place no one . . . no American, no Russian . . . will ever think to look for you . . . not in a million years."

He frowned at the pretty thing. "Where is this place?"

Her eyes were a little wild as she beamed at him. "It's called Disneyland. Didn't you want to go there?"

Chapter Ten

NIGHTMARE IN RED

In his dream, Jack Harrigan was no longer working for the State Department; he was with the CIA, its director, Allen Dulles, having personally asked for Harrigan's transfer, dispatching him on a dangerous foreign assignment.

Right now Harrigan was in Hungary—or a dreamscape version of it anyway, in black-and-white and splashed with shadows like an old crime movie, the sound of a zither plunking, as the spy walked along—a Luger in a hand stuffed deep in a trenchcoat pocket—cutting down narrow, strangely-angled, rubble-littered streets, the perspective all wrong. He was in a hurry to meet his contact, who had valuable information that could save the world; but the CIA man couldn't remember who that contact was, or where in this Caligari world he was to meet that informant.

Then, out of the dark recess of a bombed-out doorway, stepped a beautiful blonde—*Marilyn Monroe!*

Her dress was skin tight and blood-red; it looked painted on, but the paint wasn't dry, the effect liquid, like blood, and her full lips were damp too, painted the same startling color in a world otherwise black and white. Her high heels were black and her flesh creamy white, making a startling contrast against the gray, decayed, bullet-pocked wall behind her.

Suddenly Harrigan remembered: *she was his informant!*

He leaned into the recess of the doorway, as if to kiss

her; instead, he asked, "What do you have for me?"

Her forehead tensing with concern, the movie star spoke, or anyway her blood-red lipsticked mouth was moving . . . but no sound came out.

Harrigan leaned closer still. "What are you saying?" he demanded.

Lovely eyes tightened in fear. And the moist red, luscious lips moved again . . . silently.

Frustrated, the spy shook his head, saying, "I'm not hearing you. . . ."

Suddenly Marilyn reached out and grabbed him by the shoulders and shook him—shook him with unusual strength. As her lips moved again, Harrigan finally could make out what she was saying, but she sounded . . . strange.

"Wake up!" she demanded, her voice deep and husky.

Harrigan—the slumbering State Department agent, not the fantasy CIA spy—now realized he was dreaming, and fought to wake up, to climb out of the dream world, but Marilyn would not let go of him, and it was as if his eyelids were glued shut.

After what seemed an eternity, Harrigan forced his sleep-crusted eyes open, and Sam Krueger's round face floated over him like a moon with features stuck on, Mr. Potato Head-style.

"Wake the fuck up!" Krueger was shouting, shaking Harrigan by the shoulders. "K is gone!"

"Gone?" The groggy, disoriented Harrigan tried to make sense of the words. "Gone how? Gone where?"

The normally affable Krueger was scowling. "Khrushchev has gone *missing,* Sleeping Beauty! And our asses are grass."

All these words Harrigan understood, and—as awake now as if he'd just dived into an icy lake—he bolted upright in bed. The clock on the nightstand reported 2:06 a.m.—and immediately reminded him of Marilyn's prediction . . .

. . . and a promise that had been forgotten in the aftermath of the Hungarian's assassination attempt at the Ambassador.

But the dream—still vivid in his mind, not fading as so many of his dreams immediately did—indicated that somewhere in his subconscious mind he had taken her seriously. Harrigan only wished his conscious mind had done the same.

As Harrigan threw off the bedcovers, Krueger was at his side, adding gravely, "One of the bodyguards is dead."

"One of Khrushchev's KGB ones," Harrigan said, on the move, smoothing the rumpled suit that had doubled as pajamas.

Krueger was frowning in surprise. "Yeah—how did you know—"

"I didn't—Marilyn Monroe did."

"Marilyn Mon . . . Are you dreaming?"

With Krueger on his heels, Harrigan raced down the hotel corridor toward the Presidential Suite, cursing under his breath. There'd be plenty of time to fill the FBI agent in on the actress's now largely moot information.

Still, all Harrigan could think of was that he'd let the woman down—and the premier. After the attempt on Khrushchev's life at the Ambassador Hotel, and the fuss that had followed, he'd been bone tired. He knew he never should have gone to bed, he should have babysat K all night and followed up MM's lead, but fuck! He'd been bushed, goddamnit—how much could one man withstand? He wasn't superhuman.

Rushing toward Khrushchev's room, Harrigan asked Krueger if any of the extra security he'd requested had shown up.

"After you hit the sack, you mean?"

Harrigan glared at him. "Yes—after I hit the sack."

"Nope," Krueger said, shaking his head. "Nobody. Not federal, not local. Not even a Campfire Girl."

Even doing advance work in Des Moines-fucking-Iowa—not exactly a hot-bed of agitators—Harrigan had been able to round up at least five thousand officers to protect Khrushchev. Here, only a few hundred men had stood between the dictator and disaster. They'd been lulled by the finality of the junket, seduced by the California climate . . .

. . . and, once again, Jack Harrigan had been caught with his pants down around his ankles.

Harrigan entered the outer room of Khrushchev's opulent suite; right in his path was the sprawled body of the uniformed KGB agent who'd been guarding the premier's bedroom door.

"Get on your walkie-talkie and get some more bodies up here," Harrigan told Krueger. "Live ones."

Harrigan knelt briefly over the KGB officer, who lay on his back, arms casual at his side. The right lens of the man's wire-framed Coke-bottle glasses was spiderwebbed and blood-spattered, but enough visibility remained through the lens to make out the black gore-ringed hole where his eye should have been. The Russian's gun was still holstered. The man had not expected this—either he was one of the conspirators himself . . . tied off as a loose end by a fellow conspirator . . . or he'd been caught off-guard by someone he trusted.

The poor dead bastard wasn't the only one who'd been caught off-guard tonight. As Krueger used the walkie-talkie out in the hallway, Harrigan stepped over the corpse and crossed the outer area of the suite and entered the bedroom through its door, which yawned open, the wood around the lock splintered by the "key" of a bullet.

Quickly the State Department agent surveyed the sleeping quarters.

Feathers littered the mattress, the pillows shot to hell, several bullet holes on the bedcovers as well.

He yanked back the blankets and sheets, and found no sign of blood anywhere. Harrigan read the scene—in the darkness, the assassin had approached the bed and just started shooting, not realizing that the premier was no longer there.

Krueger approached. "We have men on the way, but Jack—there's another dead guard out in the bushes."

"Another Russian? KGB?"

Again mildly surprised that Harrigan knew this without being told, the FBI man nodded. "The guard who was supposed to be watching the fire escape. . . . We got a coup on our hands?"

He placed a hand on the FBI agent's shoulders. "Let's not get ahead of ourselves, Sam. We have to search these grounds and the whole goddamn hotel, to see if we have any more dead Russians layin' around."

"I already have that in motion."

"Our people only—*not* K's!"

Krueger nodded. "Strictly Secret Service. . . . But so far, two dead Rooskies is all we got."

"Isn't that enough?"

Krueger's face was pale as milk—spilt milk. "What if a certain other Russian stiff turns up?"

Harrigan's laugh was devoid of humor. "Then, Sam, you and I may be the first Americans ever sent to Siberia."

Harrigan was staring at the open window onto the fire escape, the heavy velvet curtains billowing gently from the autumn night breeze.

"If it weren't for the bullet-riddled bed," he said to Krueger, "I'd make this a kidnapping."

"But it isn't—it's an assassination attempt gone . . . please God . . . awry."

"I agree. But then . . . where's Khrushchev?"

Krueger shrugged. "If I were him, and thought my own people were after me, I'd run and hide. You try *under* the bed, Jack?"

Harrigan just looked at Krueger, who'd been kidding of course . . . but then the FBI man did check under there. . . .

Oleg Troyanovsky rushed into the bedroom just as Harrigan was turning away from the window. The previously unflappable translator—wearing only hastily thrown-on trousers and a blue silk pajama top—had unruly hair and wild eyes.

"What have you done?" the translator demanded.

Harrigan let out a breath. "We haven't done anything—your people, your KGB guards, got themselves killed."

"Your incompetence has cost us dearly!"

"Our incompetence? If you people hadn't insisted on using your own staff—"

Troyanovsky got right in Harrigan's face. "You try to shift blame at a time like this! Don't you know what this means?"

"Not yet I don't. Before you came in, I was starting to conduct an investigation. This is a crime scene, and I'd like you to move out into the hall. We'll be setting up some kind of task force HQ, and—"

"Well, *I* know what it means!"

Harrigan raised his eyebrows; if the man had a theory, he'd like to hear it.

But all the translator had to offer was more frenzy: "It means war between our countries! And that means annihilation for us both!"

Harrigan grabbed the frantic man firmly by the forearm.

"Pull yourself together, goddamnit," Harrigan said. "Stop and consider—maybe whoever is behind this *wants* us at each other's throats!"

The translator blinked, looking somewhat embarrassed, and his composure began to return.

Harrigan took command. "We've got to contain this," he said to Krueger and Troyanovsky. "The Secret Service will continue to handle the search of the grounds and this facility. I want the KGB to stay put."

The translator's eyes tightened. "Why would you close us out of this? It is *our* man who is missing. . . ."

"I'm not at liberty to disclose everything I know, Mr. Troyanovsky . . . but those two dead KGB agents may have been part of an assassination conspiracy. We don't know who, among your people, can be trusted."

Troyanovsky brooded on that for a second, then said, "This will go down hard."

"Too bad. Leave it at this: we already have two dead Russians; we don't need any more. . . . Mr. Troyanovsky, has Mrs. Khrushchev been informed?"

The translator shook his head. "She is still asleep . . . the children, too. How is it you say? Ignorance is bliss."

Harrigan thrust a finger at the man's silk-pajamaed chest. "Who among the entourage knows what's happened?"

Troyanovsky shrugged. "Only me."

"Fine—and we've got to keep it that way. . . . If anyone asks, the premier couldn't sleep, and is out on a moonlight stroll with his two bodyguards."

Troyanovsky considered this for a while; finally, he nodded solemnly. "You are right. To protect the premier, we must . . . as you say . . . contain."

"Thank you, Mr. Troyanovsky."

A thin smile allowed itself to appear on the Russian's handsome face. "You might be interested to know, Mr. Harrigan, that the premier has a liking for you. He respects you."

"I appreciate that." Harrigan found a small smile of his own. "I'm not sure I deserve it, but I appreciate it."

Krueger, who had stepped to one side to answer a walkie-talkie call, now sidled up next to Harrigan.

"You've got to come with me," Krueger told him.

"Now?" Harrigan asked irritably. "Sam, I have just a few things to do here, in light of this situation—can't this wait?"

"No," Krueger said, in a manner that conveyed Harrigan's single option in the matter.

Out in the corridor, when an elevator arrived and Harrigan began to step on, Krueger fell back.

"Are you coming, Sam? I mean, it's your party, isn't it?"

"Not hardly," Krueger said, planted firmly on the other side of the elevator doors. "He'll be waiting for you in the basement."

"Who will?"

"Company man."

"Jesus Christ," Harrigan muttered as the doors swooshed shut. That was all he needed—CIA intervention; or maybe his dream was about to come true, and Allen Dulles was waiting down there to transform him from goat into hero. Somehow that seemed just a little unlikely, and the rapid descent of the elevator only added to the sick feeling in his stomach.

The elevator doors slid open in the basement of the Beverly Hills Hotel to reveal a man leaning against the opposite wall smoking a cigarette in a holder, smoke curling upward in a near question mark.

Harrigan didn't know the man—and yet he did.

Lanky, at least ten years older than Harrigan, the spook looked like a high-rent undertaker in his black Brooks Brothers suit with the crisp white button-down shirt and thin black tie, his dark Brillcreamed hair parted on the side. His eyes were china blue and almost pretty, an anomaly in a once handsome face ravaged by time and dirty jobs that somebody had had to do.

As Harrigan stepped out of the elevator, the man switched the affectation of the cigarette-in-holder to his left hand, extending his right.

"John Munson," the man said. "Would you like to see my I.D.?"

"You show me yours," Harrigan said, shaking the clammy hand, "and I'll show you mine."

They held up their respective I.D. wallets—this was no situation in which to cut corners—and Harrigan said, "I figured you guys'd be lurking around."

"Our accommodations aren't as nice as yours," Munson said, taking a draw from the cigarette-in-holder, ironic amusement seemingly etched permanently in his features. He gestured and showed Harrigan the way, down a narrow hallway past doors marked LAUNDRY and HOUSEKEEPING, where the pink decor of the fabled hotel continued even in its bowels. In the narrow, windowless, claustrophobic confines of the basement, however, the color reminded Harrigan of Pepto-Bismol—some of which the queasy agent could have used about now.

The two men approached a final door, STORAGE, which Munson opened, Harrigan following him inside.

Bigger than a broom closet, though not by much, the room had walls lined with metal racks, loaded with cleaning supplies and hand tools; a few mops and brooms leaned casually against a wall, disinterested bystanders.

A card table took up the rest of the room, where sat a chubby man in white shirtsleeves and another thin black tie, headphones straddling his bald head like a bad comb-over. On the table, next to a sweating bottle of Coke and a half-eaten corned-beef on rye dripping with hot mustard, a large tape recorder whirred, in the process right now of being rewound.

"Khrushchev's room?" Harrigan asked, gesturing toward the machine.

Munson nodded. "We put the bug in right after his people swept it."

The combination of smoke, cleaning fluid, and corned-beef on rye was not helping Harrigan's stomach.

"We swept it, too," the State Department man said.

"No, the guy working for you was really working for us. He was installing devices, actually, not just checking for them. Hope you don't mind."

"Anything to help a brother agency."

The hand with the cigarette holder gestured, making abstract smoke patterns. "I think you'll find this . . . of interest."

"You mean, you've got everything on tape," Harrigan said, perking, realizing what that spool might hold. "You know exactly what went down in that room!"

"Well, now," Munson said slowly, sighing smoke, invoking an old radio catchphrase, "I wouldn't say that. . . ."

Harrigan waited for the CIA agent to continue.

"You see, we've been keeping an eye on a certain Chinese assassin for some time. . . ."

Harrigan grunted. "China—should have known. That lead from Formosa. . . ."

"Actually, not *Nationalist* China—Red."

"Red!" Harrigan was stunned.

". . . At any rate, this hitter is a freelancer named Lee Wong; but our operative lost track of him in Hong Kong last month. We considered him a good candidate for use in a K hit, and figured, if such an attempt were to be made on the trip, California with its ample Oriental population made sense for where he might surface."

"Red China," Harrigan said to himself, as if tasting the words, trying to get some recognizable flavor out of them. "They wouldn't dare . . . would they?"

Another sigh of smoke. "Mao Tse-tung is reportedly furious over Khrushchev's visit." Munson made a melodramatic gesture with the cigarette holder. "Views it as a 'sell-out'—the Russians consorting with the enemy, so to speak."

Harrigan was frowning, shaking his head, damn near incredulous. "And that's enough for Mao to start World War III over?"

Munson smiled wickedly. "It might be—if China were on the sidelines, waiting to come out on top."

And now Harrigan had to nod—he could see the terrible "sense" of it. . . .

"We have it on good authority," Munson continued, "that relations between Russia and China have atrophied, although both countries make a concerted effort to lead the free world to believe otherwise."

But now Harrigan was shaking his head. "What in hell makes you think that, Agent Munson? I work the State Department beat, remember—and I've seen nothing but co-operation between Russia and China."

"That's because the State Department—at least on your level, Agent Harrigan—is unaware of Khrushchev's refusal to give Mao the bomb."

Harrigan's eyebrows shot up. "The A-bomb? Mao wanted Russia to share atomic secrets with them . . . ?"

Munson shrugged. "They *are* supposedly allies. You can see how Mao might consider such a refusal . . . less than gracious."

"Jesus, Joseph, and Mary. . . . Well thank God for that much. Maybe Khrushchev means it, all this disarmament talk."

"Perhaps he does," Munson said. "And the failure to share with China, shall we say, one from column A? That discourtesy isn't the only breach between the Red giants—there's also Khrushchev's denunciation of Stalin . . . his determination to erase any memory of the former dictator—who is still revered in China, after all. That is seen by Mao as an outright act of betrayal."

"That I can understand," Harrigan said, half a smirk carving itself in his cheek. "Mao and ol' Joe Stalin have a hell of a lot in common."

"Aptly put," Munson said, nodding; then he drew on the cigarette-in-holder and, as if suggesting a round of golf, said, "Let's play the tape."

The two men looked at the chubby technician, who during their discussion had returned his attention to his sandwich; he switched on the machine with a mustard-smeared finger.

As the tape began to play, Harrigan leaned closer to the machine, but for a few agonizingly long minutes, nothing but hum, mere room tone, could be made out.

Then, finally, came a faint murmur.

"He's talking to himself," Munson whispered.

Harrigan's eyes had heard it too—the premier was talking, all right. . . .

"The fat bastard knows *English,*" Harrigan said through tight teeth. "That son of a bitch!"

"He is a cute one," Munson admitted, then held a

"shush" finger to his lips, though another humming minute of silence followed. Then Munson cocked an ear.

"Now he's getting out of bed," Munson asserted. "He's going to the window . . . opening the window . . . getting some air, perhaps . . ."

Harrigan leaned in further, straining ears that had long since paid the price of his firing handguns.

"Sounds like *two* people talking," Harrigan commented.

"That's what we thought," Munson said, nodding, "but we couldn't be sure. . . . Who would he be talking to, and in English? It's not a bodyguard."

As the tape played on, the voices diminished. Then suddenly a *crack!* and *snick!, snick!, snick!*

The remaining tape returned to room tone.

The chubby technician stopped the tape, and returned to his sandwich.

Harrigan was silent for a moment. "I want to hear it again," he said. He plucked the sandwich from the technician's thick fingers. "And crank it up, this time. Starving kids in Korea don't have headphones, you know."

The chubby tech frowned, but—after a nod from Munson—complied.

As the tape replayed Harrigan's heart began to race.

"Is that a woman's voice?" Munson asked.

"Goddamn," Harrigan said.

"We had no reports of K being any kind of letch. No women, before. What do you make of—"

Harrigan was grinning. "I'll be goddamned if that scatterbrained blonde didn't save all our asses!"

Munson gave Harrigan a puzzled look; even the chubby guy seemed interested.

"What scatterbrained blonde?" Munson asked.

"The one in bungalow seven," Harrigan said without

glancing back—he was already halfway out the door, praying a Chinese assassin hadn't beaten them to the punch.

That K wasn't already dead, with Marilyn Monroe another casualty on the floor of that comfy bungalow, her brains truly scattered.

Chapter Eleven

MAD TEA PARTY

Washed in the ivory glow of a full moon on this clear starry night, the homely portly man and the lovely young woman—looking a bit like father and daughter, or perhaps uncle and niece—sat in a large teacup.

The pair had the Mad Hatter's Tea Party attraction to themselves, that whirling ride of colorful Volkswagen-sized cups-on-saucers, which was motionless at the moment, and . . . like everything else in the vast amusement park around them . . . shrouded in darkness but for the occasional security light. Across the way, its garishly painted movie-flat-style façade muted in the wee hours, stood Mr. Toad's Wild Ride, free of laughter and screams, draped in an eerie stillness, while the turrets of Sleeping Beauty's Castle loomed starkly over all, its fairy-tale majesty turned ominous and medieval by night.

In her jeans and knotted-at-the-navel plaid blouse, Marilyn Monroe—sitting close to Nikita Khrushchev—shivered, and not merely from the cool night breeze. Beyond them, a gentle wind sang in a ghostly voice as it swirled the dust off the hard-dirt floor of the midway, carrying off candy wrappers like captives. A crushed Mouseketeer cap, one of its ears ripped askew, lay discarded on the ground.

Evidence that people had once been there.

It was as if the bomb had dropped, Marilyn thought, and she and Khrushchev were the only ones left alive in a city whose buildings still stood, but where life had been snuffed out by radiation. It was as if, beyond the vast orange groves, Los Angeles had vanished, destroyed in one horrific second, leveled in a white flash, leaving only piles of ashes on bare bones. . . .

"You'll think me silly," she whispered to her gnome-like companion, "but I'm . . . frightened."

With a smile of surprising warmth, Khrushchev took her hand; his hand was warm too, and firm, giving her comfort.

"I also am frightened," he admitted, without shame, his voice as strong as his face was placid. He might have been a suitor, holding his sweetheart's hand, under a moonlit sky.

They had been mostly silent during the twenty-five-minute drive from Beverly Hills, taking the all-but-deserted Santa Monica Freeway south, to the Disneyland exit. Khrushchev did not question her idea to hide him at the amusement park, but she'd explained her thinking, nonetheless.

"We need to get you out of the city," she said, "and then in the morning, when there are crowds at the park . . . do you know our expression, 'safety in numbers'?"

"No," he said, "but it is good one."

"It is," she nodded. "In the morning, we'll contact the authorities . . . and the press . . . and you'll be safe, from whoever it is that's after you."

Khrushchev did not share his thinking with the actress, but he agreed with her strategy—right now he could not know *who* was involved in this conspiracy. Was it a coup? Or had his "loyal" KGB men been bribed by an enemy, the Nationalist Chinese perhaps? By morning his own troops would rally, and that agent Harrigan—about the only American he trusted right now—would have sorted much of it out, the surface at least, though the twisting undercurrent of a conspiracy might remain concealed. Certainly the premier was not about to go to the local police, who were the minions of Mayor Poulson, who himself could have put the assassination attempt in motion, out of some misguided sense of patriotism.

"Will your family be all right?" the actress asked with touching concern, looking over at him as she drove.

"I believe so. They are not targets. Only I. . . . Will we hide among the people at Disneyland?"

"Oh, there's no one there now—it's closed."

"And how will we get in?"

She smiled a little. "We'll sneak in."

"Won't there be guards?"

"No. Not even a night watchman. The local police keep an eye on it, but there's no security staff or anything."

"Los Angeles police?"

"No—Anaheim."

"Anna who?"

"Anaheim . . . it's a city. Not a city really—a little town. That's where Disneyland is close to."

Marilyn had been a guest at the amusement park—built on one hundred and sixty acres surrounded by orange groves—when it had opened just four years ago near tiny Anaheim. She'd been given an after-hours tour by Walt Disney himself—Mr. Disney had great affection for her, ever since she'd posed gratis for his artists who were designing Tinkerbelle for his movie *Peter Pan*—and had left the park when things were closing up and the security people were leaving. Mr. Disney had mentioned to her that the Anaheim police kept an eye on Disneyland for him, after dark.

She hoped things hadn't changed since then.

As she had exited the freeway and onto an asphalt road that led to the park, Khrushchev leaned forward, peering through the windshield, straining to get a first glimpse of the extraordinary American landmark.

Marilyn had been going over and over the assassination attempt in her mind, and assumed her companion had been doing the same. But right now—as they approached the train-station front entry to the park, the immense empty asphalt parking lot at left—the premier seemed unconcerned with the threat on his life, and more like just another impatient kid, anxious to get to Disneyland.

"Is locked," he had said disappointedly, as they passed by the dark entrance, its front gate shut tight for the night.

"Don't worry," she replied, waving this off, "that's not our way in, anyway." Remembering her own visit, and how she'd been smuggled inside from the back, she was heading around behind the sprawling acreage.

Following the Disneyland railroad line, the lane curved around the property, which was protected by a chain link fence ("I do not think that this we can climb," Khrushchev opined). Marilyn drove slowly—with only the moonlight to guide her—and it seemed to take forever, with no view of the park at all, merely a vague sense of trees and foliage.

Finally the chain link fence ended, giving way to a carefully planted border of bushes and trees. At the back of the park was a dirt access road—a service and employee entrance—which branched off at left to some Quonset hut equipment sheds, and curved to the right where soon a waist-high metal gate barred the way.

"That," Nikita said, "we can climb."

And they did, after parking the Buick back behind some tall bushes, the premier graciously lifting the actress up by her small waist, so that she could hop over the barrier; and then he climbed over himself, surprisingly nimble.

Marilyn took the lead as the unlikely couple strolled in

the moonlight, first across the railroad tracks, and then across landscaped grass to the midway, where a pole offered signs pointing in various directions.

Marilyn, a veteran of Disneyland, explained their options. To the left was Tomorrowland, with a spaceship ride and exhibits by major American industries. To the right lay Adventureland, where riverboats churned along a tropical river (when the park was open, that is); and Frontierland, with stagecoaches and paddle-wheel steamers. Straight ahead was Fantasyland, the home of Sleeping Beauty and Never Never Land.

"Let us rest," Nikita suggested.

On the midway, next to a carousel, was the Mad Hatter's Tea Party attraction, which had caught Khrushchev's attention—he smiled as he surveyed the surrealistically oversize cups, decorated with modern-art squiggles. And it was there they now rested, sitting in a teacup, whose center was a circular wheel for children to hold onto, when the party was going strong.

Finally, Marilyn broached the subject they had both avoided, the elephant in the living room no one was mentioning (a Dumbo attraction nearby may have sparked this comparison in her mind). And they began to openly discuss . . . to confront . . . the assassination attempt that had brought them to the slumbering Magic Kingdom.

"It just *couldn't* have been America that did this terrible thing to you," Marilyn said.

"No?" Nikita grunted a humorless laugh. "America hates me."

She shook her head. "That's not true—some people fear you, maybe . . . but that's how you want it, isn't it?"

That made him smile a little; he shrugged a partial admission of guilt.

"Anyway," she continued, "it's not our way—assassinations just don't happen here."

"Oh? Tell that to your President Lincoln."

"That was a long time ago, Premier Khrushchev."

He touched her hand. "Not so formal, please. Call me Nikita. We are friends."

She placed her other hand over his. "Then you must call me Marilyn."

"Marilyn. Is lovely name."

"Nikita has a certain . . . poetry, too."

He chuckled. "That is first time I have heard such."

Somewhere crickets chirped . . . real ones, not Jiminy.

Tentatively, Marilyn said, "Those men tonight . . . they weren't Americans. They were *your* people . . ."

"Working perhaps for you."

Her forehead tensed. "I . . . I wish you wouldn't say it that way. It sounds like you think I sent them, personally."

The sublimely ugly face melted into an apologetic smile. "Sweet child, I did not mean this."

"I know . . . I know." Marilyn shook her head. "And you're right—someone must have hired those two . . . the ones I heard talking. But someone *else* double-crossed them."

He frowned in confusion; his eyes almost disappeared into his face. "What is this . . . 'double-crossed'?"

Marilyn looked up at the sky, and the moon and a million stars stared back; she felt very small, but surprisingly—considering their situation—safe. Their discussion of death and double-dealing seemed oddly abstract.

She told him, "Double-cross is when someone you trust puts a knife in your back."

Nikita let go of her hand and turned his massive body away from her. Muttering to himself, though still speaking

English, he said, "Who could this someone be?"

"In your case?"

He looked at her, mildly surprised she had responded to his rhetorical question as if he'd posed it to her. The premier of Russia normally did not, after all, turn to actresses for political insights.

"Well, let me think for a second. . . ." She placed one platinum-painted fingertip to her lips, and furrowed her brow, a child in class racking her brain for just the right answer.

He patted her hand. "Dear friend, I only meant—"

"My best guess would be Red China."

The eyes of the fat man sitting in the oversize teacup were large as saucers. Then he threw back his bucket head, and laughed heartily.

"What's so funny?" she asked.

"This answer—I am . . . impressed you would offer your . . . opinion. But this is not good opinion. Meaning no offense."

"Not a good opinion, huh?"

"Surely you know that the Chinese, they are fellow communists, our comrades."

"And here I thought you got it when I explained what a double-cross was."

The premier's smile faded, and his eyes narrowed again. "What do you mean by this?" he asked, something sharp in the previously friendly voice.

Marilyn shrugged, folding her arms over her bosom. "It's just that I've found in my life that it's the people I trust *most* who end up hurting me."

Nikita grunted and folded his own arms and lapsed into a brooding silence. Was he displeased with her remark? She decided to change the subject.

"You know," she said, "I read the speech you gave in Moscow to the Twentieth Congress . . . after you took over from Stalin?"

He frowned, skeptically. "This is not possible."

"Oh but it *is* possible. I read every word of it."

His mouth dropped open. "Even I," he said, astonishment widening his eyes, "do not have a complete transcript of this speech. I did not write—I speak for six hours, from my mind." He tapped his skull with a thick finger. Then he leaned close to her, the eyes in his face like ball bearings. "Where did you get this?"

Another shrug. "From the State Department."

Nikita just stared at her.

"If you want a copy," she said, "I could probably get you one."

His smile was wry but his eyes were admiring, and not just of her beauty. He spoke in hushed tones. "We are first in space, yes. But in spying . . ." He shook his head. ". . . you Americans always win."

Matter-of-factly, Marilyn explained: "I told Agent Harrigan that I just had to read that speech, before I'd agree to meet you. . . . I just had to know."

He squinted at her, curiously. "Know? Know what?"

She touched his chest, the silk of the pajama top smooth as a baby's bottom. "What was in your heart, silly." To this day she wished she'd insisted on such research on the President of Indonesia.

Nikita said nothing, his face empty . . . and yet filled, for the first time, with a humanity that revealed the man behind the world-leader façade.

Marilyn reached out and took his hand and squeezed it. "Your anguish . . . it was genuine." Her voice was hushed, reverent. "I'm not embarrassed to say it made me cry."

Nikita turned his face away from her. And when he looked back his eyes seemed moist, or was that only the reflection of moonlight?

For several long moments, neither said a word.

Finally, Nikita Khrushchev spoke.

"When I was younger, Stalin was like a father to me." Another humorless laugh rumbled his chest. "But at end, he was sick . . . sick in his head. You could only trust him like . . . like you could trust ice in late spring." Nikita heaved a world-weary sigh.

She said nothing, waiting for him to go on.

He did. "Lenin warned Central Committee. On his deathbed he say, do not pick Stalin as my successor! Because he knew this man was ruthless and would abuse power. But old fools do not listen. Imagine this! To not listen to father of our country! If George Washington said, 'This is man you should not trust,' . . . you would not trust that man, am I right? . . . But they thought *they* knew better than Lenin." He smirked disgustedly, adding, "As my people say, long whiskers cannot take place of brains."

Again Marilyn said nothing, sensing his need to talk.

"So many, many Russians died in purges," Nikita said, shaking his head, sorrow in his eyes. "Best we had—doctors, teachers, engineers . . . all killed as 'Enemies of People.' You see, Stalin—he was afraid of intelligentsia. They might question his directives."

He smacked a fist into a palm, making her jump a little.

"And military!" he said, eyes flaring. "He executed most of Old Guard in Red Army—honest men, good men—men I have serve with, who go to their deaths not knowing why. I tell you, dear friend, it is wonder we defeated Germany."

She was shaking her head in dread. "But . . . but how could he be so . . . vicious . . . ?"

"How could Hitler murder so many? When madness starts, it is hard to stop." Nikita lowered his head. "I should have seen it, what was happening. My lids were open, but my eyes . . . my eyes, they were closed."

Marilyn rested a hand on his shoulder. "You mustn't blame yourself for what somebody else did."

"Once," Nikita continued, as if he hadn't heard her, "I go to see Stalin. I say, 'Comrade, I have reports that the people in Ukraine are starving, we must do something.' Well, Stalin did not want to hear that collective farms were not working. 'Nonsense,' was all he said. So I got on train and go down there."

She listened intently, fascinated by the frankness of this man, this powerful man.

"When I arrive," he was saying, "I start to . . . poke around. I go to this rundown shack outside village. There I find woman standing behind wood table with butcher knife in hand. On table is slab of cut-up meat and she poke knife at me, afraid I will take her meal. I say, 'Dear lady, I do not want your meat. I want to know how you are and if you have food.' She looked up at me with crazy eyes and she say, 'Already I have eaten Little Maria. Now I will salt down Little Ivan. This will keep me for some time.' "

Marilyn gasped.

Nikita nodded at her unspoken question. "It is as you imagine: this woman had gone crazy with hunger and butchered her own children."

"But . . . but I *can't* imagine," Marilyn said, horrified, covering her mouth with splayed fingers.

Nikita sat, frozen with the terrible memory.

After a moment, Marilyn managed to ask, "What . . . what did you do then?"

"What would any man do? I ran outside and emptied

stomach in snow." He let out a breath, swallowed. "Then I go back to Moscow to see Stalin. But my plea for more food to Ukraine, it falls on deaf ears. He was rude and most insulting and called me dubious character." Nikita looked down at the hands in his lap. "Millions of people died of starvation that winter . . . and many of dead became only food the living could get."

"Oh, dear God," Marilyn gasped.

"God?" He raised an eyebrow. "We have proverb—'Pray to God if you must . . . but take care of your garden.' "

Marilyn, horror-struck, said nothing.

"Afterward," Nikita went on, "Stalin began to look at me as troublemaker. I find out later Secret Police going to take me away, and have me eliminated . . . but I come down with pneumonia, very ill, in bed for six months. By time I get well, Stalin has change of mind—that happened with him, many times—he even reassigned me back to Ukraine."

Marilyn felt numb; she hugged herself, shivering. "Someone should have killed him."

Nikita laughed hollowly. "Ah, this coming from citizen of country where there is no assassination? . . . Forgive me . . . I hurt your feelings . . . I am sure some tried to kill Stalin. But Stalin, he was very clever in his madness. He rarely left his dacha—which had more and more locks on it each time I came. Whenever I would return to Moscow, he would have me over for dinner. I would dread these affairs, because he would say, 'Oh, look, Nikita Sergeyevich, here is your favorite dish—herring.' That meant I was to taste it to see if it was poisoned. If I stayed upright in my chair, then he would have some, too."

Wide-eyed, Marilyn asked, "Did you always taste it?"

"How could I not?" Nikita said with a fatalistic shrug. "These dinners, they were frightful. They go on for hours, because Stalin, he was terribly lonely. Usually American movie afterward, brought by Minister of Cinematography, fellow named Bolshakov. He was supposed to interpret, but didn't know English, so instead he would say, 'Now the man's leaving room . . . now he's walking across street,' and Stalin would yell, 'I can see that, you idiot! But what does he *say?*' So I was ordered to translate."

She smiled a little, the first time in a while. "Did you ever show any of my films?"

Nikita shook his head, made a face in the negative. "Stalin had huge library of films, but mostly he watch cowboy pictures. He would curse at them, but always order another—cowboys, only cowboys."

"Do you screen anything besides 'cowboy pictures'?"

"I *never* show cowboy pictures! . . . Except John Wayne. John Wayne I like. . . . This summer I saw your *Some Like It Hot.*" He gave her a shy, sideways look. "If I may say . . . you were *prih-krashs-nuh!*"

Marilyn beamed; the word wasn't included in her limited Russian vocabulary, but she would take it as a compliment. And his opinion meant the world to her. "That's very kind of you to say," she said, almost as shyly.

Nikita grasped her hand again, giving it a firm pat. "Why don't you come to Moscow?" he said, and he gestured to the sleeping park around them. "You could be much bigger star in Russia! You could make your own movies. Produce, direct, choose only script you approve. . . . I see how they treat you here. . . . It is disgrace."

Marilyn's smile turned wistful. "I wonder. . . ." What would her life be like in Russia? She gazed up at the stars, musing, "Dostoevsky said Mother Russia was a freak of nature—maybe that's why I identify with her . . . because that's what people say about me."

Nikita blustered: "Such stupid people are *wrong!* Why, Miss Monroe . . . Marilyn . . . you are the most beautiful, talented woman in any country!"

The compliment stunned her.

"But I," he said, his voice nearly inaudible now, all the bravado gone, "must be 'freak' to one so beautiful."

Marilyn squeezed his hand, shaking her head slowly. "You know, that's one thing men never seem to understand about me," she said. "What's on the outside doesn't attract me—it's what's on the inside."

She moved closer to him and whispered in a devil-like ear. "I think I know how to make the cold war a little warmer. . . ."

He turned his homely face to her, not sure of her meaning.

So she explained by kissing him on the lips. Softly. Sweetly.

When their lips parted, she could see, even in the pale moonlight, that his cheeks were flushed. The effect she had on men never failed to amaze her. Or amuse her.

After an awkward silence, a flustered Nikita asked with forced gruffness, "And what is so great about teacup?"

Marilyn eyed him curiously. "What do you mean?"

Nikita gestured around him dismissively, as if it hadn't been his own childish interest that had brought them to this attraction. "What is so wonderful about sitting in teacup that would make people pay money?"

"Well, you don't just sit . . . you spin."

He frowned in confusion. "Spin?"

She twirled one finger in the air. "You know, in a circle? But the ride has to be turned on. Needs power."

He gave her half a smile. "Power is my specialty."

She laughed. "Maybe not this kind."

"You mean, electricity?"

"Uh-huh."

"But I know electricity," he exclaimed, puffing himself up, "is like brother, like sister."

"Really?"

"Who do you think built Moscow subway?"

Nikita scooted on the seat around the circular wheel, and stepped out of the little opening of the cup onto the wooden platform.

Tugging down her knotted shirt, Marilyn did the same.

"You'd have to get the cover off of that," she said, standing on the edge of the platform, pointing to a metal box on a short pole next to the ride. "And it looks locked."

"What if I have key?"

"Key?"

Nikita stepped down off the ride and again Marilyn followed. The Russian removed one of his heavy brown shoes and gave the box a tremendous *whack!*

And the cover fell off its hinges.

Marilyn gasped a laugh, then said, "But that's private property!"

"I have . . . how is it called? Diplomatic immunity!"

Inside the box were two buttons, one red, the other green. Marilyn, at Nikita's side, said, "In our country, red means 'stop' and green 'go.' "

"In our country," Nikita said, eyes twinkling like a mischievous elf, " 'red' has other meaning. But, please—instruct me."

"Okay," she said, and pushed the green button. Behind them the ride began to creak and groan.

"Oh, it's starting!" Marilyn said excitedly.

Nikita was frowning, though. "Do we attract attention?"

"No—we're a million miles away from the real world. Come on . . . don't be a 'fraidy cat."

She grasped his hand, and they hopped up onto the

moving platform, which was increasing in speed, and jumped into the first twirling cup that came by.

At first Nikita's eyes were huge and he seemed terrified. But then Marilyn giggled at him and grabbed onto the steering wheel and gave it a twist, making the cup whirl.

Soon a grinning Nikita Khrushchev was gleefully crying, "*Wheeeeeee!*"

And the sight of the premier of Russia, behaving like a kid, made Marilyn Monroe break out in gales of uncontrollable laughter.

"This," he yelled, "*is* special teacup!"

"Oh yes!" she shouted back. "But how are we going to stop it? I'm getting . . . getting dizzy!"

After another minute or so, sensing Marilyn was on the verge of seasickness, Nikita said in her ear, "For you I will stop this special cup!"

Struggling out of the spinning thing, Nikita made his way across the wooden platform floor, weaving like a Cossack who couldn't hold his vodka, then hopped off the edge of the ride, and disappeared.

After a moment Marilyn felt the teacups begin to slow, finally coming to a stop.

A breathless Marilyn staggered over to join Nikita on the ground beside the now-still teacup ride.

"That was what I call *fun,*" she exclaimed, pushing her tousled blonde hair back in place.

"Yes, is what we call fun, also," Nikita admitted. "What box can we break now?"

Marilyn laughed, but shook her head. "We really shouldn't, you know. . . ."

Nikita gave her a surprised look. "Why not? I was promised Disneyland. Is only fair."

"Well. . . ." She eyed him as if he were a precocious

child. No one was around for miles—they were alone in the huge park . . . what was the harm? "All right," she said. "But just to preserve world peace."

"Is noble goal." Nikita thrust a thick finger, pointing across the midway to where colorful flags flapped in the gentle breeze over a faux-brick front. "What is this ride?"

She laughed. "Mr. *Toad's* Ride . . . his Wild Ride, to be exact."

He seemed skeptical. "And who is this Mr. Toad?"

"Well . . . a toad is sort of a frog. You know what that is, don't you?"

He made a face. "Bah—frogs and mice. . . . Why is everything in Disney's land small forest creatures?"

She shrugged. "Because they're *cute*."

Nikita grunted. "Frogs are to be eaten and mice killed."

"Come along," Marilyn said, looping her arm in his, "and I'll tell you about Mr. Toad. It's a good story."

"I doubt this. Most good stories are by Russians."

Mrs. Arthur Miller ignored this, and, as they walked toward the ride, she began, "Mr. Toad was very rich, but he was an irresponsible fellow . . ."

"I have known such a man," Nikita interrupted. "But he was snake named Stalin. He would not want to take Wild Ride, believe me. He would hide under table."

She kept walking him along. ". . . and one day Mr. Toad got his hands on an automobile. Only Froggy didn't know how to drive, at least not very well."

Marilyn continued the fable as she and Nikita approached the ride's dark entrance, unaware that someone else had already slipped inside.

Someone who, like them, was an uninvited guest at the Magic Kingdom.

Chapter Twelve

APARTMENT ON MAIN STREET

Walt Disney was depressed.

This was not one of those suicidal bouts of depression the fifty-nine year-old movie mogul had suffered in the early days, back when the weight of his growing studio had been so crushing. It seemed, ever since his friend and employee Ward Kimball had got him interested in scale-model railroading, he'd no longer had to fight that sort of battle with himself.

The railroad at Disneyland was an offshoot of the scale-model railroad he'd had constructed around his home in Holmby Hills, much to his wife Lillian's consternation (cutting through her beloved gardens as it did). Between this hobby, and his in-house masseuse at the office (and the occasional belt of booze), Walt had managed to avoid the specter of another nervous breakdown.

Nonetheless, these last few years, he'd been sparring with melancholia, if not outright depression, despising growing older, a process emphasized in the mirror each day ("Mirror, mirror . . .") by his thinning, graying-on-the-sides hair, his increasingly droopy eyelids, his jowly cheeks, and his spreading paunch. The public might like the image of "Uncle Walt," but in his mind, Walt Disney viewed himself as the same vital young animator who had built on meager drawing talents and abundant entrepreneurial instincts to create a Hollywood kingdom.

Having the State Department yank the rug out from under the planned festivities for Premier Khrushchev had really hacked Walt off royal. Would he be reimbursed for the expense and trouble he'd been put to? No! Would he look a fool in the press, after he'd courted so much attention for the Russian visit? Yes!

One of his great pleasures, as the "mayor" of Disneyland, was to meet and greet world figures, and he relished the chance to show off his park, his personal personification of the American dream, to the world's most famous Red.

Walt would have got a particularly big charge out of showing off his Disneyland Navy. Under his hands-on supervision, old-fashioned cannons had been affixed to the steamers that churned through the Adventureland's jungle and down his version of the Mississippi, and he had assembled the paddle-wheelers—along with his Jules Verne submarines—in the Tomorrowland lagoon with an eye on presenting them to the Soviet leader, with tongue in cheek, as "the tenth largest battle fleet in the world."

Not that losing the publicity of a Khrushchev visit was anything that concerned him . . . crowds remained strong, fed by the Disneyland TV show, even if the Davy Crockett fad had finally burned out, replaced by Mousekeeter caps and the God-given puberty of Miss Annette Funicello.

The only negative remained the ongoing complaints about the high price of admission (fifteen dollars, which included a book of ride coupons). Walt had to charge what he did because the park cost a lot to build and maintain—he had no government subsidy, after all! The public was his only "subsidy." Hadn't he mortgaged everything he owned, put his studio itself in jeopardy for "Disneylandia" (as it had originally been called)?

Walt glanced at the fancy version of a Mickey Mouse

watch on his wrist: it was approaching two a.m., and he still hadn't gone to bed . . . just sat there with his bottle of Scotch and pack of cigarettes, puffing like one of his prized scale-model steam engines, going over Bud Swift's latest draft of *Pollyanna*, a fine piece of sentimental craftsmanship which had brought a tear or two to his eyes.

Seemed like everything made him cry these days.

Sometimes he just had to get away to this apartment, his private personal retreat, free from Lillian and Holmby Hills. He had chosen the decor himself—lavender-, red-, and pink-flocked wallpaper, thick red rugs, lush upholstery, heavy drapes, wind-up phonograph, china knick-knacks, faux gas lamps, brass bed, the furnishings Victorian all the way.

"Hell, Walt," Ward Kimball had said, one of the few who dared kid him like this, "what fella wouldn't feel at home here—darn thing looks like a New Orleans whore-house!"

Walt had just laughed and held his temper in check, but the remark had cut him: he had done his best in the apartment to replicate the living room of the Disney family farmhouse back in Marceline, Missouri. Unfortunately, he hadn't been able to make much use of this hideaway lately; brother Roy had gently broken it to Walt that a rumor was rife among Disney employees that Walt was using the apartment as a love nest for unceasing assignations with various young women.

The rumor was ridiculous, unfounded—he was not a womanizer, had never been sexually driven; like any studio boss, he could have had one starlet after another, if he so desired, and when he happened to walk through a dressing room where shapely girls were in various states of nakedness, he remained unimpressed: if you'd seen one naked girl, you'd seen them all.

But the rumors had to be quashed—he insisted on moral behavior from his employees at the park, and a single "damn" or "hell" would get a staffer fired on the spot—and, now, only occasionally did Walt use the apartment above the fire station adjacent to city hall, here on Disneyland's Main Street.

That first six months he had spent all his days and nights at the park. Lillian had accompanied him at first, until one morning a guard at the Monsanto exhibit refused to let Mr. and Mrs. Disney inside, before opening. Walt had shown the guard his driver's license, and had been admitted . . . but the guard still refused Lillian. Walt fired the son of a bitch, of course—anyone who'd paid to visit the park deserved the same courtesy given a guest at the Disney home—but Lillian was highly insulted.

After that, Mrs. Walt Disney refused to go to Disneyland.

Walt, however, hated to leave the place, and had the private apartment installed, to give him twenty-four-hour access to the nostalgic world he'd created, which he found so preferable to the real one. Often, during the day, he would amble along Main Street, chat with visitors, tousle the kids' hair; but just as often crowds of autograph seekers would make that impractical. Instead, he would sit locked in his Main Street apartment and stare out the window wonderingly at the Americans from every state and every walk of life who were strolling down his boulevard of unbroken dreams.

And bittersweet tears of joy at this manifestation of his imagination, tinged with the sting of a lost youth and forever bygone America, would stream down his face and pearl in his mustache.

He looked out into the darkness, only a few security lights providing pools of occasional illumination on his

Main Street, which represented to Walt the heart of a small Midwestern town from his childhood. He had designed the park so that, at first blush anyway, it provided a trip into the recent past—his past.

With the railroad defining the borders of the park, its main station was plopped down right at Disneyland's main entrance. From here, visitors—starting at the small square with its town hall and fire station (over which his apartment nestled)—would wander down the archetypically American Main Street, whose storefronts bore such familiar names as "Elias Disney, Contractor" (Walt's father) and "Main Street Gym, Christopher D. Miller, Proprietor" (his grandson).

Main Street provided an operating base for concessions, too, but (no matter what anyone thought) Disneyland wasn't about money to Walt. He wanted to create a home away from home for all Americans, and hence had—with his cartoonist's instincts—seen to it that everything on Main Street was built slightly smaller than life-size, to create a sense of friendliness, intimacy, a childlike world.

At the end of Main Street, an unlikely sight for small town American beckoned: Sleeping Beauty's castle. Walt had dangled this "weenie" (as he put it) to keep people moving, to propel the park's visitors onward, visual magnets pulling them into the next world of attractions.

Following this route clockwise, visitors moved from Main Street, finding themselves in Adventureland, then Frontierland, Fantasyland, and finally Tomorrowland, the logical conclusion to a journey that had begun in the nostalgic past. But—unlike a movie, where a viewer was drawn through a linear sequence—Disneyland could be enjoyed however the visitor pleased: a left turn, a right turn, changing the sequence of events and the "story" being told.

This concept delighted Walt.

But for all of the lavish lengths that he'd gone to, to bring each of his "lands" to life, Walt himself remained most happy, most at home, with Main Street. Right now he sat on the overstuffed sofa at the window, a black cigarette in one hand, glass of Scotch in the other, staring down at the dark street—empty of people, let alone horse-drawn streetcars.

His advisors had been after him to add a security force at the park, and he was considering doing so—perhaps he'd dress them like Keystone Kops—but he felt convinced that Disneyland was secure after dark. The Anaheim police did their drive-bys, didn't they? In four years there had been no break-ins, no vandalism—that would have been un-American. That thought was just fading when the two figures in black moved down Main Street, into his God-like view.

Walt sat forward, eyes wide as Mickey Mouse. The window had been cracked open—no air-conditioning in his apartment, they didn't have that back at the turn of the century, you know—and he could not only see the men, but hear them.

He could not, however, understand them: it was some Oriental language, Japanese, Korean . . . ?

No, *Chinese*. . . .

Long-sleeved black t-shirts and tight trousers, black gloves, only their faces showing, the slender young men were Oriental themselves. One seemed to be in charge, and was pointing off toward Adventureland, then gestured forward, to Sleeping Beauty's castle.

In their hands, their right hands, were weapons—automatics, affixed with extended snouts that Walt supposed were designed to silence their fire.

At that moment a distant but distinct mechanical

grinding sound froze the two men, and caused Walt to sit up in alarm. Was that . . . one of the *rides?* On the midway?

The men in black conversed again in their foreign language—not loud, but not whispering—and then the leader used a word that was not Oriental, nor was it English, though this was one word in the flurry of percussive gibberish that Walt Disney recognized: *Khrushchev.* Then the two men split up, going in their separate directions, moving quickly.

Walt stood slowly (his arthritis allowed nothing else), and he covered his mustached mouth with a hand.

What could this mean? Why were two foreign intruders, with guns, stalking his park in the wee hours? Why would they mention the Russian chairman's name, when Khrushchev was no longer scheduled to visit the park? Or did the two Oriental gunmen think Khrushchev *was* still coming to visit, tomorrow, as originally scheduled, and had sneaked in to be on hand to assassinate the premier when the sun came up . . . ?

He was not afraid—he was surprised, but also he was angry, a cold fury unlike the volcanic resentment he'd expressed at the canceling of the Khrushchev visit. His Magic Kingdom had been invaded—and one thing you didn't want to be, in Walt Disney's world, was the son of a witch out to get Snow White or Sleeping Beauty.

Walt mentally kicked himself for putting no telephone in the apartment—no phones at the turn of the century, either, and anyway he didn't want to be disturbed here—and dug his key chain out of his slacks pocket. A backroom behind the concession stands across the way had a working phone.

But who should he call? The Anaheim police? Or the State Department? Even without Khrushchev on the grounds, the foreign intruders at the park would seem to be the business of the American government, after all. Had he added that agent—what was his name, Harrison?—to the names and numbers in the little black book he carried?

Walt dug that out, too, knowing it was time to leave the charming past and re-enter the dangerous present.

Under the moon's watchful ivory eye, revolver in hand, Jack Harrigan—with cadaverous CIA agent Munson on his heels—raced across the manicured lawn of the Beverly Hills Hotel, dodging the heavy foliage as if avoiding shell holes on a battlefield, heading for bungalow number seven.

Although it was well after two in the morning, a light in the front room shot rays out around the edges of the drawn curtains, tiny beacons of hope in Harrigan's very dark night.

The State Department man ignored the bell, pounding on the door instead with the ball of a fist, his gun in-hand behind his back. "Miss Monroe, it's Jack Harrigan. . . . Open up!"

No sound came from within.

He banged again.

Impatient, Munson said, "Damnit man, I'll break a window. . . ."

Like a safety patrol boy at a grade school, Harrigan held his out a hand in "stop" fashion. "No—I hear something. Wait. . . ."

And then the lock clicked.

The door cracked open, revealing wide, brown eyes that were not Marilyn Monroe's, peering back out at them from behind the chain-latched door.

The secretary.

"It's May, isn't it?" Harrigan asked, forcing a smile, not wanting to frighten the woman further. "Forgive me, but I've forgotten your last name."

"It's Reis," she said quietly, guardedly. "May Reis."

"Do you remember me, Miss Reis?"

Her face bisected by the chain, the secretary nodded.

"I'm with the State Department," he reminded her, "and this gentleman is another government agent . . . his name is Munson. It's important that we speak with Miss Monroe."

The secretary shook her head, eyes narrowing. "She's not here."

Harrigan glanced behind the woman, taking in what he could of the living room through the cracked door. Munson's breath was hot on his neck, an over-eager suitor.

"Where is she, Miss Reis?" Harrigan asked.

"I don't know."

"Is she inside—with Mr. Khrushchev?"

The secretary's eyes grew wide again . . . with fear possibly, and perhaps something else. . . . The burden of a secret? Harrigan was certain she knew where the missing pair had gone.

"She's not here," May Reis insisted. "They're not here."

They're not here!

"Has she taken him somewhere?" Harrigan demanded.

The woman said nothing, her mouth a tight line, her face blank but for a twitchy nervousness about the eyes.

"Please let us in," he said firmly.

"No."

"Miss Reis, this is a matter of national security, of international importance."

"Do you have a warrant?"

"I don't need a warrant in a case of crisis like this. Open the door, or we'll open it. Understood, Miss Reis?"

The woman closed the door. Harrigan could hear the chain being unlatched. Then the door opened again, wide this time.

The two men stepped inside the lavish, white-appointed bungalow, Harrigan keeping the weapon behind him, Munson leaving the door slightly ajar.

Harrigan approached May, who had retreated to the beige sofa, but she didn't sit. Her chin high, the little woman wore a blue robe and fuzzy slippers, her short, brown hair disheveled, dark circles rimming troubled eyes.

Munson went into the bedroom, returned moments later, shaking his head.

"So they're not here," Harrigan said, and returned his weapon to its shoulder holster.

"I told you they weren't," the secretary said, not successful at hiding her alarm at the sight of the gun.

Folding his arms, planting himself before the petite woman like a sentry, looking down at her gravely, Harrigan did his best to intimidate the secretary, to shake her professional cool. "We have to find them, and soon—their lives are at stake."

"Lives . . . ?"

"Didn't Marilyn tell you? Somebody tried to murder Premier Khrushchev tonight . . . in his bed, here in the hotel."

May collapsed onto the couch, sitting there numbly, staring at hands clasped tightly in her lap. Harrigan waited with strained patience, aware that Munson was pacing behind him, mindful that the CIA agent would use a more forceful tactic on the woman if Harrigan failed in his approach.

Finally the secretary spoke. "Marilyn told me not to trust anyone . . . not even you, Mr. Harrigan. . . ." She looked up sharply at Harrigan, her distress turning suddenly to anger. "This is your fault!"

"My . . . ?"

"*Why* didn't you listen to her?" the secretary demanded.

"You pretended to take her seriously . . . but you lied to her. You shrugged her off, because she was just some, some . . . dumb blonde to you!"

Munson stepped past Harrigan and loomed menacingly over the woman. "Lady, we don't have time for your soap opera—where the hell are they?"

Eyes and nostrils flaring in fright, May reared back on the coach. Harrigan shot Munson a look, and the CIA agent backed off.

Harrigan took a seat next to May.

"Marilyn was right," he admitted, his voice gentle. "The attempt to kill Khrushchev took place at two o'clock this morning, just as she'd predicted, based upon what she overheard . . ."

May was nodding at his words.

". . . and, yes, it's my fault. I wasn't there to stop it. I promised her, and I let her down. . . . I let both of you down."

Harrigan hoped that this admission of culpability would soften the woman, but her lips remained a tight, stubborn line.

Harrigan sighed. "And now she's helped the premier, and made herself a target, as well. This is an assassin, Miss Reis—a highly skilled, completely ruthless killer . . . and he's after both of them, right now."

The secretary stiffened, turning toward him on the sofa. Her eyes were friendly, but still she shook her head. "Marilyn said they'd be safe, where she's taken him . . . that nobody could ever find them . . . and in the morning . . ."

Munson broke in. "The fact that we didn't find you with your throat slashed means the killer didn't need the information you're sitting on."

She blinked. "What?"

Harrigan touched her arm. "Agent Munson is correct. The assassin would have broken in here and made you reveal what you knew. . . ."

The woman stiffened. "I would never have told him."

Harrigan knew an assassin like this would have the information out of her in about ninety seconds, but he said only, "I believe you, but you would have died protecting Marilyn. That the assassin did not bother you means he is already on their trail . . . that he most likely followed them, wherever they've gone."

The woman's eyes filled with terror. She stared searchingly at Harrigan for what seemed forever but was in reality about five seconds, during which the State Department agent waved the CIA man back.

"They're at the amusement park," she said, finally.

Harrigan frowned in disbelief. "Where in hell?"

"Disneyland." May Reis swallowed. "Marilyn took Premier Khrushchev to Disneyland—you wouldn't, so she did. . . . They went in a Buick . . . a blue rented Buick sedan. Please, Mr. Harrigan . . . please . . . make it up to her. Help them."

Harrigan's frown deepened, as he turned away from the secretary's earnest, moist-eyed gaze. Could this be true? It seemed ridiculous to him, although considering Marilyn Monroe was the mastermind here, maybe not. . . .

That was when Sam Krueger blew in. "Jack—that phone's going to ring in a second . . . and it'll be for you!"

"What?"

Krueger planted himself near that front door, hands on hips, smirking. "Pal, it's the chief of the Anaheim police."

"Anaheim . . . ?"

On the end table by the couch, the phone rang.

Harrigan reached for it, hand hovering over the receiver,

and looked curiously at Krueger, who snapped, "It's for you, I said."

A crisply professional voice on the other end of the line said, "Agent Harrigan, this is Chief Coderoni at Anaheim."

"Yes, sir."

A pause, then: "Mr. Disney asked me to call."

Chapter Thirteen

ROCKET TO THE MOON

Hands on his hips, Nikita Khrushchev stood in front of the entrance to Mr. Toad's Wild Ride, gazing up at the façade where a portrait of a frog—in human clothes, hands on his hips—grinned down at him.

This amused Nikita—or, that is, he was amused by the grotesque humorlessness of these odd things that Americans found funny.

In the darkness, Marilyn's hand touched his. His eyes turned toward the attractive woman; the American fascination with Marilyn Monroe was much easier for him to fathom than a comical toad.

"I think the control box is over there," she said, nodding toward the inside wall of the castle's alcove.

She walked him there and, once again, Nikita removed a heavy brown shoe and brought this portable, multi-purpose tool slamming down on the steel box, springing its silver cover, which fell to the sidewalk with a metallic clunk. He peered back over his shoulder at Marilyn, who looked about apprehensively, a hand covering her mouth, as if someone might have heard them.

A jolt of memory froze him for a moment.

He was reminded of Galina, his first wife, that sweet young thing who had stood just so, watching nervously as he broke the lock to a government grain facility during the Ukrainian famine of 1922, so that he could provide food for his family. The children survived; Galina had not.

Nikita touched the girl's shoulder. "We're alone here. No need be frightened."

She smiled and shrugged. "Besides—diplomatic immunity, right?"

"Is right."

Nikita returned his attention to the metal box and flipped the toggle switch.

Suddenly the small castle was ablaze with lights, and from someplace—he couldn't tell where exactly—music blared, voices singing slow and low at first, then becoming higher pitched, like a phonograph playing too fast.

What did the words of the strange song mean?

Why were the people singing on their way to nowhere? And not just nowhere, but nowhere "in particular!" English—such a terrible language, so cluttered with the refuse of other languages, no poetry at all.

And besides, what sort of fools go somewhere they don't know they're going?

Then, to Nikita's breathless amazement, double doors flew open—at the right of the alcove—and an automobile came bouncing out, an old-fashioned one . . . he recognized it, an American Model T, jostling to a stop in front of them, chugging and wheezing like a living thing.

Marilyn, giddy with laughter, shouted above all the noise and clatter. "Come on, Nikkie! Get in!"

"Nikkie! Who is Nikkie?"

"You are, silly!"

And she gave him a nudge with her elbow.

Maybe he *was* Nikkie, and maybe he was silly, too, because Nikita—though he wasn't certain he wanted to, and like the singers knew not where he was going—followed her valentine of a bottom up into the two-seater, climbing aboard.

Going nowhere in particular.

Marilyn pulled a metal bar back across their laps.

Nikita was alarmed by the absence in the Model T of a key element in the operation of an automobile; even that teacup had had one! "Where is wheel?" Nikita asked, raising his voice above the chugging and clanking din.

"There is no wheel, silly!"

"With no wheel," Nikita informed her, patience strained, "we cannot drive car."

Marilyn gave him a sideways look. "Nikkie, *we* don't drive the car . . . Mr. *Toad* drives the car. It's *his* wild ride, remember?"

He recalled her story about the foolish frog.

"Then this is bad ride," Nikita concluded. "Frog, he is terrible driver. You yourself say this."

Giggling, Marilyn slumped down in her seat. "No," she responded, "this is *fun!*"

"More of your fun?"

"More of *our* fun, Nikkie! . . . Better hang on!"

And the car jumped forward on some kind of track, Nikita clenching the metal bar tightly—and his teeth.

The duo went rattling along toward another set of doors at the other end of the alcove, yet the car made no attempt to slow down. In fact, if anything, the automobile was increasing its speed.

Thinking that Americans had a sense of "fun" as strange as their sense of "humor," Nikita braced for the crash. But at the last moment, the doors yawned inwardly open, and the car zipped through.

The premier of Russia sighed with relief; his stomach felt funny, like when, as a child, he had gone sliding down a steep, icy, snowy slope on his backside.

The automobile was hurtling along at a great speed, or

so it seemed, lurching at every turn along a cartoon countryside. Nikita could make out part of a bright yellow haystack, coming up ahead, and a big barn, its red doors shut tight.

"Look out, Nikkie!" Marilyn yelled, and buried her face in his chest. He threw his arms around her and fought the urge to close his eyes; but he believed he understood this ride now, and—he was no frightened child, after all—he bravely kept his eyes open wide, comforting the scared girl in his arms.

Once again, at the last moment, the red doors burst open, and the two passengers in the Model T sailed through the barn amidst flying, clucking chickens and frightened, mooing cows.

Nikita frowned—the lighting was dim, but . . . were the animals *real?*

As the pair in the auto emerged from the barn, Nikita turned to look at Marilyn, who had tears in her eyes from laughing, which proved infectious: he joined her with his own loud, raucous laughter, until his sides ached.

Unlike the foolish spinning teacups, this ride had such wonderful tricks!

What would happen next? he wondered.

A faint whistle seemed to answer his question.

In Marilyn's nearest ear, he shouted, "What is that?"

Her response was to raise her eyebrows and shrug; but her smile was knowing. . . .

The whistle came again, this time louder. This whistle, it was familiar . . . it reminded him of the whistle of . . . a *train!*

Suddenly, the car veered off the road—he wasn't sure how this was accomplished; it had happened so fast!—and then they were careening and rumbling down train tracks. Nikita stared ahead in astonishment at the unmistakable bright white light of a locomotive, coming straight at them, the chugging of its engine growing louder and louder, its whistle blowing a warning, *"WHOO-WHOO!"*

As before, the automobile continued onward into the mouth of danger itself—my, this Mr. Toad was a brave fellow!—bumping along the tracks, ignoring a crossing guard where red lights flashed blindingly, and loud bells sounded a warning of the approaching train.

Marilyn covered her eyes with her hands as the train—the noise now deafening—continued to bear down on them, its headlight growing huge, the train mere yards away. But this time Nikita would not be a child fooled by tricks. . . . The automobile would surely swerve off the tracks at the very last moment.

Only, it didn't—he was startled to see the car hold its ground, the big bright light of the train now only a few feet away, and he gasped as they seemed to pass right through the train, as if it were only a ghost . . . or were they the ghosts?

In his seat, Nikita craned around quickly and saw that the "train" was only a big light running on its own track above them, accompanied by the recorded sound of a real locomotive.

So that was how they pulled off this trick! How clever, these Americans! What a smart man, this Disney was. The premier threw back his head and hollered with glee.

But his laughter echoed ominously as he filled his eyes with new surroundings: the world about them had turned red as blood, and smoke hissed with sinister contempt from out of rock walls. Here and there small black creatures with horns on their heads, and pitchforks for tails, danced mockingly.

Nikita understood at once that this meant they had been "killed" by the train, and gone straight to hell. He laughed all the harder, tears streaming down his cheeks.

But Marilyn was no longer laughing.

She was sitting up straight, and tugged at his shoulder, pointing out a figure that had stepped from the darkness of hell. While the dancing demons were clever puppets, this latest "trick" was a disappointment to Nikita.

Was the figure in their path supposed to be the devil himself? If so, he wasn't very frightening. Where was his costume? Black clothing? This was a devil? Where was his pitchfork, his horns, his red flesh?

"Of this I am not scared," Nikita grumbled, looking at Marilyn . . .

. . . but she appeared to be. "He's not supposed to be here!"

Nikita looked again at the figure, clearly a real man with jet black hair and now, out of the smoke, emerged an Oriental cast to cold features.

The devil in black was holding a handgun, an automatic with noise suppresser, pointing it at them, taking aim. . . .

With a lurch, Nikita threw his massive body over Marilyn just as the weapon fired.

Unlike the other illusions on this ride, the automatic sounded real, its muffled report echoing in the chamber—real, too, was the searing pain Nikita felt in his left shoulder, and the spreading dampness that followed.

Nikita stood in the seat of the trembling Model T, at least as far as the metal bar would allow, and as the auto glided by the assassin—who was taking aim again, about to fire a second time—Nikita used his good arm, his right one, to backhand the bastard.

The blow was powerful, tremendous, worthy of a provoked Siberian bear, and the assassin tumbled backward into the smoky darkness, as if swallowed up by hell itself.

The Model T burst through the double doors into the cool outside world, the automobile slowing, ending Mr. Toad's wild ride . . . and theirs.

Not waiting for the auto to stop, Nikita and Marilyn scrambled out, running from the miniature castle, only to head in different directions, each pausing in mid-stride to look back at the other.

"We go to Buick!" Nikita said.

Marilyn rushed to him, and with two hands took him by the good arm, tugging him. "No! That's what he'll expect," she said in a rush. "He followed us here, right? So we go the *opposite* direction."

She took him by the right hand, and led the way. They fled down the midway, away from the revealing lights of the Toad attraction. He slipped a hand into his pocket and withdrew the straight razor, keeping it hidden in his closed hand, not wanting to further alarm the young woman. He kept up with her, even as pain shot through his wounded shoulder, a sensation Nikita ignored—he had suffered much worse at the battle of Kharkov.

Soon the path they were on grew dark, and Nikita wondered where they were going, when a large signpost sprouted like a skinny tree among the sleeping flowers, one word on its rocket-shaped face: *Tomorrowland.*

That was where he had wanted to go most of all in Disneyland! Soviet Intelligence had told him to keep a sharp eye out for any new technology he might spy there.

The path curved to the right, and they were rounding the bend, when a fantastic sight stopped Nikita in his tracks.

Silhouetted against the night sky was the top of a rocket ship, like a sleek white bombshell striped red and blue, with the letters TWA on its side. *So they* did *have rocket launching pads here! Why had his son-in-law not told him!*

As Nikita stood transfixed, mouth agape, Marilyn tugged at his pajama sleeve. "Come on," she whispered. "This is no time for sightseeing—we have to find a place to hide!"

Nikita picked up his pace as the path curved around a manmade waterway, only to halt once again in amazement.

They had come to a lagoon where several old-fashioned steamboats were docked; but more importantly, many submarines were submerged but visible there—never would Nikita have imagined that a whole fleet would be hidden away in a "children's" park! This explained much about the "last minute" cancellation of his visit to Disneyland. This Eisenhower was more clever that he had thought.

"Nikkie!" Marilyn whispered urgently, beckoning him with a finger, eyebrows riding high on her forehead. "Hurry!"

He caught up to her. Soon the pathway came to an end at a large white building where a movie-type poster bore a picture of the sleek spaceship, as well as the words:

ROCKET
TO THE
MOON

Blast Off
Aboard a Rocketship
On a Thrilling Trip
To the Moon
And Return to Earth

So clever—concealing the rocket right out in the open, just another "attraction," another "ride." Soviet Intelligence had much to answer for.

The structure displaying this and other

"TOMORROWLAND" posters had a peculiar modernistic shape, with a curved roof and two big round balls growing out of it, reminding Nikita of the two-headed giant in a Russian fairy tale. He had supervised the design of many new facilities in Moscow and considered this so-called "building of tomorrow" very impractical . . . unless the domes held some technological secrets and were perhaps laden with explosives.

While Marilyn ran to the front entrance of the futuristic building to see if they could get inside, Nikita turned his attention to what was next to it: the spaceship. That razor still clasped in his hand, he stayed alert as he approached the craft, which rose dramatically into the sky, nose poking at the stars on this clear, moonswept night.

Upon closer inspection, however, the spaceship didn't seem as tall as it had looked from a distance—standing seventy feet at best—not like their towering Russian rockets. And this one had little circular windows running all the way from the bottom to the top—what could be the purpose of these? Why would any ship need windows where its rocket boosters were? Who would be looking out?

Nikita moved beneath the craft, between its three legs, and gazed up.

And where *were* the rocket boosters? There didn't seem to be any. . . . Could the United States have developed some new technology, abandoning the use of highly flammable rocket fuel to propel their ships into space? Atomic energy? Magnetism?

As Nikita pondered this unusual spacecraft, Marilyn returned to his side.

"The doors are all locked," she told him, edgy. "And I don't think your shoe would make much of a 'key'. . . . I don't know what to do . . . where to go. . . ."

She followed his gaze up the side of the rocket.

"Yes, yes you're right!" she said. "We can hide in there!"

Nikita just looked at her. "You know how to get inside rocket?"

"Sure," she said with a little shrug. "I went up, once."

This information surprised Nikita. Never were Russian citizens allowed in Soviet spaceships, which were restricted to scientists and only the highest-ranking military and government people.

"A kid fell down and broke his leg," she told him, "so Mr. Disney boarded it up . . . come on."

As she grabbed his hand, Nikita held back. "Mr. Disney must be a powerful man to close down a government rocket."

Marilyn blinked. "Nikkie, it's not a real spaceship."

"Is not?"

She shook her head; he could tell she was trying not to smile. "The ship's an observation deck—you can see the whole park from there."

Now he did feel silly.

"Another ride," he said.

"Sort of . . . only it doesn't go anywhere."

Nowhere in particular.

Silly and disappointed, he felt. He supposed the submarines didn't go anywhere, either. But he didn't ask.

"There used to be some stairs up to the deck," Marilyn was saying, pointing upward to where the base of the craft was nailed shut, regular boards that had been painted white to fool the eye. "If you lift me, maybe I can pull some of those boards down."

Nikita could see spaces between the wood that had been haphazardly nailed together. Although his shoulder ached, Nikita crouched, hugged his arms around Marilyn's hips, and lifted her up.

In the process, she must have touched his bloodied pajama top, because she gasped and wriggled from his grip.

"Oh you're hurt," Marilyn exclaimed. She obviously hadn't noticed before; in the darkness the burgundy pajama top merely looked damp, not red. "Oh, Nikita, why didn't you say something . . . ?"

"Is nothing. As they say in your western pictures, he winged me. . . . We must get in spaceship."

"But . . ."

"Will be much more than arm if we don't get inside ship."

He bent again, hoisting Marilyn as high as he could. She squirmed a bit as he held her, working at the boards; then he heard wood cracking, and two pieces of lumber fell by his feet, thumping to the cement.

When he lowered Marilyn, her face was long with concern.

"Nikkie, you're *sure* you're all right?" she asked.

He nodded.

"Can you . . . can you lift me again? I think I can get up inside."

After another hoist from "Nikkie," Marilyn pulled herself up through the opening.

"What do we do now?" she whispered down to Nikita, her pretty face visible between the opening in the boards. "I'm not strong enough to pull you up."

But an idea had already come to him. Quickly he removed his trousers from over his silk pajama bottoms, slipping them over his shoes.

He tossed the tan pants up to her. "Tie these around strong board," he instructed.

"Oh. I get it."

Nikita, using the legs of the slacks, began to climb them like a rope, favoring his right arm. Marilyn still was unaware of the razor, which he had tucked in his pajama breast pocket. The board, around which the trousers was wrapped, moaned in protest at his weight, but held.

Soon, inside the spaceship, Nikita was back in his trousers as he and Marilyn stood on a sturdy platform, taking in their surroundings. A wooden stairway, off to one side, rose dizzyingly from one landing to another, all the way to the top.

"Let me see your arm," Marilyn said. She unbuttoned his pajama shirt and gently pulled it off his massive shoulders.

"Is nothing I tell you," Nikita said gruffly. But he found her tenderness touching.

"I think the bullet just grazed you," she said slowly, examining the wound on his upper left arm.

"Yes, as I say, I am winged."

"But it's still bleeding."

She took his silk pajama top and tried to tear off the unbloodied sleeve to make a bandage; however the material was too slippery to tear, and—she pointed out—probably wouldn't stay knotted, anyway.

"I know," she said, letting the silk top fall from her fingers. "We'll use my shirt. . . . It's cotton."

Marilyn unbuttoned her blouse and took it off. She wore nothing underneath.

Embarrassed, Nikita looked away, but the glimpse of her full, perfect breasts would reside forever in his memory.

"Don't you just hate underwear?" she commented casually. They both were, at the moment, bare-chested. "It's so unnatural . . . and I go along with nature."

Yes she did, he thought, sneaking a sideways peek at those supple white breasts.

Marilyn tore a sleeve from her blouse, then—gently—wound the plaid fabric around and around his arm, tying it snugly.

"There," she said at last, taking a step back, examining her work, hands on her hips, famous bosom on display. "Is that better?"

"Is wonderful." A Russian woman would have blushed and covered her naked self. The ones that he knew, anyway.

She slipped back into the now one-sleeved blouse, buttoning but not bothering to knot it this time, letting it hang loose. "Are you ready?"

He blinked.

"To climb, Nikkie?"

"Yes. Yes! To top."

Marilyn turned toward the wooden stairs. "We should be safe up there."

Nikita followed her up, pausing briefly at each landing to look out its small circular window. As he climbed, he could see more and more of the amusement park, a sprawling world of rides and buildings and foliage, cloaked in the blue-ivory of the moonlit night.

At the top of the stairs he found Marilyn seated on a platform floor, her back against the curved wall of the cone of the ship. She was trying to look calm, self-composed, this he could tell; but he knew she was still frightened. Nikita settled in next to her, putting his good arm around her protectively, drawing her close to give them both warmth against the chill of the night.

"We'll be safe here," she repeated, her voice muffled against his bare chest.

"Yes, here we are safe."

She yawned. "Oh . . . sorry. I'm just . . . so tired. . . ."

"Now you will sleep," he said.

But he would not. He would stay wide awake. Because as he'd climbed he had seen, out of one tiny window, the Oriental assassin in black, the bastard who had shot at them in Mr. Frog's castle, coming down a pathway into Tomorrowland.

And in time, the man would find the broken boards on the ground, and discover their hiding place.

So he let the young woman nestle against him and sleep, and he kept guard—razor at the ready.

Chapter Fourteen

THIS HAPPY PLACE

Within minutes of the disclosure by May Reis in bungalow number seven—and the phone call from the Anaheim police chief, on behalf of Walt Disney—three black sedans streamed out of the Beverly Hills Hotel driveway and onto Sunset Boulevard, little traffic in the pre-dawn morning hours to hinder them, as they sped toward the Santa Monica Freeway.

Each vehicle carried its own swiftly-formed posse of State Department agents, Secret Service men, and Khrushchev's own guards—minus, of course, the two (deceased) KGB traitors; none had been briefed in detail, although the attempt on the premier's life was known by all. Jack Harrigan, behind the wheel, with CIA agent Munson on the rider's side, took the lead, as the sedans chased each other, keeping a reckless pace, along the highway to Disneyland.

Harrigan had left a Secret Service agent he trusted, Chuck Simmons, to stay behind and handle the slain Russians . . . and to maintain a strict press blackout. While Harrigan had been organizing the interdepartmental posse, FBI Special Agent Sam Krueger—who at the moment was in the sedan just behind Harrigan's—had dealt on the phone with the Anaheim police, instructing them to be waiting at the gates of the amusement park, to enter only if they heard gunfire, and not to disclose details of the situation to anyone except the top personnel involved on the call itself.

And no sirens!

Among the short list of crucial things Harrigan wanted to avoid was attracting public attention, or springing a leak to the press, or arriving at the scene of a Wild West Show already in progress by some rinky-dink out-in-the-boondocks police force.

As Harrigan swung the sedan, its tires squealing, off the freeway and onto the asphalt road to the park, he could see the round domes of the black and white squad cars flashing red up ahead, streaking the night scarlet.

Harrigan brought his vehicle to a jerking halt in front of the three black-and-whites and one unmarked vehicle parked in a semicircle, noses in but headlights off, pointed toward the locked gates of the darkened Disneyland, the park's train station looming beyond. Behind him, the brakes of the other sedans screeched, then car doors slammed like sarcastic hand claps in the night.

A uniformed policeman—a captain, according to his badge—approached Harrigan, as the State Department man scrambled out of his car. Big, burly, bucket-headed, the officer presented a comfortingly businesslike demeanor. At his side was a smaller, thinner cop, a lieutenant whose narrow face with close-set eyes and mouth-breather expression gave Harrigan no confidence at all.

In the background, milling around the squad cars, were half a dozen other uniformed officers, their casualness telling Harrigan that they were more than literally in the dark.

From out of the unmarked vehicle, a navy-blue Chevrolet, stepped a tall, rangy plainclothes officer in his fifties, his brown hair cut short and flecked with gray. He wore a brown suit and crisp, darker brown tie and looked like an executive, his badge holder tucked into the breast pocket of his suit coat, the shield gleaming in the moonlight. He, like the captain, had a reassuring air of professionalism.

Harrigan stepped forward to meet the man halfway. "Chief Coderoni, I presume."

"You must be Agent Harrigan."

They shook hands; the two had spoken a number of times on the phone, previously about the planning and then cancellation of the Khrushchev visit, more recently—less than half an hour ago—about the situation here at the park.

"How much do your men know, Chief?"

"My Captain here, Ed Keenan, and Lt. Willits, have been fully briefed. The other men, not at all. We get calls out this way from time to time, you know."

"Yes, I understand there's no security force at Disneyland."

"Not after closing, not even a night watchman. We keep a pretty close eye, though—park's a real boon to Anaheim."

Harrigan had no time for small talk. "Gather everyone around," he ordered.

The chief seemed to have no compunctions about relinquishing his leadership to Harrigan—that, at least, was a relief. Wasting time jockeying for position, pissing on trees to mark territory, was out of the question.

In a circle hastily formed in front of the locked gates of the amusement park—beneath a sign that read: *To all those who come to this happy place, welcome . . . Walt Disney*—Harrigan quickly told the diversified group about the attempt on Khrushchev's life, and Marilyn Monroe's involvement.

"We have good reason to believe they're inside," Harrigan finished. "And we have excellent reason to believe two assassins—probably Chinese—are inside, as well."

"One of them is Lee Wong," Munson added, and showed around a picture of the angular face, dead-eyed Chinese hit man. "He's freelance—ruthless as hell. He will kill you in a heartbeat, gentleman—your last. We don't know who the other one is, but it's not unusual for assassins to work in teams."

The government agents took in all of this in stride, but the local cops, for the most part, looked like non-swimmers contemplating being thrown into the deep end. The chief and his captain, however, revealed nothing but a coolly competent manner.

That mouth-breather lieutenant, on the other hand, responded by dropping his jaw further, an appropriate enough response to the critical state of things, but then the man belatedly stammered, "You . . . you mean, *the* Marilyn Monroe?"

The captain stepped up, perhaps to draw attention away from his dopey crony. "Unless they climbed over, I don't think anybody's got inside this way," he said, gesturing with his head toward the gate. "Lock's intact."

Harrigan nodded. "Is there another way into the park?"

"Uh, there's a road goes around the back," the lieutenant responded, attempting to redeem himself. "It's a service entrance and some of the employees use it, too."

Harrigan dispatched Krueger to go in the back way and keep in touch via walkie-talkie; that efficient, burly captain—"I know this park inside out"—volunteered to go along, and the FBI agent and a carload of support headed off, just as Chief Coderoni slipped up alongside the State Department man.

Speaking *sotto voce,* Coderoni said, "We may have another problem, Agent Harrigan."

"Which is?"

The Chief grimaced, then whispered, "Mr. Disney was supposed to meet us here—to let us in . . . and there's no sign of him."

Harrigan processed that for a moment, then got Krueger

on the walkie-talkie and informed him of the stray movie mogul who was somewhere inside the park, along with two assassins, a sex bomb, and the premier of Russia.

Harrigan instructed the chief to leave some of his men behind to watch the front gate. "They can raise us on this," he said, handing Coderoni a spare walkie-talkie. "Gather 'round again!"

The G-men and local cops did so.

"We're going in," Harrigan said, "in four teams. Special Agent Krueger is already heading in, to take the back way— that's Team Number One. The rest of us will split up at the end of Main Street. Team Number Two will head to the left, Team Three to the right, Team Four'll continue on straight ahead. Place is set up like the points of a compass. We'll converge at the rear of the park, at the midway."

"How about a password?" the lieutenant asked.

"What?"

"So if we run into somebody, splittin' up like this, we don't shoot their head off."

That wasn't a bad suggestion, considering the source.

"Make it 'Armageddon,' " Harrigan said.

Around back, Sam Krueger had discovered two parked cars in the bushes near the metal gate that half-heartedly barred further passage to Disneyland.

The captain was the first to reach the abandoned cars: a blue Buick and a green Ford, both late models.

"This one's a rental," the officer said, shining his flash-light on the back license plate of the Ford.

"This is Marilyn's," Krueger said, kneeling beside the Buick, noting that the tires had been slashed. Clearly these assassins didn't want their prey to get away.

The captain assigned one of his men to stay with the cars, "in case the assassins return," a tactic Krueger approved.

The FBI man used the walkie-talkie to bring Harrigan up to speed.

Harrigan took the info, and instructed Krueger to continue on into the park; right now the State Department agent was in the lead, the three teams—men with drawn handguns and flashlights and walkie-talkies—following him slowly up Main Street, a replica of turn-of-the-century storefronts, Victorian in a cartoony, postcard sort of way.

At Harrigan's side, the chief said, "No sign of Mr. Disney. . . . Thought he might meet us here, if not at the gate. He has an apartment right there, you see."

The chief was pointing to a mock fire station.

Harrigan shuddered—a foreign agent murdering Walt Disney would be almost as bad as Khrushchev buying it on American soil; wars had been fought over less.

They cautiously proceeded in, only the moon and a few security lights providing any illumination. Eyes darting from storefront to storefront, the former Secret Service agent felt he was going down a Hogan's Alley, one of those academy training exercises where at any moment a cardboard gunman might "jump" into a doorway.

But any gunman who leapt from these doorways would hardly be cardboard.

In the meantime, Krueger's group—the Anaheim captain, two Secret Service agents, one KGB, and a cop, also armed with walkie-talkies and flashlights, were fanning out from the rear of the park, jogging past a pagoda and park benches that sat peacefully among the rhododendrons in the moonlight.

Then Krueger noticed a halo of light shining through the trees up ahead—could that be the sun coming up? No, too early for that. . . . He picked up his speed.

The FBI man broke away from his group, running

toward the light, finding himself on the midway, where various rides were shut down and dark, like slumbering beasts at a zoo.

All, that is, but one. . . .

"Jack," Krueger whispered urgently into his walkie-talkie, "I've got something over here . . . Toad's Wild Ride. Lights are on like she's open for business."

The communicator crackled. "Copy."

Krueger had just signed off when he noticed several dark splotches on the ground, ahead of him. He knew what they were even before he knelt and touched one—still damp!—and his heart sank even as his breath quickened.

An out-of-wind Harrigan appeared at his side. "Jesus, Sam—don't . . . don't tell me that's what I think it is?"

"It's not catsup off somebody's hot dog."

They followed the blood trail with their flashlights, twin paths that led into the alcove of the ride. Harrigan splashed light on an empty Model T car.

"Looks like the blood starts here," he said.

Krueger leaned in, having a closer look at the car. "Shit—Jack . . . there's a bullet hole in the back of the seat. . . ."

Harrigan, noting the puncture in the car's vinyl padding, said, "Armageddon is right."

"What?"

"That's our 'password.' Don Knotts back there insisted."

By this time, the others in Harrigan's group had caught up with them.

"Watch where you step!" Harrigan said, flashing his light on the blood trail. "We're trying to find where this goes."

Flashlights flickered across the ground like giant lightning bugs.

"Looks like it goes back the way we came," the lieutenant said.

"No," Krueger said. "The trail leads there. . . ."

And the FBI man pointed toward Sleeping Beauty's Castle, silhouetted against the night sky like some gothic illusion.

As the group headed off in that direction, Harrigan wondered who the blood belonged to.

Khrushchev? Marilyn? One of the assassins?

Or maybe Mickey Mouse's daddy?

It sure as hell wasn't some kid who got a bloody nose on Mr. Toad's Wild Ride.

He was pondering that when he began to hear the screams—the shrill screams of a woman in danger.

Chapter Fifteen

WILD FRONTIER

A rough hand slipped gently over the mouth of the slumbering Marilyn, and an elbow nudged her, waking her from a deep sleep. Groggy and disoriented, for a moment—as on so many mornings, after swallowing too many Numbutals—she at first didn't remember where she was, sleep having mercifully removed their peril. Then the moon face of Nikita Khrushchev—stern, determined—came into focus.

The premier's frowning expression was not directed at her. Pointed ears perking like a dog's, he stared intently at the square hole in the floor where the stairwell led to this upper landing in the rocket's nose cone.

She stiffened in his arms: *had the assassin found them?*

Slowly, Nikita removed his hand from her lips, and together they listened. For a long, agonizing minute or more, she heard nothing other than their own shallow breathing. Then it came . . . faintly, but unmistakably, from below, as if that hole in the floor were speaking to them—the creak of a foot.

Marilyn's heart was a trip hammer. They were trapped, no way out, cornered without a weapon. Her eyes darted in panic around the small curved-walled enclosure, the dreary insides of a futuristic tomb.

There wasn't even a plank to pry loose.

Trembling, Marilyn clung to Nikita's arm. She looked at him and realized that the eyes in the otherwise resolute face glimmered with something that might have been fear. He had said, back in the teacup, that he too was frightened. . . .

What can we do? her eyes asked him, terror mounting.

His eyes, however, turned suddenly hard and black, like the lumps of coal stuck in a snowman's face. He slipped something in his pants pocket—she didn't know what, and couldn't exactly ask—and then he smiled at her, his expression seeming to say, *I have idea.*

Gently, he withdrew himself from her, then reached along his trousered leg and began to untie one of his heavy, thick-heeled brown shoes.

He whispered in her ear: "Distraction" was all he said. Then he looked significantly toward her bosom, and gave her a small smile and an arched eyebrow; Marilyn understood and smiled a little herself and nodded.

Crawling quietly away from him, like a baby only quieter, she positioned herself directly opposite where the stairs emptied out. Re-staging one of her notorious calendar poses, she leaned against the wall, tucking her legs to one side, bringing an arm up to cradle her head, thrusting her ample bosom out. She looked at Nikita for his verdict.

His head bobbed, but he mimed his fingers along the buttons of his pajama top, and she mouthed, *Oh!*, and unbuttoned her blouse, exposing most of her bosom in a teasingly provocative way. The moonlight conspired with her, streaming in from the little round window, providing her with a nice soft-focus key light. Too bad a photographer wasn't around, to show just how sumptuous a pin-up girl Marilyn Monroe could still be in her thirties.

Nikita—moving in remarkable silence for so large a man—positioned himself in the shadows to one side of the staircase opening; he got on his knees with a shoe in his right hand, poised to strike from the darkness.

She shot him a look, as if to say, *Well—how is this?* And,

briefly, as he glimpsed her posing there, he wore a stunned expression she'd seen countless times on many a man.

Which made her think this strategy just might work. . . .

Nikita gave her an approving nod; and Marilyn gave him an encouraging wink, before half-closing her eyes, then breathing deeply, affecting slumber.

Suddenly she was no longer frightened. It was as if a movie camera had started to roll, and the fear that clenched her before she was on set, and working, had vanished. She was doing what she did so well: acting out a scenario, playing a part. . . . She did not allow herself to realize this might well be the most important role of her life.

Marilyn Monroe would be the first thing the killer saw, as he stealthily climbed the last flight of stairs, his head cautiously rising above the opening in the floor, eyes piercing the darkness in search of his victims . . . then—if she was any judge—those eyes would pop at the sight of the semi-nude Marilyn, her blonde hair shimmering in the moonlight, bedroom eyes seductively closed, sensual lips parted provocatively, white creamy skin inviting a man's touch, full breasts half exposed under the open plaid shirt. . . .

He wouldn't stand a chance.

A thought jumped into her mind: *unless he was gay!*

Long seconds ticked by, as wood below them creaked, the sound of feet on stairs soft, subtle, yet building as the party-crasher drew nearer. . . .

Through her slitted eyes she saw him, an Asian face on a head that sneaked itself up into view, a hand with a gun in it, a bulky thing, nosing up over the edge of the hole in the floor; then dark eyes fastened on her and opened wide, his mouth gaping, too . . .

. . . and a shoe flashed out of the darkness and she

opened her eyes wide as that brown hammer came around and smacked the intruder in the forehead, hard, and the open mouth yelped in pain and the eyes narrowed with the same thing. Nikita slammed the shoe down again, this time on a mostly out-of-sight gun hand, apparently knocking the weapon from the man's grasp because she could hear it fall clatteringly down the stairwell to make a distant *thunk* at the bottom.

Somehow the assassin managed to swivel toward Nikita, in a posture that suggested a martial arts move might be next; but the premier dealt firmly with the matter, *Nyet!*, whamming the shoe down on top of the man's head like he was driving a nail, finally dislodging him from the stairs, sending him toppling down a flight, plunging out of her view, *whump*ing to the landing below.

Nikita was moving quickly, nimbly, amazingly so for such a corpulent man, and a wounded one at that; he was already out of sight, heading down to the landing below when she leapt to her feet and rushed to the stairs, and looked down. The assassin was sprawled on the landing, on his back, like an overturned black beetle, groaning in pain, a red welt the shape of a heel rising on his forehead.

Nikita, finishing his two-stairs-at-a-time descent, seemed about to leap on the man, as Marilyn—halfway down the stairs herself now—saw a glint of steel in the killer's hand, winking at her flirtatiously.

She yelled, "Nikkie! He's got a knife!"

As Nikita jumped back, again with unusual grace, the assassin sprang to his feet, and smiled at his target, showing him a long, slender blade, threateningly thrust forward in an assured hand.

Afraid for her friend, Marilyn—a bystander on the stairs—wondered desperately what she could do to help. . . . She remembered the assassin's gun, but it had fallen somewhere below . . . and she could hardly reach it in time, even if she did get past the two men who faced each other now, like western gunfighters.

Nikita withdrew something from his pocket—Marilyn wondered if this was the object he'd slipped away, before arming himself with a shoe, minutes before.

"I do not want to kill you," Nikita said conversationally. "Is better for trash like you to live . . . and talk."

But the assassin wasn't talking; maybe he didn't even understand English.

Then the man did understand, obviously—as did Marilyn—why Nikita was so unafraid: the premier, with a confident flip, threw open the blade of the straight razor, and now its sharp, glistening edge was doing the winking . . . and nothing flirtatious about it.

The two men with blades circled one another on the landing, waiting for the right moment to attack—the assassin, small but nimble, skilled in hand-to-hand combat and wielding a knife, wore a confident smirk, Nikita's weapon not seeming to give him any worry . . . and Nikita—determined, armed himself now, but tired, wounded—made a very big target.

Marilyn refused to play the damsel in distress, hovering helplessly on the periphery . . . she had to *do* something!

The actress ran back up the stairs and went to the small round window in the cone of the ship, and—using one of her own shoes—knocked out the glass on the first try. She leaned her head out through the jagged teeth of the broken window and began to scream—big, blood-curdling shrieks that could summon someone, anyone, who might be at the park.

Soon Marilyn was growing hoarse, her voice cracking

with each new scream, realizing that she couldn't keep yelling much longer, when finally a figure below—running down one of the curving pathways—revealed itself.

Then came another figure . . . and another . . . racing down the path.

Marilyn cried out again, managing one last shriek, but this one was tinged with joy.

"We're in here!" she yelled. "Hurry! Hurry!"

And the men—Agent Harrigan, and policemen, Secret Service, and uniformed KGB—streamed toward the spaceship like ants to a picnic.

Marilyn extracted her head from the window and rushed back down the stairs, onto the landing where the two warriors were on the floor now, locked in a deadly embrace, the man in black on top.

The assassin was trying to stab Nikita in the throat, Nikita holding the man's hand back with one hand, his own blade in the other hand, wrist pinned to the floor by his adversary. They grunted and squirmed and then the killer kneed Nikita in the side, and the pain-wracked premier lost his grip on the razor, which the assassin swept away with a hand releasing itself from Nikita's wrist, sending the razor skittering into the darkness, even as the blade of the knife drew closer to the premier's throat. But this allowed Nikita, his hand freed, to deliver a short yet powerful blow, a fist to the chest that sent the assassin reeling back, off of the Russian. . . .

"Stop!" Marilyn shouted, jumping up and down like a child in a tantrum. "It's over! They're coming!"

But even with the end drawing near—Marilyn could hear the shouts of men far below—she could see that the assassin would not stop until his grim task was finished.

The two men, both winded—only one of them armed

with a blade now—again squared off. Marilyn looked frantically around for that fallen razor and could not find it; at the same time the assassin was putting some distance between himself and the premier, and she felt certain would hurl the knife. . . .

Nikita saw her, threw her a conspiratorial signal by the tightening of his eyes, circling further, maneuvering until the assassin's back was to her.

Then Marilyn threw herself on the man, covering his eyes with her hands, locking on with her legs, holding on with dear life, praying this would buy Nikita a few precious seconds to bring this monster down.

Though he was small, the assassin was lithely powerful, and with a growl of rage he flung her off, pitching her roughly against the curving wall, where she slid down in a pile, the air knocked out of her.

But Nikita took advantage of this latest Monroe distraction and leapt at the man, knife or no knife, and grabbed him by the throat, and—his face split with a terrible smile Marilyn would never forget—the premier of Russia twisted the would-be assassin's neck with bear-claw hands until there was an awful, terminal . . . *crack!*

The killer—his eyes wide but empty—crumpled to the floor, his body twitching once before going limp, his head at an impossible angle, knife tumbling with a *thunk* from impotent fingers.

Marilyn, shakily on her feet now, covered her face with both hands and began to sob: the horror, the jeopardy, the emotions, all catching up with her.

Nikita came to her and held her tenderly.

"Is all right, now," he said softly, stroking her hair. "Is all over. . . . You are very brave woman. Braver than many Russian soldiers. You I owe my life."

She looked at him through her tears; his eyes were as moist as hers.

"That goes for me, too, Nikkie," she whispered.

And there on the landing of the moon rocket at Disneyland, in the presence of a common enemy the Russian man and the American woman had worked together to defeat, their lips met in what was not a passionate or lustful kiss, but meant so much more than just friendship.

The pandemonium of an army of men swarming up onto the landing brought their embrace to a close, and Marilyn discreetly buttoned her blouse.

Suddenly Agent Harrigan was at her side. "Miss Monroe, are you all right?"

She nodded weakly.

Khrushchev's KGB agents had surrounded him, and the men were joyously giving their leader hugs, speaking in Russian, some laughing with relief, the premier beaming, emitting a chuckle or two. One of them found his absent shoe and helped him on with it.

An American agent was leaning over the dead assassin.

Typically, Khrushchev's mood changed.

"This assassin," he said gruffly, gesturing to the corpse. "Who is he?"

A tall cadaverous man stepped forward with an answer. "John Munson, Premier Khrushchev," he said, meaning himself not the corpse. "Central Intelligence . . . and that's Lee Wong. We were tracking him in Hong Kong until he dropped out of sight a month ago."

"Nationalist China send him?"

"We believe this is Chairman Mao's work, sir. . . . Perhaps we should reserve the debriefing till we're off-site."

Marilyn blurted, "See, Nikkie—what did I tell you? Red China!"

Harrigan and Munson exchanged bemused looks—several of the men were turning to each other to mouth, *Nikkie?*—but Khrushchev only grunted, nodding solemnly.

Harrigan spoke, "Let's get you and Miss Monroe down off this thing . . . and get that arm looked at."

As Marilyn was helped down the flights of stairs by an attentive Harrigan, she heard Khrushchev and Munson chatting like old friends, coming down behind them.

"Maybe," the premier was saying, "we could help each other."

"How do you mean, Mr. Khrushchev?" the CIA agent asked.

"We are first in space, yes? But you are first in espionage. Perhaps we could share . . . information."

"Go on."

"I believe we get many secrets from same sources. Why not we combine forces, and cut down bill?"

There was a pause. Then the CIA agent responded with a laugh. "You know, Premier Khrushchev—if you don't mind my saying, that's a hell of an idea."

"Ah, I have been to hell already tonight. Let us call it . . . heaven of idea."

"Fine. Fine."

Everyone had to jump down from that first platform onto the cement "launching pad," and Harrigan and Nikita were the first to make their landings, after which Marilyn lowered herself into Harrigan's waiting arms. The State Department agent began issuing orders and four groups of assorted Secret Service agents, KGB guards, and police moved off in various directions.

Then Harrigan approached the actress and the premier, his expression somber.

"I'm going to escort the two of you out of here,"

Harrigan said. "The assassin wasn't working alone, and his back-up could still be on the grounds. . . ."

Marilyn hugged the premier's good arm. "Is Mr. Khrushchev still in danger?"

Perhaps to calm her, Harrigan lightened his expression; his tone was light, too, as he said, "Just a precaution—frankly with all this activity, he's probably hightailed it over a fence the heck outa here."

Harrigan escorted the unlikely couple around one of the curving paths, heading toward the looming castle, on their way toward Main Street. Despite his assurances, Harrigan had his revolver in hand, a fact that neither Marilyn nor Nikita missed. Still, she had a real sense that the crisis had passed. At the east the sky had a faded look, the sun just beginning to make itself known.

"We'll get you to an emergency room, Premier," Harrigan said, walking between Nikita and Marilyn.

"I have had my shots," Nikita grunted.

Harrigan laughed, gently. "Nevertheless . . . we'll have that wound tended to."

Nikita said, "Has been tended to—by Miss Monroe."

As they walked, the State Department agent glanced at Marilyn, warmly—but a little embarrassment was mixed in. "I hope you know," he said, "that America . . . the whole world, in fact . . . owes you a great debt. Hell, if it hadn't been for you—"

"Any American would have done the same," she told him, and meant it.

The path was curving around a pagoda. "If there's *anything*," Harrigan was saying to her, "anything at all I can do, just let me know."

After that Harrigan encouraged no further conversation as they walked along, and despite his casual demeanor, the agent was obviously on alert, his eyes everywhere, reacting to the smallest sound.

As they were approaching the castle, Marilyn—who had been reflecting on Harrigan's offer to do "anything at all"—began to speak, intending to broach the subject of Nikita returning to the park in the safe light of day.

But she never got a word out, Harrigan cutting her off rudely with, "Quiet," as he froze on the pathway, eyes narrowed, the revolver swinging toward thick bushes to the their left.

Marilyn didn't hear a thing.

But Harrigan obviously had, because he yelled, "Down!"

The agent shoved Marilyn to the asphalt, while Nikita dropped himself like a trap door had opened under him. She looked up, terrified, and standing half-hidden in those bushes was a figure that Marilyn at first thought was the assassin in black, somehow come back to life!

But this was a different man in black, his face Asian but rounder, though the eyes were equally cold and hard and dead.

And in his hand was a weapon—an automatic with an extended snout, probably (she thought) what in the movies they called a "silencer". . . .

Marilyn took all of this in, in half a second, during which Harrigan dropped to a knee and assumed a firing position with his .38. In the next half second Marilyn realized, with a terrible certainty, that the assassin and Harrigan had each other in their sights, that one or both men would surely die. . . .

Then another figure lurched within those bushes, behind the assassin, swinging something that might have been a golf club but wasn't, smashing it against the assassin's neck and back, sending the man in black pitching forward out of the foliage, to lay sprawled like an offering at Harrigan's feet.

Quickly Harrigan plucked the weapon from the hand of the stunned, flat-on-his-face assailant.

From the bushes stepped a big man in a short-sleeved pale yellow shirt and corduroy trousers.

Marilyn—who, like Khrushchev, had slowly risen from the asphalt to her feet—gasped in surprise and delight.

A grinning, self-satisfied Walt Disney was standing there, breathing hard, and in his arms was an old-fashioned rifle.

"One of our Davy Crockett props," Mr. Disney explained, almost sheepishly.

Marilyn's eyes were huge. "Ol' Betsy!"

"Be sure you're right," Mr. Disney said with a shrug, "and then go ahead."

Calling in the troops on his walkie-talkie, Harrigan knelt over the unconscious figure; Marilyn hadn't seen it happen, but the State Department man had already slapped handcuffs onto the half-unconscious assailant, hands behind his back.

Marilyn made introductions, and Mr. Disney and Nikita were shaking hands and grinning at each other.

"If you're up to it," Mr. Disney said to the premier, as casually as if knocking out assassins was just another of his many responsibilities here at the park, "I'd like to show you around, some—we don't open up for a number of hours, you see."

"Now I *really* get to see Disneyland!" Nikita said, his face bright with childish anticipation.

Standing guard over his prisoner, Harrigan said, "Really, gentlemen, I don't think—"

"Jack," Marilyn reminded the agent, "you said if there

was anything you could do . . . *anything!*"

Harrigan sighed. "Then let's start with the nearest first aid station."

Mr. Disney said, "You won't need an E ticket for that." Then, beaming a wide, warm smile back at the premier, the animator settled a fatherly hand on his V.I.P. guest's shoulder. "I'd very much like to show you my Disneyland fleet, Mr. Premier—tenth largest battle armada in the world!"

"Already have seen, thank you." Khrushchev turned to the young woman at his side, a movie star who might have been a Russian peasant girl . . . and a lovely one. "Where should we go first?"

Marilyn touched a cheek with a platinum-nailed finger, giving the problem some serious thought, ignoring the rush of hard footsteps on asphalt as cops and Secret Service men and KGB agents and a CIA man came running pell mell to join them. "We've been to Fantasyland," she said, "and've already had quite an adventure. . . . Why don't we stay in Tomorrowland for a while?" She shrugged and granted them her famous smile. "After all, Nikkie—who knows what the future will bring?"

Epilogue

Da Svidaniya, Khrushchev

In October of 1959, after his ten-day visit to the United States, Nikita Khrushchev returned to his homeland. To his closest advisors he confided that he "brimmed with hope" that Russia and its chief adversary could avoid a nuclear confrontation, and even coexist peacefully.

Khrushchev's enemies, however, did not share this hope, much less his desire for detente. Irritated by the premier's praise of America, and his consideration of adopting U.S. manufacturing and farming techniques, communist party hard-liners secretly began plotting his downfall.

Later that same October, a trip to China proved revealing to Khrushchev, the premier receiving so cool a reception from Mao Tse-tung that he might well have longed for the hospitality of Mayor Poulson of Los Angeles. Although the Chinese of course insisted that the attempt on the premier's life was not sanctioned by their government—and was in fact the action of renegade, self-interested agents—Khrushchev knew better.

At the conclusion of her Disneyland adventure with the Russian premier, Marilyn Monroe returned to New York to a broken marriage, which she and Arthur Miller held temporarily together only out of the necessity to complete their collaborative movie, *The Misfits*, to be shot in the blazing Nevada desert.

Now and then, during that troubled, oppressive production,

she would hear from Nikita—letters forwarded to her on the set by the State Department in Washington, courtesy of a gracious Jack Harrigan. And after the completion of *The Misfits*, she and Nikita kept in touch, mostly by phone, often talking for hours.

Marilyn, living alone now in the Manhattan East 57th Street apartment, would ask Nikita about his wife and children and grandchildren, always interested in what they were doing. And Nikita would continue to try to persuade her to abandon America for Russia, where she could better pursue her artistic muse, creating motion pictures that she could be proud of, without studio interference.

Sometimes, in spite of suspicions that the phones were tapped—by both governments, and maybe someone else's—their conversations would venture into politics, Marilyn as always interested in world affairs. Once, when the movie star extolled the virtues of America's new president, John F. Kennedy, Nikita agreed wholeheartedly with her assessment, and recounted his first meeting with the man, at a Foreign Relations Committee Reception, when Kennedy was still a senator.

"I liked his face," Nikita told her, in a 1961 phone call (declassified in 2001), "sometimes stern but, often, would break into big, good-natured smile. I could tell he was interested in finding peaceful solution to world problems." Nikita had paused, then added, "I help put him in office, instead of that puppet Nixon."

"Whatever do you mean, Nikkie?" Marilyn had asked him breathlessly.

"You remember this U-2 pilot of yours—this Gary Powers?"

"The one who crashed in Russia and got captured—sure."

"Yes, this one. Well, I wait until *after* the election to

release him." Nikita chuckled. "This way Nixon cannot claim that *he* could deal better with Russians than JFK."

"Well," she laughed, "I can see how that might have given Jack the edge to win."

"By at least half million votes," Nikita said proudly.

"Nikkie, you're a genius."

"Da."

Khrushchev was vacationing with his family in the Crimea, on August 5, 1962, when he received word that Marilyn Monroe was dead of a drug overdose. Devastated, he took to his bed.

Newspaper accounts that were brought to him attributed the movie star's death to probable suicide or at best an accidental fatal self-medication; but Nikita suspected otherwise. In her last phone call to him at the Kremlin, made in July of 1962, she had been enthusiastic about the Kennedy brothers, and her newfound opportunity to "really get involved in politics." He wondered perhaps if, finally, Marilyn had gotten *too* involved in politics.

A request by Nikita to the State Department to retrieve his personal letters to her was unsuccessful; no correspondence of the premier's was ever found among her belongings . . . or so the State Department claimed (Harrigan in 1961 had returned to the Secret Service, retiring during President Clinton's first term).

Khrushchev's after-hours visit to Disneyland slipped past the media and through the cracks of history; but it was nearly otherwise, thanks to Walt Disney.

Despite the U.S. government's efforts to keep the episode under wraps, Disney—who may have been a loyal American, but was after all the king of a magic realm—decided in 1960 to make a movie on the subject. Disney assigned one of his top scriptwriters to a film that would be called *Khrushchev in Hollywood*, and signed Peter Ustinov for the part, despite the actor's reluctance to shave his head.

In Disney's re-imagining (which skirted the espionage realities of the event), Khrushchev defied the State Department and visited Disneyland in secret, in various comical disguises, ducking both U.S. officials and anti-Russia demonstrators.

But it wasn't till 1965 that the screenplay was in shape and Ustinov could make time in his schedule, and so, in the end, Walt Disney pulled the plug.

When his associates, knowing how keen Walt had been on this picture, asked why he had at this late date nixed the project, Disney had only shrugged and said, "Old news."

Khrushchev, after all, was out of power.

In October of 1964, after a disastrous harvest had sent his popularity plummeting, the premier's enemies finally brought him down, though without any Stalin-esque bloodshed. Nikita Sergeyevich Khrushchev resigned from office at the age of seventy, retiring to a dacha outside Moscow, where he wrote his memoirs, living peacefully until his death in 1971.

A TIP OF THE COONSKIN CAP

Despite its extensive basis in history, *Bombshell* is a work of fiction, and liberties have been taken with the facts, though as few as possible, reflecting the needs of the narrative as well as conflicting source material.

This novel expands upon a short story by Barbara Collins, "Da Svidaniya, Khrushchev," published in *Marilyn: Shades of Blonde* (1997), edited by Carole Nelson Douglas. The invitation to write this story—taking advantage of Barbara's longtime interest in Marilyn Monroe—came from Ed Gorman and Marty Greenberg. Our thanks to Carole, Ed, and Marty.

Among the sources for the characterization of Nikita Khrushchev were: *Khrushchev Remembers* (1970), Nikita Khrushchev; *The Space Race* (1962), Donald W. Cox; *Inside Russia Today* (1958), John Gunther; *Khrushchev: The Years in Power* (1978), Roy A. Medvedev and Zhores A. Medvedev; and *Life in Russia* (1983), Michael Binyon. Contemporary accounts consulted regarding the Khrushchev visit included: *Time* magazine, September 28, 1959; *Newsweek* magazine, September 21, 1959, and September 28, 1959; and *Life* magazine, January 13, 1958, January 20, 1958, September 28, 1959, October 5, 1959, and October 19, 1959.

The authors have accumulated a large library of Marilyn Monroe material, and drew upon many books and periodicals for her characterization. The key books used were: *The Unabridged Marilyn, Her Life from A to Z* (1987), Randall Riese and Neal Hitchens; *Marilyn Monroe, In Her Own Words* (1983), Roger Taylor; *Marilyn Monroe, The Biography* (1993), Donald Spoto; *Legend, The Life and Death of Marilyn Monroe* (1984), Fred Lawrence Guiles; *The Life and Curious Death of Marilyn Monroe* (1974), Robert F. Slatzer; *Goddess, The Secret Lives of Marilyn Monroe* (1985), Anthony Summers; *The Marilyn Encyclopedia* (1999), Adam Victor; and *Timebends* (1987), Arthur Miller.

Background for Jack Harrigan was drawn from *The United States Secret Service* (1961), Walter S. Bowen and Harry Edward Neal; and *The Death Dealers* (1960), Phil Hirsch.

Sources for the characterization of Walt Disney and the depiction of Disneyland included numerous contemporary magazine accounts, various Internet web pages, and the following books: *The Art of Walt Disney* (1973), Christopher Finch; *Disney's World* (1985), Leonard Mosley; and *Walt Disney, Hollywood's Dark Prince* (1993), Marc Eliot. In addition, the DVD set *Walt Disney Treasures: Disneyland USA* (2001)—featuring documentaries hosted, produced, and written by Leonard Maltin—was particularly helpful, including interview material with Disney himself discussing the Khrushchev/Disneyland controversy. Walt Disney did have an apartment over the fire station in Disneyland, and was indeed planning a *Khrushchev in Disneyland* feature film; but certain liberties were taken here with the park and its geography, for storytelling purposes.

Other helpful sources included: *His Way, The Unauthorized Biography of Frank Sinatra* (1986), Kitty Kelley; *Out With the Stars: Hollywood Nightlife in the Golden Era* (1985), Jim Heimann; and *Mental Hygiene: Classroom Films 1945–1970* (1999), Ken Smith.

The authors wish to thank their agent, Dominick Abel. This book has been a long time coming, and readers who have heard about the project have occasionally inquired about when it might arrive; we hope—as was the case when Marilyn Monroe finally walked onto a soundstage—it will have been worth the wait.

The Authors Are . . .

. . . MAX ALLAN COLLINS, two-time winner of the PWA "Shamus" Best Novel award for his historical thrillers *True Detective* (1983) and *Stolen Away* (1991), featuring Chicago P.I. Nate Heller. In 2002 he received the Herodotus "Lifetime Achievement" Award from the Historical Mystery Appreciation Society. An MWA Edgar nominee in both fiction and nonfiction categories, Max is a leading writer of movie and TV "tie-in" novels, including the *New York Times* bestseller, *Saving Private Ryan* (1998) and the *CSI* novels. In 1995, he wrote and directed the thriller, *Mommy*; a sequel, *Mommy's Day* followed; and his third indie feature, *Real Time: Siege at Lucas Street Market*, is on DVD. Max's graphic novel, *Road to Perdition* (1998), is the basis of the 2002 DreamWorks motion picture starring Tom Hanks, Paul Newman, and Jude Law, directed by Sam Mendes.

. . . and BARBARA COLLINS, the author of numerous short stories, with appearances in such top anthologies as *Murder Most Delicious*, *Women on the Edge*, *Murder for Mother*, *Murder for Father*, and the bestselling *Cat Crimes* series. Her stories have been selected for inclusion in the first three volumes of *The Year's 25 Finest Crime and Mystery Stories*. Her short story collection, *Too Many Tomcats* (2000), has been followed by a collection of stories with her husband Max, *Murder His and Hers* (2001), and she was co-editor of the anthology *Lethal Ladies* (1997). The Collins's first collaborative novel, *Regeneration* (1999), was a paperback bestseller. Barbara worked as production manager on the *Mommy* movies and line producer on *Real Time: Siege at Lucas Street Market.*

Barbara and Max Collins live in Muscatine, Iowa; their son Nathan is a Computer Science major at the University of Iowa.